TWENTY PALACES

HARRY CONNOLLY

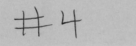

Praise for the
TWENTY PALACES
novels:

"[Child of Fire] is excellent reading and has a lot of things I love in a book: a truly dark and sinister world, delicious tension and suspense, violence so gritty you'll get something in your eye just reading it, and a gorgeously flawed protagonist. Take this one to the checkout counter. Seriously."
—JIM BUTCHER

"Connolly doesn't shy away from tackling big philosophical issues . . . amid gory action scenes and plenty of rapid-fire sardonic dialogue."
—*Publishers Weekly* (starred review),
on *Game of Cages*

"An edge-of-the-seat read! Ray Lilly is the new high-water mark of paranormal noir."
—CHARLES STROSS

"The fast pacing and over-the-top action never let go. This has become one of my must read series."
—*Locus*

For librarians everywhere.

CHAPTER ONE

I stepped off the bus into the November wind and drizzle. I'd gotten out of doors in the last three years, of course—they'd let us into the yard nearly every day—but now that I had my freedom, weather made me feel exposed and alone.

And I was glad. I was a free man again.

At the far end of the bus station, Uncle Karl leaned against the wall. I slung my backpack over my shoulder and moved through the crowd toward him, taking care not to jostle or bump anyone. Bumping up against some stranger didn't mean the same thing outside as it did in, but old habits die hard.

It had been fifteen years since I'd seen my uncle and I was startled by the lines in his face and the ash gray in his mustache. He'd worn his big blue Seattle PD uniform, gun, badge, handcuffs, and hat, and he stood as near the exit as he could without being on the other side of the door.

He wasn't going to make things easy, but that was fine. I was ready. When I got close enough, he jerked his thumb at the passenger side of a Chrysler Sebring sedan and said: "Door's unlocked." He didn't smile or offer to shake my hand, and he'd skipped right over *Welcome to town. How was your trip.*

I nodded and we went outside. I tried the passenger door and found it locked. "Other one," Karl said.

Of course. I climbed into the back seat, setting my backpack and manila folder beside me. Then I clicked the seat belt across my chest. I was a seat-belt person now. A paycheck person. If I was lucky.

Karl pulled out of the parking lot and drove through the city. I had the same view as the last time I'd ridden in a car—the back of a cop's head. At least I wasn't handcuffed this time.

"Thank you," I said. Seat-belt people were polite people. Karl just looked into the rear view mirror and scowled. "Uncle Karl, can I ask a favor? I mean, beyond all the favors you're already doing for me?"

"What is it?" His voice was as flat as a piece of sheet metal.

"The bus was late getting in, and I'm supposed to meet a guy about a job. He's a guy I knew in junior high and he said I should look him up right away before he goes off shift."

"Your aunt has dinner waiting for you."

It sounded like an accusation and for a moment I didn't know what to do. I wanted a real job as soon as I could get one, but my aunt and uncle were taking me in. I didn't want to insult them before I'd even arrived.

"Where is it?" Uncle Karl asked. "I'm sure your aunt will understand."

Not fifteen minutes later, he pulled up to the curb at a little business district not far from the house I'd grown up in. My uncle scowled at me through the rear view mirror. "Is that what you're wearing to the interview?"

I glanced down at my brown Dockers and the white button down I'd picked up in a Valley Thrift Store. Interview? I'd never been to a real job interview in my life and it startled me to hear the word. I thought I was just meeting a guy. Should I have worn a tie?

It didn't matter because I didn't have one. My second-hand backpack had my other clothes, but none were as nice as what I was wearing. "I guess so."

"Are you going to ask me to wait for you?"

"No," I answered quickly, reading his tone and expression. Uncle Karl wasn't going to be waiting around for me to do anything. "I remember your address. I'll come straight there after."

He nodded. I scrambled out of the car, leaving my backpack on the seat. I couldn't bring it to an *interview*.

The business was a copy shop. There was a clock above the cash register that said it was two minutes to seven, but Wally, the guy I'd come to see, was nowhere in sight. Had he left early?

There were two employees behind the desk—one was a teenage boy with a brush of fake orange hair and piercings through his eyebrows, the other was an aggressively bland college-age girl with her collar buttoned tightly across her throat.

The only customer was working a self-serve machine. I walked to the counter and the bland woman met me there.

"Hello." I remembered to smile. "I'm looking for Wally King."

Her face turned sour, then became Professionally Dismissive. "I'm sorry. He isn't here."

The teenager found a stack of papers to sort at the counter, moving close enough to eavesdrop. He wasn't subtle about it. I pressed on: "Do you know when he'll be in? He asked me to meet him here and give him this." I opened the manila folder. A sheet of paper floated out, slid across the top of the counter and bumped the woman's arm. "Oops," I said, suddenly feeling ridiculous. "I didn't mean to shoot it at you like that."

She glanced at the paper. It was the job application Wally had sent me, all filled out.

"No, I don't know when he'll be here." She had something more she wanted to say and despite herself, couldn't hold it back. "He hasn't been in to work for three days. We've been short-handed."

She managed to make it sound like a plea for sympathy and an accusation at the same time. The teenager spoke up. His voice was surprisingly deep. "He's off stalking his ex."

Bland Woman cut off that line of discussion quickly. "Sorry. We can't help you."

If Wally hadn't show up for three days, I figured he didn't want his job anymore—At least, he didn't want it as much as I did. "Do you have any openings? I can work any hours."

The bell above the front door jangled. "Ray! You made it!"

Wally came through the door and spread his arms wide. He was as fat as I remembered, but he'd grown sloppy, too. His face was flushed and blotchy. His clothes were a mismatched clash of yellow plaid and green stripes. Even his sneakers were mismatched. His hair, however, was carefully blow-dried and gelled into place.

I had to force myself to say it: "Wally. It's good to see

you." I let myself be hugged and slapped on the back. Wally was all smiles.

"Hey Andrea, Oscar," Wally said. "Did Ronnie fire me yet?"

Andrea seemed put out, as though Wally had ruined a speech she'd prepared. "Well, he hasn't said anything to me, but we've been short-handed all this week."

"Let's make it official: I quit. Ray here can take my place. I kinda promised him a jay oh bee."

I stepped away from Wally and focused on Andrea immediately. "I'll work hard," I said. "I need this job. I can cover any hours and I'll work hard and... I take beatings like a pack mule."

Andrea wrinkled her lip and looked over my application for the first time. "It says here you've been to jail. For Battery."

"He was probably sticking up for someone," Wally said. "Ray's like that."

"Not any more." I gave Wally a cold look, trying to back him off. "I learned a hard lesson. I don't do that anymore."

Wally walked behind the counter. "If you recommend him, Ronnie'll give him a couple shifts. Let me get my stuff from the office."

Andrea wouldn't look at me, and Oscar was watching me too closely. I'd have had better luck if I hadn't mentioned Wally at all, and damn if I wasn't going to have to walk all the way to my aunt and uncle's house without a job. "Please. Like a pack mule."

The bell above the front door jangled again. "Wally!" I turned to see who was shouting, and there, standing in the doorway, was Jon Burrows.

I felt woozy all of a sudden, as though I was starting to unravel. I staggered back against the wall. Andrea grabbed a fistful of Oscar's shirt and said: "That's him!" With her other hand, she pulled a tiny gold cross from beneath her collar and clutched it.

"Jon!" Wally called from the far end of the room. "*Stroll* on in here!"

Jon did an exaggerated strut toward him, moving away from me. "Look at me, Wally, you fucking genius!" He lifted his knees high and punched his thighs, and the motion made him turn slightly so I could see the edge of his face. His hair was too long and he was carrying a good-sized pot belly, but it was him. Even after 15 years, I knew him on sight. And he was walking.

Without even realizing what I was doing, I started toward the exit.

Wally leaned on the counter. "One hundred percent vertical, my friend."

"Friend?" Jon said. He jumped across the counter, grabbed Wally, and kissed the side of his head.

"Excuse me," Andrea cut in. "I'm sorry to interrupt, but... Would you tell me how it happened?"

Jon glanced at the cross in her hand. "It was a miracle."

"Jon," Wally said. "You'll never guess who's here."

And I was through the door and gone.

I'd barely gotten twenty feet when I heard the copy shop door jingle again. I ducked into the recessed storefront of a darkened Hallmark store. It wasn't really cover, but it was all I had.

Jon charged out of the copy shop and looked up and

down the block. It must have been darker than I thought, because he couldn't see me. "Ray!" he called. I watched him, feeling the breeze on my face. He took a deep breath through his nose, as though smelling a flower. "Ray!! RAY!!"

I leaned back and closed my eyes, keeping very still. Then, as soon as Jon went back into the copy shop, I bolted from cover and ran.

By the time I reached Karl and Theresa's house, I was exhausted. I'd run the first six blocks, then traded off jogging and walking the rest of the way, keeping to small residential streets as much as possible.

I didn't want Jon or Wally to catch up to me in a car, and they didn't. Whether that was because they didn't look for me or they didn't find me, I couldn't tell. I knew which one I hoped it would be, but what did that matter? "Hope" was a four-letter word I couldn't bring myself to say.

So when I arrived at my aunt and uncle's house, I was sweaty, disheveled, and still unemployed. It was Karl who answered the door. "Well?"

"I'll try someplace else tomorrow."

He sighed, disappointed. He also didn't move out of the way to let me in. Just as I wondered if I was going to sleep on the lawn, Aunt Theresa bustled by him and clasped my hands.

She was smaller and rounder than I remembered, and she seemed more beaten down. Her knuckles were crooked, making her fingers come off her hands at an angle, but if her arthritis pained her, she didn't show it. "Raymond, it's... Oh, come here!" She put her arms around me and gave me my second hug in years, and the first one I was glad to have.

"It's good to have you back," she said to my ear.

"Thank you."

"Come in, come in. Did it go well? Never mind, I don't care if you have the job right this second. You'll get one, I'm sure. Dinner is waiting for you, but Karl and I have already eaten, of course, since it's so late. Are you hungry?"

"Yes," I was surprised by the force behind my answer. In fact, I was starving.

"Good! I made stew because you used to love it. I hope you still do."

I told her I did as she led me through the house. The furnishings were simple, worn, and slightly dusty. Karl certainly wasn't going to run a feather duster over the place, and I was sure Aunt Theresa did what she could. As soon as I found a feather duster or whatever, I was going to go over the whole room.

She sat me at the table, then bustled to the stove. As she reached for a dutch oven, I started to get out of my chair to help, but Uncle Karl laid his hand on my shoulder. I sat again. She'd ask for help if she wanted it. Karl sat opposite me.

The stew was so good I gasped at the first bite. "See? I knew you would need some real food. Certainly better than you're used to, right?" I nodded as she sat beside me. "And another thing! You're not a guest, not here. You're family, so don't get all worried about what's proper. If you're hungry, eat. Lonely, visit. That's how I want it."

"I'm glad," I said. "And after dinner I'll take out the trash and do the dishes, right? Family."

"I like this better already!"

Uncle Karl wasn't smiling. "It's easy to start strong and then blow it. You aren't going to blow it, are you?" He didn't seem to expect an answer so I didn't offer one. "I've seen a lot of young guys try to go straight after they came out. Do you know why they fail?"

"They commit crimes?"

I regretted it as soon as I said it, but Karl pretended he hadn't heard. "They think they paid their debt in full just because they walked out of their cell. They think they have a clean slate. Truth is, you haven't finished paying your debt. People are going to keep taking pieces of you, treating you with disrespect, making you wait for things, and making you struggle for things. You think you've paid your debt, but you haven't."

"I'm not going back."

"Good, because here are the rules. No trouble, and nothing that looks like trouble. No loud music, no piles of beer bottles in the recycling, no buddies dropping by at 1 a.m. I don't care if it's a midnight prayer and needlepoint society; if it looks like trouble, I don't want it here."

Aunt Theresa scowled at him. "Oh, Karl..."

"No, it's all right," I said. "I want the same thing. No trouble."

"Good," he said. "Tell us about the interview."

"Jon Burrows was there." I hadn't meant to say it, but it came out anyway. My aunt and uncle looked at each other, and I knew they weren't surprised at all. "How long ago did he...?"

It was Uncle Karl who answered. "Sometime within the last few days. Did he say how it happened?"

The way he asked the question made me wary. I'd spent the last few years refusing to answer cops' questions, but what the hell, I was starting a new life. "He said it was a miracle, but I think he was full of... I think he was lying."

"Why do you think that?"

"His expression. His tone. The woman asking the question was fiddling with a cross at the time—I think he was saying what she wanted to hear."

Karl nodded. He took a dishtowel off the end of the table, revealing a newspaper. He passed it to me. The headline read "Miracle or Hoax?" and just below it were two pictures: One showing Jon in a wheelchair, his slack face partly covered by his long hair, and the other showing him standing in his yard, laughing. It was dated yesterday.

I was about to say that I wasn't hungry anymore, but my bowl was empty. I didn't need an excuse to get up from the table. I carried the bowl to the sink and started washing the dishes. Aunt Theresa fussed over me a bit, trying to get me to take a second helping, but eventually she gave me a hug and let me get back to work. Uncle Karl stayed behind, watching me closely.

"You can take that paper with you if you want. The key to the apartment is just beside it."

"Thanks, I will. Is there anything in the article worth reading?"

"Only that Burrows's insurance company is suing him for fraud. Listen, if this guy has broken the law—even if he's suspected of it—that makes him trouble, and you need to keep away from him. It's part of your debt."

I nodded, not looking up. I'd expected him to say something like that from the moment I saw that headline.

"By the way," he continued. "Just before you got here, a woman called. Andrea something. She said you can have the late shift at the copy shop tomorrow. Your shift starts at four, but she wants to you come in fifteen minutes early for paperwork. And bring this." He held a slip of pink paper in front of me. WHILE YOU WERE OUT! was printed across the top next to a cheerful cartoon character, and beneath that was a short list scribbled in ball point pen. I couldn't focus on it at first. "If you want the job."

I snatched it out of his hand, then set it on the counter. Hell yes, I wanted the job.

My uncle nodded at me, informed me that I'd need extensive training before I was ready to take out the trash, recycling and food compost in Seattle, and left me to finish the dishes. When the drying rack was full and the sink empty, I took the key, the newspaper, and the slip of paper into the backyard.

My apartment was above a detached garage at the far end of the yard. The stairs creaked and groaned as I climbed them, and while the deadbolt lock was sturdy, the flimsy door it was mounted in had too much glass.

What the hell. Inside, I found my backpack laying on the couch, looking oddly deflated. My clothes were in the tiny dresser beside the fold-out couch. Against the front wall was a little sink, fridge and two-burner electric stove. Behind it was the bathroom. Against the far wall was an empty bookshelf.

I switched on a lamp, casting a dim yellow light over everything. My aunt had rented this room to students looking for work and middle-aged men needing a new start. It wasn't spacious, but it was a good place to start over.

The first thing I did was set aside the papers I'd need for my new job. After that, I went into the bathroom. Through the window, I could see into Aunt Theresa's kitchen window. She and Uncle Karl were sitting at their table, and he was rubbing some kind of salve onto her crooked, arthritic hands. I turned away, feeling like a peeping tom.

Then, suddenly, I had nothing to do and nowhere to go. There was no TV or game console in the room, and I couldn't imagine going back into my aunt's house, sitting on their couch and watching whatever they were watching.

It felt like a test. Or maybe I should say it was a trap. I had a lot of ways to fill empty time, but they were all old habits that might land me in jail or get me evicted. I sat on the couch, quietly looking at nothing. In prison I'd lived on the institution's schedule and now I had the freedom to stay up as late as I wanted. It was just fifteen minutes after lights out in Chino, but I slipped under the covers anyway, feeling oddly defeated.

Tomorrow would be better. I closed my eyes and tried to sleep. I wanted to concentrate on my new job, how it would work and how I'd behave, but I fell asleep with the image of Jon Burrows standing on the sidewalk, screaming my name.

CHAPTER TWO

In the morning, I found myself once again with time I wasn't sure how to fill. The first thing I did was dig an old bicycle out of the garage below my apartment, fix the brakes, and ride to the nearest hardware store. I spent some of my dwindling gate money on a little bell, some string and a few other odds and ends.

On the way home, I passed an open library. I was surprised that they would issue me a card on the spot and let me walk out the door with a small stack of books. *Victims,* was my first thought, but I pushed that aside.

Back at my apartment, I loaded the books into the shelves, then mounted the bell outside the door. I hung the string from it and tied off the other end to an eye screw placed on the ground floor.

"What are you doing, Raymond?" Aunt Theresa walked across the yard toward me. She seemed to be struggling a bit, as though the neatly-mown grass was treacherous footing. She held a square pastel green envelope in her hand.

"I didn't want you to have to climb those stairs every time you wanted to talk to me—I know it was you who put my clothes in the drawer. Anyway..." I pulled on the string and the bell up by the door jingled. It was a clear, cheerful tone.

Aunt Theresa smiled and sighed, then patted my arm with such affection that it made me feel embarrassed. "That's so sweet of you, I'm almost sorry to give you this." She gave me the envelope. My name was scribbled on it in a heavy, cramped hand. There was an invitation inside.

I read it. "Jon is having a party tonight," I said. "A celebration. And he's inviting me?" I looked up at my aunt.

"He came by, and seemed quite disappointed that you were out."

"He wants *me* there?"

"Very much so, I thought. Are you all right, Raymond?"

"Yeah," I said, reading the invitation again to make sure I hadn't missed the word *not* in there or something. "Yeah, I guess so."

"You knew when you came up here that you'd have to see Jon again, didn't you? You knew you'd have to make peace with him."

Her brown eyes seemed to be looking straight through me. "I was going to try. But Uncle Karl—"

"I know what Karl said. He's got a sharp eye, my husband does, but he's more understanding than he lets on. You're not going to be able to avoid Jon forever, not if he's coming around here."

"I don't want to avoid him," I said, even though I'd done just that the night before.

"Of course not. You may visit him and discover you have nothing in common anymore. Maybe you'll wish each other well and go your separate ways."

"But I ought to see him."

"I told him you would be starting a new job today. He

asked if you would come by the house after your shift. He even said *please*."

"Okay," I said. We both knew I'd be going to the party. "How did he...?"

"How did he look?" Aunt Theresa said as she started back toward her house. "He looked so happy that he frightened me. He looked like a starving man just sitting down to a Christmas feast."

She went back into the house, leaving me with too much to think about.

I made sure to arrive at the copy shop fifteen minutes before the already early time Uncle Karl had given me. There were no customers, but they were both busy. Oscar was loading paper into machines and Andrea had to stop working on something at the back of the office to meet me.

"Oh good, you're early. Come on back." She led me into the office where Wally had collected his things. It was a sad little room with bare drywall and a stamped metal desk that someone had kicked the hell out of. The chairs looked like cafeteria discards and boxes of stationery were stacked along one wall. "Paperwork first, of course. All the usual boring stuff."

She handed me a clipboard and promised to come back. The forms I was supposed to fill out seemed incomprehensible to me at first, but I managed to get them finished before she returned. She read them over, approved, and gave me a green polo shirt like her own and a name tag with masking tape over the front and *Ray* written on it in blue ball point pen. When I put them on, it felt like a Halloween costume.

"Everything here is easy," Andrea told me. "Just remember

a couple things: Clean clothes, close shave, no B.O. Oscar will train you on most things while I run a big job, just be sure to push the blue legal paper. Wally over-ordered so we're offering a two-penny per sheet discount." She took a step toward me. "So," her voice was lower now. "You know him?"

"Wally? I knew him in school, but it's been 15 years."

She absent-mindedly tugged the little gold cross from beneath her collar. "Not that creep. I'm talking—"

"Oh." I suddenly understood her. "No, I mean. Not for a long time." I realized just how I'd gotten this job so quickly, and it made me want to quit on the spot. I wasn't going to spill my history to this stranger just because I needed a paycheck. "Do I have to talk about this if I want this job? Is it a requirement? Or can I just push the blue legal paper and—"

She seemed taken aback. "I'm sorry! I didn't mean to pry."

"I understand, but it's complicated."

"No problem. You don't have to... Um, hey, it's five minutes to. Come on out at four and we'll get started."

She left me standing in the room, feeling awkward and stupid, like one of the victims of the world. *You think you've paid your debt, but you haven't.*

I went out the door early and shook hands with Oscar. It turned out that Andrea was right: the job was the easiest thing I'd ever done in my life. I learned to clear paper jams, tell people I was sorry when I wasn't, and to sweep the floor. The only challenge was that the four-hour shift seemed endless. Did people really do twice this every day? I couldn't imagine it.

After my shift, I went outside to unlock my bicycle. Oscar

came out behind me and said "See you tomorrow, dude," in a way that showed he approved of me.

Andrea came out right behind him, her car keys jangling in her hand. "Heading home?"

"Yep," I lied. She told me I'd done well enough to earn more hours, if I kept it up. I thanked her and rode away.

It wasn't that late, but the streets were empty enough that my ride to Jon's place was almost lonely. I went slow—my clothes were nice if not terribly fancy, but I didn't want to be sweaty and rumpled when I arrived at Jon's. What's more, on the way I passed within two blocks of the house I grew up in, but I didn't detour to see it. My family had left years ago, and I had no interest in looking at an old building full of bad memories.

Approaching Jon's parents' house, the first thing I saw were the lights. Someone had mounted powerful lights on tall stands, which were shining on the crowded sidewalk. There was a cop car with two bored cops inside parked at the corner, and I slowed my approach. It didn't look like the party had moved into the street...

Once I got closer, I saw that the lights were plugged into outlets on the sides of news vans. And a surprising number of the people out on the streets were in wheelchairs, or pulled oxygen tanks behind them. I hopped the curb and rode the sidewalk on the far side of the street, behind the news vans and far from the house. How could I have thought these people milling around in the lights were party-goers? Many were in obvious pain, and they turned resentful, desperate expressions toward Jon's house.

I chained my bike to a tree, listening to a reporter interviewing a woman in a wheelchair. Both sounded weary and more than a little frustrated.

As I clicked the lock shut, I felt something strange, something I'd never felt before in my life. There was something wrong with this tree, but I had no idea what it was. I touched the bark and felt, among the rough exterior, that someone had carved something into it. A shape or a design that I couldn't make out because it lay in the shadow of the news lights.

I didn't know what to make of it, so I moved away. Further along the sidewalk, standing in the shadow of another, larger tree, was a small figure. At first glance I thought it was a homeless person, although I'm not sure why. Bulky clothes made it hard to guess if it was a man, woman or kid, but I didn't trust the way they stood there, watching.

The reporter was ending the interview, although the woman seemed to want to repeat her grievances all over again. I moved toward the house, noting the sign on the front yard that read PRIVATE PROPERTY! TRESPASSERS WILL BE SUED! Down the block, a bald bowling ball of a man started shouting about God and his wife and whether the one was going to the other before her time. I heard the distinctive sound of cops slamming their car doors shut.

Two camera men jumped out of their folding chairs and rushed across the street. Up ahead, a young woman was leading an older man up the front walk of Jon's house. I slowed, letting them go ahead the way I would watch a dog wander into a minefield. The cameramen stopped at the edge of the lawn and so did I, if only to avoid walking into their shots.

As the old man and his helper approached the wheelchair

ramp on the porch, the front door opened and a dark-haired woman came out. What the hell. I drew the invitation from my pocket, took a deep breath, and started up the walk.

As I got near them, I heard the dark-haired woman say: "I'm sorry, but this is private property and you're trespassing. You'll have to leave." She sounded as if she'd said that so many times that she was sick of it. "Go home."

"This may be my last chance," the old man said. His voice was shaky and frail. "If I go, I might not be able to come back."

"We can't do anything for you."

"If I could just talk to the young man—"

"Please—"

"I have money."

"Please. Go home. Please."

The old man sagged, and the young woman holding his elbow helped him struggle back to the sidewalk. "I shouldn't have come," he said to her as he passed me. "I was ready for the end. I'd accepted my prognosis. Then I heard about this young man and... Lord, I was so much better off without this *hope*."

The dark-haired woman turned to me, obviously about to give me the same speech, then she froze. "Oh. My. God. Ray Lilly."

I suddenly recognized her. "Bingo?"

"Don't you dare call me that."

"I'm sorry, um..." I blanked on her real name for a moment. "...Barbara. I didn't—"

"You should be sorry. Of course you show up now, of all times. Of course you do."

I held up the invitation. "Jon asked me to come here."

But she wasn't listening. She just kept right on talking. "And you're *sorry*, of all the things to say. After everything Jon's been through over the years while you've been who knows where, and you're here now and you're fucking sorry. I'll tell you what: You stay right there, okay? You stay right there. I'm going to go inside and get Dad's thirty ought-six, and then I'm going to show you how *sorry* feels."

So much for being invited. She marched up the stairs onto the porch, and I turned tail and ran. The cameras followed me, and I wanted to curse at them, smash them so they couldn't record me while I ran for my life. I didn't. I just sprinted for my bike, digging my key out of my pocket as I went.

The sick people cleared a space for me, but the reporters and their camera people closed in. I needed that bicycle; it was no good trying to get away from someone on foot, and since I was not not not going to boost a car on my second day in town, I would have to ride.

I slipped the key in the padlock as the reporters started shouting questions, their lights shining on me. I looked up at the tree; the news people had very kindly lit up the weird, disturbing shape carved into the bark, but it was just a strange meaningless shape to me. I opened the lock, ripping the chain from the bike and slinging it over my neck. Let them shout at me, I didn't care. As long as they stayed between me and Bingo, they were my best friends in the world.

Someone shouted "GUN!" and we all turned toward the Burrows' house. Jon was there on the porch, having just come out the front door, with others pushing through behind him. Bingo stepped to the side, a hunting rifle in her hands.

Mr. Bowling Ball sprinted across the lawn as fast as his bulk would allow, heading straight for the porch. He raised his hand, and Jon flinched, lifting his own left hand as a shield as he ducked low.

A camera man side-stepped in front of me, blocking my view. I heard a long string of pistol shots, coming very fast, then screams and shouts of terror. The crowd was too thick to fight through, so I yanked my bike away from the tree and ran with it to the back bumper of a news van, where I had a nearly-unobstructed view of the porch.

Jon was surrounded by people fretting over him. He clutched at his left hand, looking down at it, then stuffed it into his hip pocket. With his other hand, he began making unmistakable motions of reassurance, trying to convince people he was fine.

Mr. Bowling Ball lay sprawled on the grass, almost as if he was having a nice little nap. The two cops stalked toward him, their weapons drawn, but it was clear they'd already done everything to him that anyone was going to do.

I saw Bingo lean the rifle against the wall as she joined the others in the crowd around Jon. Still, she turned and scanned the crowd, while Jon did the same. I pushed the bicycle a little further along and rode away, wondering how I was going to convince Uncle Karl not to throw my ass out of the apartment once he found out I'd been less than 50 feet from a police shooting.

The ride from Jon's house to Aunt Theresa's had several uphill stretches. I ate my pride and walked the bike no less than three times, and I was ready to turn in and get some sleep when I rode down the alley and braked by the garage.

As I swung my leg off the bicycle, a van parked across the driveway suddenly started up. It startled the hell out of me, and I jumped back against the wall.

But the doors didn't swing open suddenly, and the engine didn't race. Instead, the driver slowly backed out into the alley. The night's excitement had made me jumpy as hell. If Arne and the others had seen me startle at the approach of a GMC Savana, they'd have laughed themselves sick.

I knew who it was even before the van turned and I looked into the driver's window. It was Jon Burrows. Somehow, at the party, I hadn't noticed that he'd gotten a haircut. "Ray!" he called as he rolled down his window. "Ray, you came!"

"Yeah, I did, and your sister ran me off with a gun." There were so many years between us, and I couldn't believe that was the first thing I said to him.

"Dude, I'm sorry. That was a misunderstanding."

There was more I wanted to say—being threatened with a gun isn't something I shake off lightly—but I couldn't. Not to him. "I have to put my bike away."

I turned my back and pushed the bike toward the garage. Behind me, I heard the van door open. "Dude!" Jon called to me, and I could hear him approaching. "Hey, man. Hey. Check this out."

I yanked open the access door at the back of the garage and shoved the bicycle inside, letting it crash against the wall. I was feeling threatened and reckless, as though Jon and his party invitation had brought a prison sentence to my door.

"Check this out," Jon said again. He held up a framed

photo for me to take. I did. It showed the two of us as twelve-year-old boys, wearing the T-shirt and cap of sponsored intramural baseball teams. My cap was blue and his was orange, which surprised me because, as I remembered it, we'd been on the same team. "Remember the day this was taken? It was the league championship."

And suddenly I did remember. Jon had been pitching for the opposing team, and I'd hit a home run off him to win the game. It was the sort of play that you see in the movies, and I'd felt eight feet tall as I'd rounded the bases. But what I remembered most was that, even though I'd just beaten him and won the game, Jon had smiled at me. He had been proud of his friend.

The picture had been taken less than a year before That Day. "I do. I remember this." I handed him the photo and he took it with his left hand. "Hey, what happened to you?"

"Nothing to worry about." Jon held up his hand to show that his pinkie was gone at the bottom joint. The grin on his face was hard to read. I remembered, not even an hour before, that he'd raised that hand to shield himself from Mr. Bowling Ball. Even at that distance, it had seemed whole and complete to me, but that couldn't be right, because the injury wasn't bloody or fresh—the skin looked pinched closed like a kid's clay sculpture.

But I couldn't talk about that, because that was crazy.

CHAPTER THREE

"Ray, seriously, I'm sorry about Barbara," Jon said. "I totally forgot to tell her. That was all my fault."

"No," I said, and the word nearly stuck in my throat. "No, you don't have to apologize to me. I'm the one who—"

"It's not necessary," Jon said.

"No, I mean, I never apologized to you."

"Ray," Jon laughed. "You don't have to say it. I don't want you to, okay? I don't care. Look at me." He stepped back so I had a view of his whole body. "Everything is different now. Right?"

We both turned at the sound of the sliding door on the far side of the Savana rolling open. A few seconds later, a man and a woman stepped around the front fender. The woman was tall and lean, with short hair and thrift shop style. The man was slightly taller but built like a college linebacker. He looked wary and stood too close to the woman, as though she was his favorite toy and he was afraid someone else would wind her up.

"Hey," Jon said. "These are my friends, Echo and Payton. The party broke up, big surprise, so we're going to pick up my girlfriend and head out. Come with us, Ray. I want to celebrate with my old friend."

"Nobody else is going to be shot, are they?"

Echo laughed. Her voice was deeper than I'd expected. "That's why we're going out, to get away from the crazy."

"That's not the only reason." Jon pointed at me with the framed photo. "Come with us, dude. Please."

"Well, if you're going to say 'please'...." I started toward the van, following Payton and Echo around the front while Jon climbed in the driver's door. Everyone was smiling, even Payton, who didn't seem to smile easily.

The only chairs in the back of the van were vinyl benches with the legs cut off. Payton and Echo sat together on the bench along the back doors, and I sat on the side-facing one. The floor was littered with burger wrappers. Gross. I looked over at Jon to tell him he needed a trash bag for his ride, and saw that he was sitting in a wheelchair.

"Oh, shit."

Jon turned toward me. "Oh hey, don't freak, Ray. I haven't had time to trade it in for one with gas and brake pedals. I mean, I don't need it now but someone else will."

"You think so?" Echo asked from her back seat. Jon laughed.

We rode in silence for quite a while. The front passenger seat was empty, but no one suggested I take it so I sat quietly while the radio played some kind of trip hop I'd never heard before.

After twenty minutes, the van slowed. "Oh you're kidding me," Jon said. He turned off the music.

I rolled to my feet to look out the windshield, but Echo was quicker. Looking over her shoulder, I could see a crowd on the sidewalk ahead, lit by a silent turning police light.

They were holding handmade signs aloft, marching back and forth. The nearest sign read "Healing Not $tealing"; I didn't bother looking at the others.

There was a second, smaller group of people on the other side of a strip of yellow police tape, all huddled together as if for protection. They clustered near the entrance to the taped-off building; the sign above the door read HILLTOP PHYSICAL THERAPY CENTER. One of the women threw her arms around an older woman nearby, then broke off from the group and ran under the tape to the van.

Echo leaned over and opened the passenger door for her. She jumped inside, a tiny woman about my age with a turned-up nose and a nest of tight brown curls. She leaned across the van and gave Jon a quick hello kiss. "They're shutting us down."

"Because of what we did?" Jon said, his voice loud with outrage.

Echo hugged her. "Oh, sweetie, I'm so sorry." Jon took hold of her hand. I stepped back in case Payton wanted to join the hug, but the curly-haired woman broke free and looked me in the eye.

"You must be Ray. I'm Macy. Jon's said so much about you. I'm glad you've decided to come." There was something startling in the way she spoke to me, as though I was the most interesting thing in the world. She could have been a politician. "How was the party?"

Things got quiet after that. Payton had moved from the back bench to the side one, probably to be as close as possible to Echo. I moved to the back bench while Jon pulled into traffic and Echo began to describe what had happened on the lawn. I knelt, staring out the back window as we pulled away.

There, standing absolutely still in the midst of a crowd, was Wally King.

"Oh my God!" Macy shouted from the front of the car. I spun and saw Jon's face in the rear view mirror as he put the index finger of his left hand to his lips to quiet her, then winked. She glanced back at me, obviously upset but she fell silent.

Jon put his left hand back on the steering wheel. I settled onto the bench to look them over. Under normal circumstances, I wouldn't have any problem with a group of friends who were carefully not saying something in front of me. It's expected. But there were cops involved now, not to mention gunfire. I needed to be careful around these people.

Macy sighed. "Sweetie, would you mind?"

"Not at all," Echo answered. She took a small case from behind Jon's seat, opened it, and took out the two halves of a flute.

"Something happy!" Jon said as she put them together. "We're still celebrating. Nothing is going to stop this celebration." She began to play a happy tune that made me think of green meadows and guys with turned-up green shoes, even though every pot hole interrupted the music, ruining the effect. Macy grabbed a paper bag off the dashboard and dug out some damp-looking fries.

We drove for a while longer before I felt the tell-tale sharp turn and sudden bump of a vehicle pulling into a parking lot. "Hell yeah," Jon said. Echo put away her instrument, and a few seconds later, Jon was shutting off the engine and squawking the parking brake in place.

Everyone piled out of the van. I could see my breath in the chill night air. Jon threw his arm around my shoulders. "Wait until you see what I have planned for us."

Macy grabbed his wrist and pulled him away as Echo moved into his spot, standing close enough to command my attention. It was a well-timed switch, almost as though it had been orchestrated. "Big baseball fan, are you?" Echo asked.

"I used to be." We had come somewhere outside the city. There was a single large building in the center of the parking lot; it looked like some kind of huge sports bar. Jon had chosen a spot near the back, past a scattering of Hondas, Toyotas, and Fords—not the most upscale models, but worth a lot when stripped down for parts. Not that I did that anymore.

"We spent part of the day out at a field by Jon's house. He hit the ball as we chased it. I could see the appeal for him, but..."

I laughed and looked over her shoulder. Jon and Macy were speaking very closely, very quietly as she examined his damaged hand. Payton was just behind Echo and me, and he wasn't smiling anymore. "I gotta admit, I lost my taste for it. It's been a while since I followed a team."

"Well that's not allowed!" Jon said, bursting in on us. "Ray, ten minutes, that's all I ask. Ten minutes and you'll be ready to throw in with the Mariners again."

I liked the way he was smiling at me. It made me feel good. "Hell, you can have eleven."

Everyone laughed. Echo jumped at Payton and threw her arms around his beefy neck, and he lifted her off the ground with one hand as we walked. Macy came forward and slipped under Jon's arm on the other side. I was the odd man, but it felt okay.

The inside was dark and cavernous. Dings and clangs of dozens of arcade games could barely be heard over the blaring butt rock. Jon turned to Macy and yelled "Food!" over the din. She, Echo, and Payton yelled it right back, then headed toward a narrow counter at the back of the bar.

Jon took my elbow. "Come on! Let's go home!" He dragged me through the bar and out the back door.

There was a sturdy weathered picnic table chained to the back of the building. Beside it was a long, high chain link fence. It stretched twenty feet up, with huge squares of canvas hung over the far side. Then I noticed it had a roof, like an enclosure for a giraffe. A cage.

I almost had time to get angry, but then I noticed a machine at one end. Jon offered me an aluminum bat from a rack. "What do you think, huh?"

I couldn't help but smile as I accepted the bat. "Pretty cold out here. Even the pros have given up the game until spring."

"Screw them. I'm going to be out here all winter. Maybe I'll even try out for the M's."

"Great way to get rid of those news vans."

Jon laughed as he got a second bat from the rack. The back door opened and Macy, Echo, and Payton carried a startling amount of food to the picnic table. They laid out red plastic baskets full of french fries, burgers, and fried chicken strips, then began to eat. The women tore into the chicken as though they were starving, and the smacking noises they made were disgusting.

"Whoa," Payton said. "Hungry, babe?" He took a shaker

from his pocket and sprinkled a pale white powder over his fries. Macy and Echo reeled away from him, holding their noses and gasping for air.

"Jesus!" Echo said. She had tears running down her cheeks. "You and your garlic powder."

"What? It purifies my blood."

I watched Macy and Echo as they wiped away tears, trying to decide if they were play-acting to bust Payton's chops. They didn't look like it, but I was standing almost between them and I couldn't smell a thing.

Jon snatched a burger from the table. "You first, buddy."

I went into the cage and stood beside the plate. The night was cold and so was I. Still, it felt good to stand here after so long. This was a sacred spot.

Jon dropped a token into the coin slot and the pitching machine began to whir. It was a spinning rubber wheel with a ball feeder. The pitches were going to come quickly, without warning. "It's been a while," I said. "I haven't even warmed up."

"No excuses!" Macy yelled. "If you hit every pitch, I'll introduce you to one of my girlfriends."

I looked up at her just as the first pitch zipped by. Everyone laughed. Echo leaned toward the chain link. "Guess you're stuck with hand lotion and an old sock, huh?"

"No one understands me but my socks."

The second pitch came in much too fast for me and I swung so late I shouldn't have bothered. I was more prepared for the third pitch; even though my swing was still rusty, I managed to tip it foul behind me. It felt good.

"Foul!" Macy yelled. "Somebody help this boy!" She

yanked open the door and marched in. There was something about her expression that told me it was all in fun, so
I shrugged, handed her the bat, and stepped out of the cage.

The next pitch whizzed by while we were switching
spots. When Macy stepped up to the plate, her stance was
all wrong: knock-kneed and tilted too far to the right. Her
skinny little hands were too far down the bat and too far
apart. She obviously wasn't a player or a fan.

"Put them into the upper corners," Jon said. The next
pitch came in even before he'd finished his sentence. Macy
chopped it into the upper left corner. "Other side," Jon said.
She hit the next pitch into the upper right corner. "Left corner." She did it. "Right corner." She did that, too.

I stared at her, dumbstruck. Her stance and grip were all
wrong, but her swing was quick and scarily accurate. If they'd
asked me to put money down, I'd think I was being scammed.

"Left si—no, right side!"

She tried to change her swing as the ball came in, but she
hit it a foot and a half from the upper right corner. "No fair!"

Jon laughed, and so did she. "Boring!" she exclaimed. She
dropped the bat as she walked out of the cage.

"My turn." Echo rushed into the cage and grabbed a bat
just as another pitch zipped by.

I was about to ask Macy where she'd learned to hit like
that, but she ran to Jon, threw her arms around his waist
and tilted her head back for a kiss. I turned away from them,
went to the picnic table and picked up a couple of fries.

Payton was already standing there. Just as I was trying
to figure out how to ask what he knew about Jon's cure, he
spoke: "You're wondering why she's with me."

"What's that, big guy?"

"You're wondering why a woman like Echo is with a guy like me. Well, she *is* with me. Don't forget it."

It was one thing for a cute girl to bust my chops, but a challenge from a guy like Payton had to be answered. If he thought he was going to make me back down, he was in for an unhappy surprise, not to mention a broken bone or two. "Don't forget what, now? Because I'm not listening to a word you say."

That was what he wanted to hear. He squared off against me and stuck his finger in my face. "Maybe you should clean out your ears, asshole."

"Hey!" Jon called. "What's going on?"

I didn't look away from Payton. "Dude is telling me all about how great his relationship is."

Jon rounded on Payton. "This again? Payton, he's my friend, and we're celebrating tonight. Can't you—"

"I'm waiting!"

We all turned to the batting cage. Echo was standing at the plate, bat cocked at a crooked angle, waiting for a pitch.

Payton took a token from Jon's hand, mumbled an apology, then walked over to feed the machine. Jon turned to me. "Ray, I'm sorry. Payton's cool; you don't have to be scared of him—"

"No sweat. I wasn't."

"Shit. Look. I don't care what Payton says, and I don't care what Barbara says, either. Or my parents. You and I were friends for a long time, and what happened was hard on both of us."

"Harder on you."

"Yeah, it was, but you know what would have made it easier? Having my best friend around. I kinda missed you, buddy."

I had no idea how to respond. I'd come back to town knowing I'd have to make my peace with Jon, but the last thing in the world I expected was for him to make it so easy. "I, uh... I never had a chance to say I was sorry—"

"And now you don't have to! Seriously, don't. Like I said, everything is different now."

Jon was my oldest friend in the world, and he had every reason to hate me. I owed him a debt I could never repay. But here he was acting like none of that mattered. A flush of gratitude ran through me that was so strong it made me feel dizzy.

"Okay," I said. "Everything does seem different. You're right. So, Jon... What happened? How did you get this cure?"

CHAPTER FOUR

"Aw, Ray, if there's one person who deserves an answer to that, it's you, but I can't, buddy. I promised. This person gave me my legs back, right? And all I had to do in return was not tell anyone who I got it from or how it was done."

"That's cool. No problem."

"It's the *only thing* the guy asked in return."

"Hey, I take the question back. No problem."

He was about to say something else when there was a loud clang from the cage. Jon spun around with surprising speed and stalked over to the chain link.

Echo crouched at the plate with her butt out way too far and one of her feet almost out of the batters box. She didn't know how to stand any better than Macy did. The next pitch came in and she smacked it. The ball flew in a line drive straight at the pitching machine, struck it at the top of the rubber wheel and rebounded straight into the air.

"Hey!" Jon yelled. "Don't you break that machine!"

"Relax," Payton said. "She didn't do it on purpose."

The next pitch came in and Echo hit it onto the exact same place. Jon threw himself wildly against the chain link. "DON'T YOU BREAK THAT MACHINE!"

Echo didn't even glance at him. The next pitch came in

and she hit it squarely on the pitching machine's guard, two inches lower than her previous shots.

She gave Jon a sly look, and he burst out laughing. That was what she was waiting for; she tossed the bat aside and said: "Your turn."

Jon went into the cage like a man entering a chapel.

Echo turned to Payton. "Put a token in for the man, hon, then get us some more cheese and chicken."

"More?" He dropped the token into the machine, then went inside to do as he was told.

Macy and Echo turned toward me. Each took one of my arms, and I let them push me back to the bench until I was sitting down and they were standing over me.

"I was Jon's therapist," Macy said. "From before. He talked about you all the time. Ray this. Ray that."

"So where have you been?" Echo asked.

"Shoveling snow at the North Pole." It came out sharper than I'd planned, but I didn't like the way they were trying to stand me down, even if it was just for fun. "Are therapists allowed to date their patients?"

"Nope, but once he was cured we didn't need to hide it anymore."

"And he's a big improvement over the charity case she was dating before," Echo added. "I'll bet there's a lot of job security in arctic snow shoveling."

"Smart bet."

Macy leaned closer to me and lowered her voice. "Jon said you were in jail."

I looked away from them, into the parking lot where Jon's van was parked. I didn't want to have this conversation.

"Only the last few years. And before you ask what it was like or why I was sent up, don't. Please."

"What was it like?" Macy asked.

"Why were you sent up?" Echo asked.

I didn't look at them. Being challenged and tested was an everyday part of prison life, and my instincts told me that I should back them off. But I wasn't living a prison life anymore. You think you've paid your dues, but you haven't.

"My friend started a bar fight. He was hitting on a woman while her husband was sitting right there. The woman turned out to be the lieutenant governor's sister-in-law, but we didn't know that at the time. When the husband shoved him, I jumped in and popped him a good one."

"Gotta tell you," Echo said. "I'm on the husband's side in this."

"Yeah, but the other guy was my friend."

"You went to jail for a single punch?"

"I went to jail because I put a guy in the hospital. Plus, the cops thought my buddy and me were boosting cars, and they threatened serious jail time if I didn't testify against my friends."

Echo folded her arms over her chest. "You should have testified."

"I'll remember you said that if shit ever comes down. Look, did you see the picture Jon had today? His mom took that on the day of the intramural championships. It seemed pretty important when we were 12."

"And you hit the winning home run off of Jon."

I was surprised Macy knew about that. I had almost forgotten it myself. Jon really had talked about me. "The thing is, after the ball sailed over the fence, Jon smiled at me. He'd just lost the game, but he was proud of what I'd done. He was always on my side."

"And you spent a lot of time at his house," Macy added. "He said his mom fed you breakfast every day before school, and lots of dinners, too."

A sudden vision of Jon's mother came into my mind—her leaning over me, smiling, as she set a bowl of cereal in front of me. Across the table, Bingo would complain about "cold soup" but I loved it. I'd watched Mrs. Burrows carefully, searching for some sign that she resented me and my space at the table, but I never saw one. "There wasn't a lot of breakfast at my house. There wasn't much dinner, either. Most of the home-cooked meals I ate were at Jon's house. That's where I learned that people can have normal conversation when they eat with their family. His backyard is where his father taught me to throw a baseball. When his kid sister misbehaved, I saw how they..." I almost said *punished misbehaving kids* but nothing that happened to her met my family's definition of *punishment*.

"So it wasn't just Jon, then," Echo cut in. "You were friends with the whole fam."

"Yes, I was."

Macy nodded, thoughtful. "And a few months after that game, you shot him."

"What?" Echo said. "Seriously? You're the one who shot Jon?"

"It was an accident, of course, right?" Macy's tone was sympathetic; I had never gotten much sympathy from people who knew the story and I sure as hell didn't want it now.

She continued: "Boys and guns in the same house, no safety training, no trigger locks, no gun safe. *I know* whose fault it was that Jon was shot, even though Jon's family laid all the blame on Ray."

I could remember the sound of the gun going off, and the sight of the blood, but what I remembered most of all was my refusal to believe that Jon had been shot and my own desperate search for an excuse that would make it someone else's fault. "Some debts can never be repaid."

Everything is different now. I walked away from them and started toward the batting cage, where Jon was still hitting balls. Above the canvas, in a neat line along the top of the fence, was a perfect line of baseballs wedged into the chain link. Jon smacked another one and I saw the metal deform as the ball slammed into it, sticking in place.

I turned to Macy and Echo. "What is going one with the four of you?"

"Four?" Echo answered, smirking. "Payton's an athlete. He can't afford to 'risk' his body."

Macy sniffed at the air like bloodhound. "God, what is that smell?" Then she spun and hopped onto the picnic table. "Trouble."

Echo sprang up beside her. The gate of the batting cage banged open as Jon dropped the bat and joined them. All three stood tall, as alert as prairie dogs, staring into the parking lot. Payton emerged from the restaurant with an armful of food but as soon as he saw the others, he scattered the baskets onto the table and climbed up beside them.

I followed their gaze and saw a tattered silhouette standing beside Jon's van. "I saw that guy outside your house."

"That's not a guy," Echo said. "It's a woman."

"We should call the police," Payton said. "She may be another kook with a gun."

No one took out their phones. "Why can't people leave us alone?" Macy asked.

I stepped in front of them. "Jon, I'll check it out. Don't worry, buddy. I won't let anything bad happen to you."

Jon glanced me. He seemed startled and pleased.

Macy took his arm. "We'll wait inside by the front door. You guys bring the van around." Jon tossed his keys to Echo.

"We should call the police." Payton repeated.

It seemed like a reasonable suggestion for seat-belt people but the others ignored him again. Echo started toward the van. "Come on."

Jon and Macy retreated inside. Payton and I hurried after Echo.

The stranger side-stepped away from the van. As she entered the light, I saw by the shape of her face that she was indeed a woman, though I had no idea how Echo could tell from so far away. She had red hair cut very short and wore a black fireman's jacket with reflective green and silver stripes. At first glance I thought she was homeless, but then I saw her hiking boots were expensive and looked fairly new.

Then I came close enough to see that her neck and wrists were covered with tattoos. Beneath her big jacket, she was tiny, almost frail. It was hard to judge her age at night and at that distance, but I guessed she was around 40. Maybe she was another terminally-ill patient trying to get her hands on Jon's mysterious cure.

She watched us approach, her posture tense; I could see we weren't going to have a friendly chat.

Payton held out his hands. "Can I help you?" His voice was deeper than usual. The woman didn't seem intimidated.

She opened her fireman's jacket. I froze. If she started shooting, we were too far away to rush her and too close to run.

But she didn't take out a gun. She wore a vest covered with ribbons, all alligator-clipped to her clothes and grouped by color. She plucked a white one free and threw it at Payton.

The clip struck his chest and bounced off. He caught it and held it up. The ribbon was decorated with the same design I'd seen on the tree outside Jon's house.

"You aren't infected," the woman said. Her voice was small and girlish, but also strangely flat.

She plucked another white ribbon and threw it at Echo, who snatched it out of the air. The design immediately flared, turned black, and gave off a jet of black steam and iron gray sparks. Echo threw the ribbon onto the asphalt.

"But you are," the woman said.

CHAPTER FIVE

Payton's anger was quick. "Hey! You could have hurt her!" He stepped toward the woman and reached for her arms.

The tiny woman grabbed him with both hands and pressed him over her head. It wasn't some kind of judo move—I'd seen plenty of those. She simply muscled Payton into the air.

Then, in the same motion, she tossed him aside. He landed hard on the parking lot, six feet away.

"What the hell?" I blurted out. I couldn't have picked up Payton that way but somehow she had done it. It must have been adrenaline. Must have been.

Echo crouched low, facing off with the woman. They looked as if things were going to get deadly serious.

Hadn't I just gotten out of prison for a fight that got out of hand? I stepped between them. "Let's calm down a minute."

The little woman didn't like that advice. She stepped toward me and threw a punch. I slipped it easily. She threw another punch, then another, but I danced away from her. She had a hitch in her shoulder that telegraphed her swing and she kept aiming up at my jaw—she'd have had better luck going for my stomach. It was closer to her level.

I tried not to think about what she'd done to Payton, and how it would feel if she did it to me. "Come on, lady, calm down. Calm down."

But she kept coming, her face grim. Then I struck something with the back of my heel and fell against a lamp post.

The corner of the woman's mouth twitched upward as she threw an overhand right.

I ducked, barely dropping under her punch and sprawling to the side. Her fist hit the metal post with an absurdly loud *thoom*. She had to have broken every bone in her hand.

A blue ribbon had been crudely sewn into the back of her coat. It had another strange, compelling design on it. Acting on an impulse I didn't quite understand, I tore it free, then scrambled away from her.

My shadow was moving strangely. I looked up and saw the light pole toppling over.

I rolled out of its way. The woman jumped aside, too, barely getting out from under it in time. The metal post crashed against the asphalt, scattering broken glass.

"What the hell is going on?" I said to no one at all. None of this made sense. She couldn't have destroyed a metal lamp post with one punch, could she? She couldn't have felled it like a tree with a right cross. It had to have been damaged already. It had to be a set up.

I didn't know what to believe, but I knew I wasn't the victim of a prank. I looked up at that strange, grim-faced little woman and repeated myself in a voice gone shamefully high with fear and confusion. "What's going on?"

She came toward me, supremely confident and completely

pitiless. "You picked the wrong friends," she said in her tiny voice.

Payton slammed into her from the side. It was a full-body blind-side tackle worthy of an all-star college linebacker. He drove the woman into the asphalt and for a moment she disappeared beneath his huge frame. My hair stood on end at the sound of it; I thought Payton had murdered her right in front of me. Then momentum carried him over and she rolled on top of him.

"You, too," she said, her high, flat voice still calm.

She held Payton's hand against the ground and punched his elbow. His sleeve went flat beneath her fist. She sprang to her feet and stomped on one of his ankles. It, too, flattened beneath her.

Payton drew a breath to scream, but the woman shrugged out of her jacket—I glimpsed a huge, complex glyph drawn into the lining—then she draped it over the big man. Payton's eyes and mouth suddenly glowed, and he fell unconscious.

Echo slammed into the woman from behind, knocking her off her feet and smashing her head-first into the side of Jon's van. The panel buckled under the impact. Echo landed a blindingly fast punch to the woman's kidneys.

The woman threw her elbow back, but Echo darted away. Then she pounced again, bouncing the woman off the side of the van and rocking the vehicle a second time.

I stared at them, unable to believe what I was seeing. Jon's van looked like it had been side-swiped by a car, but the little woman seemed unhurt. Echo whipped her fists against the woman's face and neck so fast I could barely see her move. She was a blur, but the stranger was taking the punches

without much effect. She covered up to defend herself, then
tried to counter with a punch of her own.

She couldn't connect. She was moving at human speed
while Echo had gone far beyond that.

I struggled to my feet, feeling dizzy. Either I was going
crazy, or something terrifying, miraculous and obscene was
happening right here in the parking lot. It was as if the veil
had been parted just a bit, and I was seeing the freakishness
and fury at the heart of the world. I hoped I was hallucinating. I hoped I was going crazy.

The little woman threw a punch at Echo, missed, and
struck the side-view mirror. It tore off the side of the van,
spinning over my head and out into the darkness.

Something sharp struck my cheek. I brushed at it. It was
a tiny sliver of glass, beaded with blood.

The sliver fell away. I wasn't holding the blue ribbon
anymore and I wasn't sure what I'd done with it. I studied
the tiny red smear on my index finger. That's real. My blood
was real. The scratch on my cheek, smaller than a shaving
cut, was real.

I looked back at Echo and the strange little woman. Real.
I wasn't going crazy or hallucinating. I was seeing this, and I
had to come to grips with it if I was going to survive.

Echo landed a kick on the woman's belt buckle, slamming
her against the van. The woman grabbed the sliding side
door and ripped it free, swinging the huge hunk of metal
at Echo.

Echo vaulted over it.

The woman let go of the door. It flew out of her hand,

skidding across the asphalt in a shower of sparks, straight for Payton's body.

I leaped at him and rolled him out of its path. It skidded by us, grinding against the asphalt. I stopped my roll suddenly—the exposed, sputtering wires of the shattered lamp post inches from my face.

Echo kicked at the woman's legs, knocking her to the ground. The woman pulled a red ribbon from her vest and threw it into the air. It burst into a dazzling flash of light in front of Echo's face.

Blinded, Echo staggered back, her hands like claws over her eyes. The woman rolled into a crouch and charged.

Echo took a deep breath through her nose, then struck out with both fists. She hit the woman full on the chest, sending her tumbling backwards.

She struck her head against the fallen metal lamp post and came to a stop two feet from where I was lying.

"Dammit!" she said, more out of frustration than pain. Then she did the thing I feared most. She noticed me.

"Did you think I forgot about you?" she asked. She plucked a white ribbon and threw it at me. It struck my chest and flashed silver.

The woman was startled. "What the hell?"

I threw the ribbon back at her. She caught it easily, and the design flashed silver a second time.

Then all her tattoos and ribbons glowed silver, spilling out of her sleeves and cuffs—even through the fabric of her clothes, as though she was covered with glowing tattoos. For a moment, she shone like a star and was beautiful.

Then the light faded, and she became shabby and merciless again.

"Wait here for me," she said, then stood and whipped her coat onto her shoulders.

Echo rubbed her eyes and blinked her vision clear. She and the woman charged each other. The woman threw a red ribbon at Echo.

Echo ducked below it, charging forward on all fours for a moment. The ribbon passed harmlessly over her. Then she sprang back to her feet just as it exploded in a burst of fire.

The force of the blast lifted Echo into the air. She collided with the little woman, her clothes burning.

They fell backwards onto the asphalt. The woman wrapped her arms around Echo. "Gotcha!" she cried.

Echo went wild, frantically lashing out with her fists and nails at the stranger's face and neck, but the woman didn't let go. She drew back her fist and punched Echo once in the stomach.

Echo collapsed against the asphalt, stunned. The woman sprang to her feet and shrugged off her jacket.

I ran toward them. I had no idea what I was supposed to do, but I ran anyway.

The woman draped her jacket over Echo and pinned her arms beneath it. Lights flashed in Echo's eyes and mouth. She screamed like she was on fire.

I charged at the tiny woman, lowering my shoulder down the way Payton had. But at the last second, I eased off—I couldn't bring myself to use my full strength against her, no matter what I'd just seen.

She saw me coming and braced herself. I bounced off

her as if she was a tractor tire and fell back on the asphalt. I moved my shoulder just to reassure myself that I could. I was useless.

"Dammit," the woman snapped. "I'm trying to cure her."

That made me pause. Was Echo sick? *Infected,* the woman had said. Was Jon infected, too?

Echo screamed again, but the sound was strangled as a bulge appeared at the top of her throat, moving toward her mouth. She looked like a snake vomiting an egg.

Echo's mouth opened wide and a pair of long black filaments emerged from it. They twitched and wavered like long grass in a hurricane. Then a set of needle-sharp black points appeared, pushing out of her throat. They were all connected, I suddenly realized, like a small tree branch. Another set appeared, then another, like thorn bushes growing out of her. They were each half as thick as my little finger, and they curled up out of Echo's throat and braced themselves on her lips.

Legs. They were legs. Something was crawling out of her.

Echo thrashed. The little woman could barely hold her still.

"If he gave you a weapon," the woman said, "use it!"

I didn't have a weapon. I didn't even have the ability to move.

Something wet and the color of new phlegm pushed past Echo's teeth. It looked like a grub or a maggot, but with those strange, crooked, spiny legs. And it was as big as a cat.

Wings uncurled from its back and began beating the air. Blood sprayed off them. Echo fell still.

The thing turned toward me and leaped.

CHAPTER SIX

I fell back. The creature landed on my chest, needle-sharp legs stabbing through my jacket. It snapped at my mouth with pincers and—

There was a tremendous flood of energy from the pocket of my jacket—it felt like I was hiding a high-powered generator in there. The worm was flung straight up into the air, and the energy subsided.

The creature beat its wings and stopped itself falling. It glanced at the tiny woman then turned and flew away, struggling to stay aloft.

"You let it get away?" the woman said, incredulous. "Why didn't you attack?"

I knew I should have answered her somehow, but I couldn't tear my eyes off the retreating creature.

It had been inside Echo. That *thing* had been inside her. I thought back to the batting cage—to Echo's amazing quickness and coordination. Macy had been just as gifted. And so had Jon.

Did Jon have one of those things inside him, too?

I reached into my pocket and felt what had given me that tremendous surge of power. I'd dropped the stolen blue ribbon in there at some point without realizing it.

"Hey, dipshit!" the woman said to me. "Is this your first time? It can't be."

I turned to her. The streetlights shone directly onto her face and I got my first good look at her. She was younger than I'd originally thought, probably under 25. Her plain face looked delicate. She had no makeup, no hairstyle, no jewelry that I could see.

She had turned her attention to me and it was like being stared at by a live wire. She was full of power, and she was irresistible.

"My first time? Yes, it was." Echo was absolutely still. Her lips were split and torn from the passage of the creature but she wasn't bleeding. Her neck was misshapen and collapsed like an empty bag. "She's—"

"Cured," the woman said. "As cured as her kind can be. Let's get after that thing or I'll have to cure the whole damn city."

I knelt beside Echo. She couldn't be dead. I touched her chin and her head rolled toward me. A pool of blood spilled out of her mouth onto the parking stripe. I jumped back.

Damn.

The strange woman grabbed the back of my jacket and pulled me along. "Come on," she said. "We'll help the others later."

Somehow she had the idea that I was on her side. I craned my neck to look at Payton. He was still breathing. I wanted to run back into the bar and call an ambulance for him, but I didn't. I kept my mouth shut and did exactly what the woman told me to do.

She marched me toward a high fence at the edge of the lot. The woman was alert and careful, watching for the return of the creature. She didn't seem concerned with me.

I considered cold-cocking her, but she had already smacked her skull against the metal lamp post. If that hadn't hurt her, nothing I could manage would. I looked at the back of her head and neck, half-expecting to see a set of switches there. All she had were more tattoos.

"It looked weak to me," she said. "I don't think it could have gotten far. Keep your eyes peeled."

"Are you sure it went this way?"

"Can't you see the blood?" She pointed to the parking lot. I almost said no, but then I saw it: A line of dark droplets barely visible in the light of the distant street lamps.

"What are you, undercover?" she asked. "What have you found out?"

"The world is scarier than I thought."

"Funny." Her tone suggested that she hadn't laughed in years. "He didn't give you a weapon?"

"No, he didn't." I had no idea who "he" was, so my answer was an honest one.

"Where are the others?" she asked.

"I don't know."

"Jesus. He keeps you in the dark, doesn't he?"

"Oh, I'm in the dark, all right. What is that..." I couldn't say *creature* or *monster*. Those words were ridiculous. I was afraid that, as soon as I said the word *monster* aloud, I would stop believing everything I'd just seen. "...that thing?"

"Don't know. Don't care. It has a physical form now. Mostly. Let's just kill it and move on." We reached the fence.

The trail of blood continued on the other side. The worm had gone over here.

The woman grabbed the bottom of the chain link and pulled up. The metal groaned and warped. When she was done, the fence was twisted enough to allow us to slip beneath it. The thing had gone over; I was going under.

"Tell me what you found out so far," the woman said. "How many more were there like her?"

That was a question I did not want to answer. Or was she testing me? She had seen me at the house earlier. She probably knew about Jon already, but not that Macy and Echo had apparently received the same cure.

If you could call the thing in Echo's body a "cure."

It didn't matter. I wasn't going to inform on my oldest friend, or anyone else. I was loyal.

I still had to tell her something, though. I couldn't just lie, not without knowing how much she already knew. Hell, I still wasn't clear on what I "knew" myself.

The stranger had already slipped under the warp in the fence. I followed, taking my time as I slid on my belly over the dirt. I considered saying that the mysterious, non-weapon-distributing "he" deserved to hear the information first, but I just didn't know enough about the situation. What if "he" was this woman's boss? Her ex-husband? Her—

"Well?" she said. I had delayed too long.

A heavy piece of metal fell somewhere across the yard.

"That way," she said. I went in the direction she indicated, creeping around a low brick building while she went the other way. I was glad for every step that put distance between us.

The lights were now so far away that I couldn't tell if I was still following the trail of blood. I had to detour around a pile of something I couldn't make out in the dark. I laid my hand on it and immediately recognized a brake pad. They were auto parts. I didn't know for sure if the yard was still operating, but the rusty grime under my fingers suggested not.

I inched forward carefully, not wanting to trip and cut open my head on a lump of metal, and not wanting to run into either the strange woman or the... *thing*. The stolen blue ribbon had repelled the creature, but would it work a second time? Better not to gamble on it.

I couldn't hear the tattooed woman's footsteps anymore. I looked behind me; the parking lot was well lit and there were no silhouettes between it and me. Time to get the hell out of here.

There was a groan from up ahead. It was a man's voice, hoarse and trembling. I stupidly edged around a wrecked car toward the sound.

The old man lay on the asphalt, half-lit in a shaft of reflected light. My vision had adjusted well enough to make out his general form. He lay stretched out on his side, facing me, as though he'd tripped over one of the empty bottles by his feet.

I moved toward him. "Come on, dude. This is a bad place for you to be right now." God, he stank like a urinal, but I grabbed his arm and tried to lift him to his feet. With luck, I'd be able to get him back through the warp in the fence before I passed out from the stench.

As the old man shifted position, the reflected street light fell on the *thing* clinging to the back of his tattered jacket.

I grabbed the old guy's jacket and tore it off his shoulders. The huge worm jumped backwards before I could throw the jacket over it. It snapped open its wings and fluttered a foot or two off the ground.

I yanked at the old man's arm, dragging him across the concrete. The worm fluttered toward us, zeroing in on the old man. I heard a scuffled footstep behind us and turned to see the tiny woman approaching. She had a green ribbon in her hand.

"Wait!" I shouted. "Just wait!"

She didn't wait. She threw the ribbon straight at me.

I dropped to the ground, thinking I should have run away when I had the chance.

The worm fluttered toward me and the old man both, but the ribbon intercepted it, striking it dead on. There was an explosion of green fire. The *thing* burned up to nothing without making a sound.

A blast of icy air struck me just before I was engulfed by green flames.

But they didn't hurt. Again, the ribbon in my pocket hummed with power. Flames surrounded me, licking against my skin, my clothes, even my eyes, but they felt like a wintry breeze. Nothing painful.

The homeless man beneath me wrenched in agony, then seemed to dissolve. The flames suddenly receded.

The old man had been burned down to a pile of smoking bones. He hadn't even had time to scream.

There were greasy ashes stuck to the front of my clothes. I tried to brush them away and they stuck to my hands. My nostrils were filled with the stink of burned oil and charred meat. Revulsion flooded through me as I looked down at my palms, and that revulsion immediately changed to rage.

I leaped to my feet. "You killed him!"

The woman turned and started to walk away. "I saw the creature warded away from you. I assumed you were protected."

The stolen ribbon in my pocket... No. No, I couldn't think about that yet. The woman was still walking away. Hadn't she heard me? I followed, determined to make her understand. "You killed that old man! If you'd given us another second and I would have gotten him away."

She waved me off. "This was easier."

"EASIER!" I grabbed her elbow and spun her around.

Mistake. The woman slapped her hand over my face. She was small and as light as a child, but her hand squeezed me like a vice. Her strength astonished and terrified me. She could squeeze until my teeth broke off and fell into my throat. She could push until the hinge of my jaw shattered and the bones stabbed into my brain.

"If you don't change your tone," she said, "I'm going to mess up that pretty face of yours. I'm a *peer* in the society. *You* don't talk to *me* that way."

She grabbed my arm and marched me around the building. We weren't going to the hole in the fence; she walked straight up to the gate, grabbed the padlock holding it shut and twisted. The lock burst. A few seconds later, she was marching me down the street away from Jon, Macy and Payton.

"Where are you taking me?" My voice sounded thin and frightened. I hate being afraid.

She didn't answer.

Damn. If only I hadn't lost my temper. If only I hadn't tried to save that man's life. He would have been just as dead and I would have gotten away from this crazy fucked-up woman. For a little while, at least.

I wanted to shoot questions at her: What the hell was she and how could she do what she did? What had come out of Echo? What the hell was going on? But I kept my mouth shut because she'd mistaken me for someone else, someone in this society of hers. She seemed to think I was a junior member, something below "peer." If she found out I was nobody, she could do to me what she did to Payton....

No.

To hell with that. This strange, tiny, tattooed woman scared the piss out of me, and I hate being afraid.

"I changed my mind," I said, unable to hold back. "It's all right with me that you murdered that guy *in cold blood.* I'm totally cool with that. Seriously. Why don't we head down to the Millionaire's Club? You could probably burn a dozen guys to death for no damn good reason. Wouldn't that be fun?"

Her only response was to set her jaw. I was pissing her off, which was a stupid thing to do, but damn it felt good. Was that good feeling was worth dying for? Apparently.

She stopped at a motorcycle parked at the curb. It was a blue and gray BMW R1200GS—a nice bike and fairly new, but it was scuffed, scratched and generally misused and neglected. "On the back."

"And if I don't?"

"Then I'll tear your legs off and throw them up on the roof over there."

Her tiny, pale eyes stared at me and her lipless mouth was set in a thin, tight line. She was ready to do it and I didn't have anyone to back me up. I shrugged and climbed on the back.

She climbed on in front and kick-started the engine. "Hold onto my jacket," she said. I did. She peeled out of the street and onto the empty road.

Echo's corpse, Payton's mangled body, and Jon's wrecked van got farther and farther away. I had no idea what I'd say to him if I lived long enough to see him again. Would he believe that Echo had that creature inside her? Would he believe that this woman had forced me to come with her? Would he believe how strong and fast the women had been?

It was ridiculous. All these people needed were colorful spandex suits and they could fold themselves into the pages of a comic book.

I shifted my grip on the back of the woman's jacket, mainly to wipe greasy ashes off my hands. She should be the one wearing evidence of murder, not me.

Because, Christ, I'd been in town one day—one damn day—and I was already fleeing the scene of a double murder. I suddenly barked out with laughter as I pictured Karl's face when I told him what happened. I had ashes on my jacket—and probably Echo's blood from the thing's beating wings—and a story no one would believe. Probably it would be best if this woman broke my damn head open; it'd save me from a life sentence.

But would Jon believe me? Maybe this happened to him twice a week.

I needed to find him. I needed to get away from this

woman and tell him everything that had happened, whether he believed it or not. Maybe it would save his life.

We zoomed around a corner and she swerved across the double yellow line for a dozen yards. She was going way too fast, and the wind in my hair made me acutely aware that I wasn't wearing a helmet. Neither was she, of course, but she could probably drive into a brick wall and walk away unharmed. I hung on for my life, too tall for the small bike and whipped by the chill wind.

After a few more hair-raising turns, we pulled into the driveway of a hotel. We passed the sign before I had a chance to look at it and she braked hard at the entrance.

A valet took her key and gave her a ticket. She swung her leg off the bike and gave me a hard look. I followed her inside.

The hotel lobby was the most beautiful man-made place I had ever seen in my life. The floors were marble tile. The desk looked like it was trimmed with mahogany. To the right, a three marble steps led to a genteel little circle of plush leather couches. Beyond that, a longer flight of marble stairs led to a restaurant.

The tattooed woman marched straight through the room without a sideways glance. If she was impressed by our surroundings, she didn't show it.

I felt wildly out of place in my sooty clothes. The woman looked like a street weirdo, with her tattered fireman's jacket hanging open to reveal the swarm of ribbons clipped to her vest. We made quite a spectacle for the suit and tie crowd. Not that there was a crowd. I glanced up at the clock. It was 1:45 in the morning. Uncle Karl had probably already taken my things from my apartment and dumped them on the back yard.

A tall, slender man with a receding hairline stepped out from behind the concierge desk. He was dressed in a stylish black suit and wore a golden name tag so small I couldn't read it. I had a moment of absurd envy for that name tag.

"Ms. Powliss," the man said. His tone and expression were full of snobby contempt. "The service elevators are this way."

Ms. Powliss ignored him and marched straight to the stand of elevators against the back wall. I was grateful to have a name to hang on her. It made her seem almost human.

The concierge glanced at me but, before I could mouth the word "Help" or "Call the police," he turned away. I looked at the front entrance. What if I ran for it? What if I simply shouted *nine-one-one*?

I didn't do any of those things. As if she could read my mind, Ms. Powliss grabbed my jacket and dragged me into an opening elevator. Besides, I had no idea what she would do to the people who came to help me. She'd killed that drunk without a second thought. Would she do the same to the bellhops and cleaning staff here? And while I had no great love for cops, including my uncle, I didn't want to see them burned alive.

She pushed a button. We rode up alone. If she'd taken me to a secluded spot, I'd have known she was planning to kill me. But a four-star hotel? I figured I was either about to meet someone important or we were going to do some hot-tubbing.

The doors dinged open. Ms. Powliss lead me down a wide, tastefully decorated corridor. The wallpaper was covered with lemon-colored stripes and there were small tables with vases of fresh flowers against the wall. I supposed there was no point in smashing a vase over her head. Maybe I should offer her a daisy and kill her with kindness.

"Are we going to order some raisin toast?" I asked, trying to hide my growing fear. "Cause I'd love some raisin toast." She wasn't amused.

She stopped at a door and thumped on it hard enough to make it rattle. I couldn't tell if she was angry or if she couldn't handle all that strength.

The door swung open, revealing a man in his early fifties. His skin was pale and his eyes were vague and sleepy. His blond hair was long and fine, hanging limp around his sagging face. His shirt—he wasn't wearing pajamas, even at this hour—was pale blue silk and he wore a waistcoat embroidered with elaborate stitching. The designs reminded me of Ms. Powliss's tattoos and ribbons. His pants were cream colored and tailored. He'd probably been handsome when he was younger, but now he looked all used up. He looked weak. And rich.

"Annalise, how good to see you," he said. I couldn't place his accent. Something European, but I'm not much for accents. "How goes the hunt, my dear?"

"I don't report to you." Annalise shoved me toward the door. The European released the door knob, letting me bang it open with my shoulder. I stumbled a few feet into the hotel room, trying to keep my balance.

"Callin, keep your wooden men out of my way. I nearly killed him. And next time you put someone in the field, let me know first."

"That's interesting," Callin said. "Because I do not have any wooden men."

"What?" For the first time, Annalise's tough exterior broke, replaced by genuine confusion and worry.

Callin looked me over carelessly. "Not since Hubert died in '93."

Annalise's expression turned back to anger quickly. "You're lying," she said. "No one else would send a wooden man here without telling us."

"He doesn't belong to me," Callin said. "Are you sure he's one of us?"

"Look." She tossed a white ribbon at me.

I tried to duck out of the way, thinking she was about to set me on fire again. The ribbon homed in and struck my shoulder. The glyph on it immediately glowed silver.

"See?" Annalise said. "He's carrying our—"

"Before you say anything imprudent," Callin interrupted, "you are not missing something, are you my dear?"

Annalise grabbed the tail of her jacket and pulled it. She saw the torn threads where the stolen ribbon used to be. "Well, I'll be damned," she said. When she looked up, her expression was icy and dangerous. "Sorry to bother you, Callin. I'll take him and go." She took a step forward.

Damn. I backed away. Maybe there was a fire exit in the next room, or—

"I will handle it, child," Callin said. He shut the door in her face.

I stared at the blank white door and the man beside it in shock. I expected Annalise to kick it open any second, but it didn't happen. Either she didn't want to raise a racket in this hotel, or she had to defer to the sickly-looking guy beside me.

Callin leaned against the door and watched me with a placid smile. He didn't look very scary, but neither had Annalise before she'd started tearing off car doors with her bare hands. And if the two of them were at odds, maybe I could use Callin against Annalise and escape them both. Maybe I could even find out who they were. Jon needed to know.

"So," I said, breaking the silence. "Will you tell me what is going on?"

No answer. Callin simply stood and stared at me. He looked a little dazed, as if he was drunk. I glanced around, giving the guy time to think of something to say. The room was tastefully decorated with flowers and cream-colored lace. Everything was refined and effeminate, as though it had been put together for an elderly aunt. There was a hall, probably leading to a bedroom, and a balcony. We were too high up for me to get out that way.

"Okay," I said. "That's cool. Thanks for helping me get away from her. I'll be going now."

I stepped around Callin and tried the door. It wouldn't budge. The knob wouldn't even turn.

"Hey, man. Would you unlock this? Please?" I was trying to be polite but it didn't seem to be doing any good. I remembered Echo lying dead on the asphalt and the smoking bones of the old drunk. I needed to get the hell away before something similar happened to me. "Can't you understand me? Let me out."

Still no answer. Callin didn't even move, except to watch my movements.

"No? Then how about in here?" I strode quickly down a short hall into the bedroom. It, too, was pale and tasteful. It was almost ghostly.

And there was no door, just another balcony.

Callin strolled into the room, his body language casual and confident. While watching me very closely, he moved to the desk, closed a leather-bound journal and slid it into the top drawer.

I could have sprinted to the front door, but it was still locked. "Look, this doesn't have to get ugly. I just want to leave. All right?" I couldn't be more reasonable than that.

"You are no one's wooden man," Callin said.

I glanced over at the huge bed. "Nope. Not that there's anything wrong with that. I mean, I've been to jail."

"Annalise should have killed you after all."

That was too much. "You just said the wrong thing," I said with a bluster I did not feel. "Now open that door before—"

Time froze. My thoughts seemed to stand still. The room turned blinding white.

Then the world started moving again. I was on my back on the carpet. Callin had me by the throat.

"You will tell me everything," Callin said. He smiled, revealing a pair of long, needle-sharp fangs.

The world turned a blinding white again.

CHAPTER SEVEN

I opened my eyes. Sunlight. I was lying on my back and I could see sunlight. The light seemed important, although at the moment I couldn't figure out why. I also had a headache.

I was still alive.

I felt satin against my skin and sat up. I was lying in Callin's bed. "Oh, shit." I lifted the covers. I was completely naked—even my socks were gone.

"Oh, shit shit shit." My clothes lay on the bed table in a neatly-folded stack. I jumped out of bed and started pulling them on. Something rubbed against my neck as I pulled my shirt over my head. I checked in the mirror and saw a bandage below my left ear.

I slowly peeled the bandage back. Beneath it were two pin prick puncture wounds. Christ, was that a vampire bite?

There weren't enough *oh, shits* in the world for that.

I grabbed my jacket off the back of the chair and went through the pockets. The blue ribbon was gone, of course. Dammit. I didn't even know what it was or what it did, but it had saved my life twice. I wanted it back.

There was the desk. Callin had taken an open journal off the desk and hidden it in the top drawer. I tried to open it but it was locked.

I pulled the chair away and knelt beneath the desk. The bottom of the drawer was made of thin wood. I grabbed a letter opener and jammed it into the join at the front, then twisted.

The wood split with a crack that seemed as loud as a gun shot. Hesitation kills, so I pried further, splitting the bottom of the drawer free. The book slid out into my hand. There was a slipcase for it stuck in the back of the drawer. I yanked it out, too.

I rolled to my feet and pushed the chair under the desk. The splintered wood rested on the seat. It wouldn't be noticeable until someone tried to sit down. I hoped.

In the mirror, I caught another glimpse of my bandaged neck and peeled back the tape. Yes, the marks were still there. No, I hadn't dreamed it. No, I wasn't crazy—at least, I didn't feel crazy, whatever that meant.

The book's cover was made of plain black leather stretched over metal plates and it was creased from years of use. I opened it. It was filled with hand-written notes and diagrams.

This was a spell book. Diagrams like the ones on Annalise's ribbons were scattered over the pages, and at the top of each was a name for the spell. *Stepping through Shadows* was hand-written on one page. *Dead Speech* topped another.

I closed the book, and noticed a faint design scored into the front cover. I ran my hand over it, felt the ridges and also the power embedded in the symbol. The book itself had a spell on it.

Goosebumps ran up and down my back. Last night I'd been astonished to see people doing things I'd never seen outside of a comic book. Was this book an instruction manual to let me do the same crazy things?

I opened it again. It had been written in black ink with a ball point pen, so it wasn't as old as I'd thought at first. At least it wasn't human blood. It was also much thinner than the magic books I'd seen in the movies; it looked more like an old-fashioned diary.

I tried to read a random spell, but I was too exposed here in Callin's suite, too jumpy. I needed to go somewhere safe to study it.

The bedroom door was closed; was Callin in the front room or had he gone out for breakfast? I listened for him but didn't hear anything. If he was out there, I wouldn't be able to smuggle this book past him.

I slid the book into the leather slipcover and buckled it shut. Then I slid open the glass door and stepped onto the balcony. The city sprawled below, with Elliott Bay on one side and the gently sloping hills on the other. The sky was cloudless, for once, and Seattle was almost beautiful from so high up. A heavy black cloth had been draped over the railing, but I wasn't sure what it was for.

There was a parking garage below. The roof had painted yellow lines for cars but there were no vehicles on it, only a line of Dumpsters along the side of the building directly below me.

I held the book over the railing with the back cover flat to the ground, then dropped it. It didn't tumble, and none of the pages flew out. It struck flat on its cover in a pile of trash inside a Dumpster.

I hurried back into the room and slid the door shut as

quietly as I could. I grabbed my socks and shoes, sat on the bed and finished dressing. As I was tying the second shoe, the door opened and Callin entered.

He was wearing a robe the color of eggshells and a pair of pinstriped pajamas. He held a long envelope in his hand.

"I am glad you are awake," he said. "Would you please close the drapes?"

Beams of sunlight were shining through the glass doors, falling across my legs. I remembered the bite marks on my neck and concentrated on my shoelace. No way in hell was I going to shut out that light.

"Fine," Callin said, sounding more aggrieved than annoyed. He crossed the room, walking straight through the direct sunlight, and pulled the drapes closed.

"Disappointed?" he asked me. "Did you expect me to scream, fall to the floor and turn to ashes? Of course you are disappointed. But things are not always what they appear to be."

As a guy with two punctures below my ear, I wasn't interested in that conversation. I stood and pulled on my jacket. The wound on my neck was tender, but I ignored it.

I had a clear path to the door and I moved quickly toward it. Callin could stop me easily, but I had to try. Besides, the less time we spent near the broken desk, the better.

I heard Callin following into the front room. "Raymond, I have something to give you."

"Keep away from me!" I was startled and embarrassed by the fear in my voice. I grabbed the knob to the front door but couldn't turn it. It wouldn't open.

"Oh, stop being melodramatic," Callin said. "I have done nothing—"

I lunged for the fireplace and snatched up a poker. With all my strength, I slammed it over Callin's head.

"—permanent to you," He finished, as though nothing had happened. "I certainly didn't molest you in your sleep, if that's what you're so worried about. I simply had your clothes cleaned."

The poker was bent where it had struck Callin's skull. I tossed it aside. "You shouldn't have emptied my pockets."

"Lively one, aren't you? Hold still, if you can, and let me look at you," Callin said. He stepped toward me and reached for the bandage. I tried to back away but Callin grabbed my shoulders so quickly I didn't see him move. Then he shook me. Once. I felt the strength in that grip and held still.

Callin peeled back the bandage and inspected the wound, probing it with soft fingers. I could smell his flowery cologne and he still looked a little drunk. I glanced at the tall mirror beside the door. Callin's reflection stood beside mine, completely visible.

"More disappointment, yes?" Callin said. "You thought I might not reflect in a mirror? I hate to disenchant you, my dear boy, but I am not a *vampyre*. I do not shrink from crosses or sunlight, and I love garlic, when it is properly roasted."

"If you aren't a…" I couldn't bring myself to say this word, either.

"There are no more vampires," Callin said. He didn't pronounce it like Bela Lugosi this time. "Thanks to me. I have fought many evils over the centuries. Some of my battle scars are worse than others."

Centuries. I stared at him, wondering how much was truth and how much was bullshit.

Callin didn't glance up from the bandage. "These teeth—and the talents that come with them—are one of my scars. Like your injury, it is nothing—I don't even thirst for blood the way vampires do. The difference is that you will be perfectly healed by the end of the week and I will never be free of this curse."

Callin laid the bandage back into place, then pressed the tape against my skin. "I know a couple curses I'd like to lay on you," I said.

There was a crooked smile on the old man's face, as though he admired the empty tough talk I couldn't seem to hold inside.

"I have something to give you to help Jon and Macy." I was startled to hear him say those names. "Oh, yes, my boy. I stole more than your blood; otherwise I wouldn't have bothered. I have something to give you so that you can give it to your friends. It may, just possibly, save their lives."

"Does Annalise know you're going to save their lives?"

Callin shrugged. It was a smooth, practiced, careless motion, as though he'd dedicated years of his life to indifference. "What she knows or does not know is immaterial. Do you know what she is?"

I thought about Echo, about the smoking bones of the old drunk. I touched my jacket, feeling absurdly grateful that it had been cleaned. "One of the 'evils' you're supposed to be fighting. A killer."

"We are all killers, my dear boy. Annalise is wonderful— for her level of ability—but she is so drearily direct. But do you know what she *is*?"

I searched for the right word. *Centuries*, Callin had said. "A sorcerer." Just saying it aloud made me want to put on a pair of rubber Spock ears. "A sorcerer and a vigilante. And a peer in the society."

I was hoping for a reaction, but Callin's face betrayed nothing. "Told you about that, did she?"

"Told me what? I don't remember a thing about last night. Can I go now?"

"You may leave after you take this." Callin took the long envelope from the pocket of his robe and offered it to me. I didn't take it. "It is for Jon and Macy. Let them open it and look at it at the same time."

Damn. I wished I had a way to take back those names. "What will it do? Make them fall over dead?"

"Nothing so dramatic, I assure you. They will look at the paper inside and then they will come to see me. They will be compelled. They will also be protected, for a short while, from the influence of the creature inside them. Once they are here, I will try to help them."

"Really." Callin had been inside my mind. It made me feel exposed and vulnerable. It made me want to attack, no matter how useless that was.

"Don't be so cynical. You'll get lines at the corners of your mouth. Have you already forgotten what you learned about the nature of your friend Echo's...enhancements?"

"That was the first thing I decided to forget."

"Naturally. Jon and Macy likely have the same infestation. I don't know for certain if I can help them, but at least I will try. Annalise will simply kill them because that is the easiest way."

I remembered Annalise waving me off after killing the drunk. She was a killer, yeah, but that didn't mean Callin was much better.

"You're going to undo Jon's cure?" I said, suddenly realizing what Callin meant. "You mean you want to take away the use of his legs again?"

"I do."

"I can't do that. I really and truly cannot do that to him."

"He must lose his life or his ability to walk. Trust me, he has no other options."

"What if I opened this myself?" I snatched the envelope and held the corner as though I was about to tear it.

Callin didn't look concerned. "Then the effect will be wasted on you. I spent the entire night preparing that envelope. I will not go to so much trouble again. If you were to look at the paper inside, you would return here, to me." Callin gave me a crooked smile again. "Which I admit would not be so terrible."

Time to go. I took the envelope and headed for the door. Callin stepped around me and turned the knob. It opened for him as though it hadn't been locked at all.

"Let me give you something to think about, my boy," Callin said. "You are at a crossroads. If you avoid prison, you might live a life of car payments, lunch breaks and ever-larger television screens on which you watch other men play games. Perhaps you will find someone to share it with—a pretty woman who loves travel but eschews red meat. You could let the years pass, and then the decades, all the while allowing the memory of the conversation we are having right now become more remote in your mind, slowly convincing yourself that this opportunity wasn't real even while you resent yourself for fleeing it.

"Or you could return here and work for me. You are welcome here at any time. I could teach you many things about the world. And about yourself, too."

"I don't think your partner would like that."

"I do not have a partner. Annalise is a peer, and an unequal peer at that. She doesn't matter." Callin stepped closer. I could smell that flowery cologne again. "I've seen the inside of you," Callin continued. "I know you could be useful to me. You have a certain wakefulness that most men lack. I also know you are, as I said, at a crossroads in your life. Should you live as a model citizen, or fall back into a life below the law? Raymond, I am telling you there is a third path, hidden from most. You could be one of the few people to walk it, one of the few to touch real power and glimpse the vast, terrible beauty of the universe. I could do this for you. I could show you the world behind the world."

I stared at him. "Why me?"

"Well, it's not because you are some special Chosen One, that is certain. It's not because you are favored by destiny or the universe. In my considerable experience, there is no such thing. Any number of people might have felt the power inherent in the iron gate—the little blue ribbon Annalise was wearing—were they perceptive enough. You, however, were not only open to it at a time of great stress, you *reached out to seize it*!"

I remembered the way the ribbon protected me from Annalise's green fire and from the creature, too. "That was luck."

"There are many kinds of luck," Callin said. "Sometimes it is a random bolt out of an unblemished sky. Sometimes it is an opportunity well-exploited. Luck can be a clear eye quickly and accurately judging a situation. Afterwards, others will say 'That was a lucky thing you did,' because they don't truly understand. But I do. I am not being cute or clever when I say I could change your life. The choice is yours." Callin stepped back, clearing the way for me to go.

I started toward the elevator, looking at the wallpaper, the carpet, the flowers: everything looked hyper-real. I pressed the elevator button, feeling as though my head had been cracked open and examined. And it had.

I suspected Callin's offer would expire as soon as he noticed his broken desk drawer. Good. I didn't want that temptation. I'd seen what Annalise did to Payton, not to mention what she'd done to Echo and that old drunk—I didn't even know the guy's name. Did I want to sign up with them?

Shit no. I didn't have any romantic notions about going out and killing people. I'd just spent three years at Chino, and none of that talk impressed me.

Besides, Callin had locked me in that room, had stolen my blood and my thoughts, had put his *wet mouth* on me. Did he think I was going to forget all that and sign on to be his little helper? Fuck him.

To hell with the world behind the world. I was going to pay my debt and live a safe, normal life.

As soon as I took care of Jon's problem.

The elevator door opened. I went inside and pressed the button for the lobby. I still had the envelope in my hand.

We are all killers. Callin had said. *Annalise is so drearily direct.*

This is as cured as their kind gets, Annalise had said.

Trust me, Callin had said.

I held up the envelope. Whatever was in here, no way was I going to give it to Jon.

The elevator opened onto the magnificent lobby. My shoes squeaked as I walked across the tile to the front desk. The same concierge was still on duty. He glared at me.

"You know that woman I came in with last night?" I said.

For a moment, I thought he wouldn't answer. Finally, he said: "I'm aware of her."

I pretended his expression wasn't pissing me off. "Callin wants you to give her this next time she shows up." I took a pen from the desk and wrote *Annalise Powliss* on the front of the envelope. If the contents of the envelope were really as harmless as Callin said, nothing bad would happen to her. Otherwise....

The concierge picked up the envelope between his thumb and forefinger as though it was a loaded diaper.

I went out into the sunlight, circled the building and strode past the valet booth into the parking garage. If the attendant noticed me, he didn't say anything. I climbed the stairs to the roof.

Cars had arrived while I was talking with Callin. All around me were targets that would have made Arne drool on his collar. There was an Expedition. There was a Lexus. There was a Yukon. A Ford 250. These weren't cars you stole for the chop shop. These were cars you drove into a shipping container and resold in South America. Arne would have brought in a team, slipped the attendant a few bucks (while showing him a shiny gun), and driven them all down to the docks. An hour's work, tops.

Not that any of that mattered to me now.

I tried to pinpoint the Dumpster below Callin's window but, looking up, I couldn't see the black cloth on his balcony railing. When I was dropping the book, it would have taken me half a second to count which Dumpster it had landed next to, but I hadn't bothered. The first two I checked were empty. As I checked the third, I noticed a sign that said PRIVATE PROPERTY NO DUMPSTER DIVING. Yet another opportunity to get arrested.

Of course, smashing a poker over some dude's head would land me in jail, too. Several witnesses had seen me enter and leave the hotel, and there had to be cameras. Christ. This was my third day in town and I'd almost committed murder. If Callin had been human...

I found the book. It had hit hard, of course, and had slid between two trash bags. I vaulted out of the Dumpster and examined it. The case had gotten a little wet but the spine seemed undamaged. At least, the pages didn't spill out onto the ground when I opened it.

I laid my hand on the cover and ran my fingertips across the faint design. Like the blue ribbon, I could feel the power in it. It was like laying my hand on the outside of a generator. And somehow, I could feel the glyph reaching upward toward Callin.

I didn't know how I knew, but I knew. The glyph was a connection to Callin.

I laid the book on the closed cover of a Dumpster, then snatched a wine bottle out of a recycling bin. I broke the bottle and laid the jagged edge against the design on the cover.

I didn't know what was about to happen, but it didn't matter. I needed this book. Jon needed it. If it was a spell book, it would tell us what Callin and Annalise could do. Maybe it could even help Jon purge the worm creature, if he had one in him.

I closed my eyes. I remembered the green flame and the way Callin made the world turn white and vanish. Anything could happen next. Anything.

Jon needed this book.

I gouged the cover, slicing across the glyph. The leather peeled back, revealing dull steel, and the broken bottle immediately began to vibrate. The vibration shot up the bottle into my hand. I felt the bones and muscles in my hand and wrist tremble.

A gout of black steam blasted up from the book, barely missing my wrist. The vibrations intensified.

I shoved the bottle away. It rolled across the lid of the Dumpster, and I ducked behind the metal.

The broken bottle exploded like a bomb. I held my hand, willing it to calm down, to be still. I imagined my hand exploding, too, spraying bits of bone and flesh in all directions. Calm. Calm.

I wasn't feeling calm at all, but the pain and tremors began to ease anyway. Slowly. I stood up.

The bottle had exploded about three feet off the ground. The shards had punctured the metal shell of the Dumpster. If I'd still been standing...

The jet of black steam had vanished. I laid my hand on the cover of the book. The feeling of power was gone and I wondered if Callin could sense its absence. I tucked the book under my arm and hurried toward the street.

CHAPTER EIGHT

I hustled down the street, holding the slipcover and journal close to my chest. No one gave me a second glance.

I felt like a guy who'd stolen a suitcase full of cash from a drug dealer—I was a small fry who'd just come into some serious gold, and I knew what would happen to me if I got caught. *Annalise should have killed you after all.*

The only protection I had was in this book, if I could figure out the magic inside.

Damn. I'd thought the word. *Magic.* It was frightening and ridiculous at the same time. I touched the bandage on my neck to make sure it was still there.

No. I couldn't keep doing that. I couldn't keep doubting my sanity.

I dug into pants pockets and produced two five-dollar bills, three twenties and a handful of change. Callin hadn't taken my money, at least. The sidewalk was full of people bustling to their jobs. I tried to blend in, knowing it wasn't going to work.

My stomach grumbled; I hadn't eaten anything since last night's handful of fries. There was a coffee shop on the corner but I passed it by. The line was too long to risk for a bagel and I needed to talk to Jon.

I walked block after block, looking for a pay phone. No luck. Everyone had cell phones now. Everyone but me. I kept glancing over my shoulder as I went, but I didn't see Callin coming up on me. Every motorcycle that passed made my heart skip, but none of the riders were Annalise. If they were after me, they were taking their time.

Unless Callin had some other way to track me. Maybe there was something about the book or the bite that linked us, and he was waiting for me to lead him to Jon.

Maybe maybe maybe. I had no idea what they could do. Guessing was not only pointless, it was paralyzing. Better to do what seemed right at the moment and muddle through.

I finally found a pay phone outside a convenience store and fed it two quarters. I hadn't called Jon in fifteen years, but his parents' phone number was still bright in my memory.

The line was busy. Of course. If the outside of the house was besieged with reporters, cops, and sick people wanting cures, the phone would be, too. They'd probably taken it off the hook. At least I got my quarters back.

I hadn't memorized Theresa and Karl's phone number so I had the perfect excuse not to call. If Karl knew about Echo, he would already be looking for me and would already know I'd spent the night away from the apartment. If I turned up there, I'd be in cuffs again in no time.

I needed to see Jon. Jon would let me explain, if I could think of a way to contact him safely.

On impulse, I ran into a Starbucks and bought a bagel and a daily paper. I sat near the back door, well away from the windows, and flipped through the main and local news sections of the paper twice, then the other sections. Echo wasn't mentioned. Of course, people got themselves murdered all the time without any serious coverage, but Echo's friendship with Jon should have interested the local media. Maybe no one had made the connection, or maybe the police were asking them to hold off.

Maybe they were looking for me.

I tucked the paper under my arm and went back onto the street. Heavy clouds had rolled in off the Sound and I knew it would rain soon. I found a bus stop that would take me to my own neighborhood and waited for it.

A patrol car rolled down the block. The officer looked right at me and drove on by.

Maybe they weren't looking for me. Maybe I'd gotten lucky and I could still go back to my apartment. But good luck never lasts. I had to start acting like I had a brain in my head.

I caught a bus, picked up a transfer and, 40 minutes later, walked into the copy shop. I hadn't met any of the morning staff, of course. I went to the counter and asked for the blue legal paper. The clerk was reedy and had more adam's apple than chin but I suppose his narrow glasses were supposed to make him look smart. He also seemed to recognize me, which didn't make me happy.

I took the paper to a self-serve machine near the desk, fighting the urge to flee. If the chinless counter guy picked up the phone, I was going to bolt for the sidewalk.

I opened the journal then laid the legal paper across it. As I'd hoped, the paper covered both pages of the book.

I glanced at the first page, which had *To Look Into the Empty Spaces and See the Great Predators* carefully written across the top. Then I laid it face down on the glass, fed the blue paper into the machine, and made three copies.

The chinless clerk collected money from the last customer in line and walked over to me. "Aren't you the new night guy? Watcha copying?" He leaned over and craned his head to align it with the pages in the output tray.

I was already jittery and I didn't need some stranger prying into my business. I almost told him to fuck off, but I worked here now. "Spell book," I said.

"Really?"

"When the demonic forces of evil are out to get you," I said, letting a little more of my raw nerves show than I'd intended, "a little magic might help you fight—"

"Uh, I gotta pee." He fled behind the counter.

Maybe that had been a stupid thing to do, but there was no taking it back. I lifted the journal, turned to a new page and made three more copies.

When I was finished, I paid, fled the shop and jumped on the first bus I saw. It didn't really matter where it was going; I wanted distance between my new job and whatever was going on with me. And I still had sixty-three dollars in my pocket.

I didn't know where the bus was taking me until it turned up the Magnolia Bridge. I'd never been to this part of the city even when I lived here. Good. I stared out at the train yards passing below and marveled at how mundane it all looked.

I climbed off the bus at the first shopping district we came to and was pleased to see a small post office across the street.

Six people stood in line at the counter, but the lobby full

of post office boxes was empty. I went to an empty table and began collating my stack of blue pages.

It was calming work. I only glanced at each page, trying to avoid the temptation of studying them. Someone, presumably Callin, had numbered each page in a flowing, delicate hand. I made three stacks, the page numbers counting down. Fifty-three, fifty-two, fifty-one... It was easier than thinking.

When I finished, I took four free priority envelopes down from the wall and laid them out. I wrote *Do not open. Please hold this for me. I'll call soon. Thanks.* on a Tyvek envelope, then slipped the first stack of pages into it. On a second envelope I wrote the address for my cousin in Maine. Duncan had been the only person in my family to send me mail while I was inside. I didn't know why he'd done it, but I'd been stupidly happy to get them.

In any event, Duncan's last letter said he would be in Madrid until next summer, and that a friend would collect his mail. I put the Tyvek envelope inside the second one and sealed it. Callin's spell book would be tossed into a pile in the corner for a couple of months, and that was just what I wanted.

I slid the second and third stacks into cardboard envelopes and headed for the counter.

The smallest post office box cost more than half the money I had left, and the postage to Maine wasn't free, either, but I had to do it. I opened the box, curled one of the envelopes up tight and slid it inside. Then I took the book and the last remaining envelope into the rain, to look for the next bus home.

It took nearly an hour to get there and made me ache for my own car. My aunt and uncle were out, so I dug through their fridge and made a peanut butter and jelly sandwich. It wasn't really stealing, since Theresa had told me to help myself, but I felt like a thief anyway. I'd stock my tiny fridge as soon as I got my first paycheck.

It was nearly one o'clock by the time I climbed my creaking stairs and stumbled into my cramped living room. I ate the sandwich, feeling fear and tension draining away, leaving me exhausted. I heard a motorcycle engine from somewhere nearby, but what did it matter? I was off the street.

The cops weren't after me. If they had been, Karl or someone who dressed just like him would have been waiting for me. Since there wasn't, I knew they hadn't put my name next to Echo's yet. Payton must have lawyered up. Or something.

I'd been too paranoid to read Callin's book on the bus, but here in the relative safety of my darkened room, I felt ready. I opened the cover, feeling the torn leather and cold metal.

The stairs creaked.

I stood, grabbed my empty backpack off the floor and stuffed the envelope inside. Through the window, I could see Annalise's BMW parked at the mouth of the alley. Damn.

I tossed Callin's book, still in its slipcover, onto the couch. Now that I had copies, they could have it back. I hurried into the bathroom and swiftly, silently opened the window.

The front door of my apartment burst inward. I could hear splinters of wood bouncing off the walls and floor. I eased my legs out the window and felt for the top of the neighbor's iron fence.

"Here's the book," Annalise said from the other room. "Think you can hold onto it this time?"

"Why thank you, my dear," Callin's voice responded. "I shall do my very best."

Both of them? My hands began to tremble. My feet touched the railing; it was farther away than I'd expected. I eased my weight onto it, then jumped backwards onto the neighbor's lawn. I hit the grass hard and rolled beneath a bush.

I stayed very still, wishing I could have closed the bathroom window above. I could smell something nasty, and remembered too late the Scottish Terrier that lived in this yard.

If Callin and Annalise could track me like bloodhounds, maybe the smell of dog shit would throw them off. Then again, if they had x-ray vision, they'd see me cowering in the bushes.

My hands began to shake even more and my stomach felt unsteady. I needed to study that book, if only to get an idea of what they could do.

I backed away on my hands and knees until I reached the far edge of the yard, then I hopped the fence. I sprinted between two houses, crossed the street and went between two more to the next block. They had vehicles and I didn't, which meant I was in trouble. I had to get off my feet or off the street. If I'd had the right tools, I might have stolen a car, but I'd deliberately not spent any of my gate money on them. Of course, any of these houses I was passing might have the tools I needed in their garages...

I turned a corner and saw a bus rumbling toward me. I

didn't know where it went, but it didn't make any difference. It was better than stealing again.

I hurried to the corner and took out my transfer. It had already expired. Annalise didn't zoom around the corner and burn me down to my bones while the bus approached, so I climbed on, flashed the transfer, and took a seat when the driver nodded.

The smell of dog shit returned. I tried to check my clothes without looking like I was checking my clothes, but couldn't find the source of the odor. Great. I'd become one of *those* bus people.

After a short while, the bus reached the University District. I jumped off, thinking it was crowded enough to mix in.

There was a smear of dog shit on the back of my jacket below my right shoulder blade. I scraped it against the edge of a trash can but couldn't make it come clean. This stupid jacket had gone to prison with me and I wasn't going to throw it away. I needed a sink and some soap.

I turned a corner and crossed the street onto the campus itself, holding the jacket in front of me like a bouquet of flowers while pretending that my backpack was like camouflage among all those students.

I felt ridiculous. My life was in danger. I'd seen amazing, terrifying things—I shouldn't be worrying so much about one little shit stain. But it was a small, mundane problem that I could deal with. This little mess was keeping me sane.

I mingled with the students, trying to convince myself that I didn't stand out, even though they all looked five years younger than me and they were all wearing heavy coats against the cold November drizzle. The trees made a green canopy above us, shadowing the paths.

As boys, Jon and I had planned to go to the UW. We were going to try out for the baseball team together—Jon had even picked out a fraternity to pledge, not that I could remember the name of it now. He had planned to be an architect and I thought I'd become an engineer, even though I didn't really know what that would mean.

Instead, I'd gone to juvenile hall, met Arne and fled with him to L.A. at fifteen. I'd spent the next ten years doing stupid things for money, girls and fun.

And Jon had gone into his wheelchair. Had he still gone to college? I had no idea. I didn't really know a thing about him.

The campus looked like a park. I tried to imagine myself enrolled here, taking classes and studying to become...whatever. The idea was so ambitious it was almost threatening, especially for a guy with a prison G.E.D.

I wandered for at least ten minutes before finding a sign with a map of the campus. Five minutes later, I breezed through the security gates at the university library. Rows of bookshelves dominated the edges of the room, while a nest of desks and tables clustered by the windows in the corners. The students at the tables seemed to be falling over each other as they worked together. I didn't look at them too closely.

A sign indicated that the third floor was for silent, private study. That's what I wanted. I climbed the long, open stairway past the students packed like sardines around computer terminals on the second floor. No one challenged me or asked to see ID.

The third floor was a mirror image of the first, except that the tables had been replaced with cubicles. A sign at the top of the stairs urged me to study quietly. Glad to.

First, I went into the men's room. There was a nice resting spot on a shelf by the sinks. I squirted hand soap onto my jacket and began to wash it under the spigot. This wasn't the place to smell like a street bum.

When the jacket was clean, I rung it out. I grabbed my envelope off the shelf and noticed a cheap ball point pen sitting behind it. There was no one else in the bathroom, so I decided it was lost property and claimed it.

At the information desk, I smiled at an old hippy as I took a short stack of scrap paper. The hippy didn't seem to mind. Each was about the size of my hand—larger than I'd expected, but that was a good thing.

The cubicles were all taken, but I found a small empty table in the corner. I sat, the scrap paper under my right hand and the envelope under my left. The clock on the wall read forty minutes after one. I could spare an hour and a half looking over the book before I had to go to work but I was sure it wouldn't take that much time. It was barely 60 pages long.

If I was still going to work. If Callin's bite had told them where I lived, he probably knew where I worked.

It was too late to sweat that now. Once I knew what was in the book, I could share it with Jon. Then I could do whatever I had to do—skip town, face down the cops, whatever.

I opened to the first page. Written at the top was: *To Look Into the Empty Spaces and See the Great Predators.* Whatever the hell that meant.

Two weird but simple designs had been drawn on the

bottom of the page. Each was similar to Annalise's tattoos or the stitches of Callin's waistcoat. The design on the left was labeled *1* and the other was *2*.

I wasn't looking for something that would let me "see." I needed a way to fight Callin and Annalise. For Jon.

I needed a weapon. The fact that I wanted power to help my friend didn't change the fact that it was power I was after. Seeing the world behind the world wasn't enough, and having Callin offer to give it to me in his way wasn't enough, either—I wanted to own a piece of it. I wanted to *take* it.

I turned the page. *A Gift of Tongues,* was written at the top. This page also had two designs.

Next page: *A Path Through the Wilderness.* Below, two designs.

Next page: *The Shadow Walks Free.*

Next page: *Golem Flesh.* That was more like it. The note below the title read: *To harden the flesh.* This was some kind of protection spell.

I studied the designs at the bottom of the page. Beside them was a small stack of five lines with musical notes on them. I couldn't read music. Reluctantly, I turned the page.

The Unwinding Spectre. Callin's description was simple. *To Undo An Enemy And His Works.* Okay. Whatever that meant. I turned the page.

Ghost Knife.

"Hello," I said aloud, forgetting I was in a library. The note read: *To cut ghosts, magic and dead things.*

That was the one. I bookmarked the spell with a sheet of note paper and turned the page. Then the next. I needed something that sounded protective.

The handwriting changed partway through the book, then it changed again. More than one person had put this together. Even if one of the others was Annalise, that meant there was at least a third person in their society.

I reached a page that had the words *Steeled Glass* at the top. The designs beneath it were very simple. The notation read: *To Protect Against a Single Blow.*

I slipped another bookmark into this page.

The steeled glass spell looked so simple I considered starting with it, but hell, the ghost knife sounded cooler. I flipped back to that bookmarked page.

The designs under the ghost knife were side by side. The only other notes on the page beside the one I'd already read were a tiny scribble marking design number one as *For the mind.* Design number two was marked *For the hand.*

Whatever the hell that meant.

I copied design number two onto a sheet of scrap paper, but there was nothing special about it when I was done. It looked like Annalise's tattoos and Callin's waistcoat designs, but there was no magic in it as far as I could tell.

I drew both designs beside each other, which had the same disappointing result. Next, I drew design two directly over design one. Nothing. I switched the order. Nothing again. I suspected that was not the right method anyway; the resulting glyphs didn't look like Annalise's tattoos or Callin's stitches. Too busy.

If this crap was easy, everyone would do it. I focused in on the pages again, skimming the first and last sheets in the hope of finding some kind of instructions. If Callin and

Annalise could do it, so could I. They hadn't exactly struck me as geniuses.

Unless the book alone wasn't enough. Maybe I needed a magical pen to write it out, or a special decoder ring for the designs. Maybe I was supposed to be wearing enchanted underwear.

Whatever. I didn't have anything but the book to work with. Besides, Callin had locked up the book and the book alone. If he needed a magic pen to cast a spell—or a magic embroidery needle—he'd have locked them up together, wouldn't he? I wished I had kept the slipcover so I could search it for secret pockets or hidden instructions.

I looked at the words on the page again. Maybe they held some secret significance. I studied them closely, then held them up to the light. If there had been watermarks or faint scribbles on the pages of Callin's book, the copier hadn't picked them up. They were just words. I flipped to the spell before this one and the spell after it. The numbers were not in the same position relative to the design in the spell before, but they were in the spell after.

Okay. The numbers don't matter either. Probably. There was nothing to do but look at the designs again.

Dammit. It didn't make sense. I organized the scrap papers on the table, then laid my pen against the copy I'd made of design number one. These curved lines could be an eye, if I added a line here and here.

Something clicked. I looked at the original design again, then closed my eyes. The shape of the drawing stood out in the darkness of my mind's eye. Yep, that one looked like a rough drawing of an eye. And those lines could almost be an image of a knife. And was that elaborate squiggle right there a clawed hand, reaching for the knife's handle?

Suddenly, the image in my mind flashed white and burst into flame.

A bloom of ghostly fire erupted inside my head and quickly spread to my entire body.

CHAPTER NINE

I jolted in my chair, frozen with pain. Flames raced down my body. My heart was on fire. My guts were on fire. Tongues of flame erupted from my mouth and nostrils. My blood must have been boiling....

But at the same time, a deep animal part of my brain knew, even through the pain, that this fire was not real, physical fire. It wasn't really boiling my blood. My mind was burning. My soul was burning. The flame was killing me, but it wasn't touching me physically.

I snatched up the pen and set it on a piece of blank scrap. I moved it slightly, making a tiny little comma of ink, and I felt the fire flow down my arm, through the pen into the paper. I kept the pen moving, carefully reproducing the second design. "For the hand."

The pain overwhelmed me. Spectral flames roared around my face. Every muscle in my body was clenched at once, and I would have screamed if I could have taken a breath. But on some level I knew that if I stopped this second drawing, or if I made a mistake, the fire flowing out of my would be blocked, and come backwards out of the page. It would destroy me before I had a chance to try again.

I kept going, slowly copying the glyph, willing my writing

hand not to tremble or spasm. The symbols in my mind: eye, hand, blade, glowed brighter as the fire left me, and it almost became like sharing someone else's thought, as though I had touched another mind out in the universe somewhere and we were thinking this thought and writing it out together.

I drew the last squiggle and the rest of the fire rushed out of me.

I gasped, taking shuddering breaths and letting the pen fall from my hand and roll off the table. Tears and sweat streamed down my face. I held my arms away from my body so I could be touching nothing at all.

But my clothes weren't burned. There were no scorch marks on the table, no curled blackened edges on the papers around me. More importantly, the pain was receding. I knew that wouldn't happen with a real burn.

I'd been right. The fire hadn't been physical. Thank God thank god thank god.

I noticed a young woman glaring at me like I was a nutcase. Since she was giving me a nasty look rather than spraying me with a fire extinguisher, I knew she hadn't seen the flames at all. I was the only one who could.

Okay. Magical fire.

It was remarkable, really, how quickly I'd gone from not even wanting to think the word "magic" to this.

I took a deep, calming breath, although it didn't do me much good. I was damn lucky not to be dead, or at least being loaded into an ambulance. Not to mention that fire doesn't burn without fuel. Had I torched away some part of my body I didn't know about? Had I burned up part of my soul?

I looked at the scrap paper but didn't dare touch it yet. There was my mark, and it held power. I could feel it humming from two feet away.

A strong hand gripped my shoulder. "You have to come with me, young fella."

A campus security guard stood over me. He was about forty-five and his face had the scarred, rounded look of a lifetime of hard fighting. I'd seen plenty of faces like it among the older inmates. Out of habit, I glanced down at his hip. Yep, he was wearing a gun.

I was still dazzled by pain and magic, and apparently wasn't moving fast enough, because the guard took my arm in one hand and lifted me. With his other hand, he reached for the scrap papers. Including the ghost knife.

"No!" I lunged for the spell, snatching it away just as he was about to grab it. The paper curled as I yanked it back, and the corner struck the guard's hand.

It passed through him as if he wasn't there. The corner hit just between the man's index and middle knuckles, then slid back toward the wrist. The white corner of the paper peaked over the top of his skin like a tiny shark fin speeding through calm water. The paper struck the man's watch, then it emerged from his arm.

His watch fell off his wrist and bounced away on the carpet. He stumbled and caught himself against the table, then stared at the spot on his hand where the ghost knife had cut through him.

His flesh was completely unmarked.

"Lordy," he said. "I'm sorry. I shouldn't have grabbed at your things like that."

For a moment, I was utterly stunned by this sudden change. Power emanated from the piece of paper in my hand like a live wire. I slid it gently it into my pocket.

"Are you okay?"

"I think so," the guard said. "You're working here, right? You don't have to go. I'm sorry I said you should. It ain't necessary."

"Well, okay." I didn't know how to respond to that. "I'll stay here and keep doing my thing."

"Let me know if you need anything," the guard said. He turned and shuffled away.

What was going on? What had I just done to him? I touched the front of my jacket and shirt, remembering the feel of greasy ashes from last night.

Screw this. I followed him. "Hey, maybe you should see a doctor or something."

"That's okay, thank you. Don't trouble yourself. Sorry to bother you." The guard kept moving away and I trailed behind him.

A second guard approached. This one looked like someone's fat grandfather. "What's going on here?"

"This man nearly collapsed," I said quickly. "I told him he should see a doctor or something, but...."

Fat Grandpa nodded and took the other man's arm, stepping forward in a way that forced me to back off. The two guards started toward the elevator, talking in low tones.

I watched them enter the elevator. When the doors closed no one had fallen over dead.

I went back to the table, took the scrap paper from my pocket and smoothed it out. I could feel the magic in it.

Annalise's ribbon had not been like this. Maybe spells feel strongest to the person who created it? I had no way to know.

Did Callin's waistcoat, which was covered with sigils, feel like this, times twenty? Did Annalise's entire body feel like this times a hundred? It boggled my mind to think they were surrounded by this kind of power all the time.

And now I had my little piece of it. Mine.

But I had to be more careful. I'd just accidentally used my spell against the security guard and I didn't really know what I'd done. What if he'd just had a stroke?

Or maybe I'd only cut the man's "ghost"—his soul or spirit or something. Maybe it wasn't dangerous at all, like a magical stun gun. I liked that idea so much that I decided to believe it.

The guard's watch lay on the carpet; I picked up both pieces. It had been cut through the band and the watch face. It was a clean, sharp cut right through the metal workings.

According to Callin's book the ghost knife cuts "ghosts, magic and dead things." The watch was a *dead thing*, of course. I held the edge of the paper against the corner of the wooden table then pressed down.

The paper crinkled and bent. It didn't work against wood.

The table was certainly dead, though. I held the paper in place again, and this time I let myself feel the power coming out of the spell. It belonged to me, the way my thumb or my ear belonged to me.

I willed it to cut, then pressed down.

The sheet of paper sliced through the table corner as though it wasn't there. The hunk of wood struck the floor with a chunky, substantial sound.

I looked at the ghost knife again. A single word kept running through my head: Power power power power.

No one else came to roust me from my chair. I looked back at the table where the woman had glared at me. Her seat was empty.

Fair enough. I turned to the other bookmarked page.

Steeled glass. *To protect against a single blow.* I moved a fresh piece of scrap paper into position and held the pen over it. I wanted to be ready this time.

Except I wasn't ready, not for that ordeal. Was I really going to set myself on fire for a spell that seemed as though it would only protect me from one attack? One bullet, one knife thrust, one punch from Annalise's padlock-snapping hands?

I rubbed my face, then looked over the page. The fire had hurt, but it hadn't harmed me in any way I could tell, while Annalise could tear my arms off if she wanted to. I had the ghost knife, sure, but I needed protection, too, so I'd have a chance to use it.

And there was Jon. If Annalise killed me, who would protect Jon?

It was a frightening thought, and not just because the word *kill* had emerged from my subconscious after churning around in there for hours. I was falling back into my old life. I was standing with my friends again, planning to fight their enemies. This was the person I was supposed to have left behind.

But this wasn't like the bad old days with Arne and his crew. Jon was a good guy, while Arne was most definitely not. I wasn't going to become my old self. I was going to be the good guy now.

Besides, I had a debt to pay. I had taken away Jon's legs. I'd taken walking and baseball and all kinds of things I didn't even want to think about.

So it would just be this time: one last time to do the right thing and square an old debt. Once this was finished, I would *really* straighten out my life, get a paycheck job and bore myself stupid with a big-screen TV.

And this next spell wouldn't be so bad. It was only pain. I hoped.

I picked up the pen and covered design number one with my other hand. I practiced the second design a couple times to be sure I'd get it right.

Then I looked at design number one, at the straight lines, hard corners and curving squiggles. Slowly, it began to make sense.

CHAPTER TEN

The fire filled me. I was a living furnace. But the steeled glass spell was simpler than the ghost knife, and the fire less intense. I finished the spell, then held it up. It didn't look like much, but neither did Annalise or Callin.

The pain receded. I grabbed another piece of paper. If I waited too long, I might lose my nerve. I called up the design again and started drawing, pouring my pain and energy into it. When I finished, I felt dizzy and nauseated. Weak. What was the use of arming myself with spells if I was going to be too wasted to use them?

Don't stop. Don't stop. Don't stop.

I grabbed a third sheet of paper. My world had become very small—it was just my pain and the design I was drawing. It was as if I'd erased everything else, and when the last of the fire poured into the third design, the flames vanished and the design faded from my thoughts. There was nothing to take its place.

I returned to consciousness slowly. My hands and feet were cold. My shirt was damp with sweat. A man bent over me, holding my elbow. He wanted me to move. I realized I was lying on the floor.

"Are you all right, sir?" the man said.

I pulled my legs underneath me and stood with all the vigor I could manage. It wasn't much. "I'm okay," I lied. "Rough day."

"Would you come with me?"

I was finally being thrown out. I stuffed the blue pages into the bottom of my backpack, then put the practice drawings in there, too. It wasn't safe to leave them lying around but I was too fuzzyheaded to figure out what to do with them. Finally, I picked up the ghost knife and the three steeled glass spells. They seemed too precious to pocket.

"Let's go for a stroll," I said, trying to be jaunty and failing miserably. My whole body tingled. Casting these spells *hurt*.

The man leading me through the bookshelves was a short, dumpy guy with a sloppy black beard. His longish hair lay across his forehead in wavy clumps. His shirt was stretched tight over a wide, soft gut. I immediately thought *Victim*, then quashed it. I didn't look for victims anymore.

He led me to the ground floor, through a door marked EMPLOYEES ONLY then down a short hallway into a small room. In the center of the room was a cheap metal table and plastic cafeteria chairs. Against one wall was a counter with a sink and microwave. This was a break room. I'd only ever seen them on TV before.

"I'm Hank," the man said. "Won't you sit down?"

I did. The table was cold against my arms. "Thanks. I'm Payton."

"Are you feeling okay, Payton?"

"I looked pretty bad, I guess. I'm fine. Tough day."

"Have you eaten?"

I wasn't sure what to make of all the concern the guy was

showing me, but I couldn't see what his angle was. "I'm fine." I hoped that would end it.

"I'll be back with some food." Hank started toward the door.

Just then I noticed a phone and a clock on the wall behind me. "Is that the right time?"

Hank checked the clock against his watch. "Yes, it is."

He left. I slumped forward and let my head strike the table. According to the clock, it was 6:45. I should have been at work nearly three hours ago.

Shit. I couldn't even make it for my second day.

I was tempted to blow it off, clear up this mess with Jon and then, when things were *really* straightened out, find a new one. But I couldn't. Being a citizen wasn't something I could keep putting off; once I started, I'd never stop.

In my wallet, I found the note Uncle Karl had given me listing the paperwork I needed for my first day of work. At the top of the paper was the shop's phone number.

I picked up the phone and called. Andrea picked up on the fourth ring and said: "Copy shop," in a clipped, flustered voice. I could hear a commotion in the background.

I didn't hang up. Instead I said: "Andrea, this is Ray Lilly. I'm sorry. I don't have an excuse for you. I'm just sorry."

"Ray." She seemed almost to enjoy the flash of anger in her voice. "Take beatings like a pack mule, huh? Come down here so I can find out for myself. And where is 555-0838?"

As she said the numbers, I read them off the telephone in front of me. I'd forgotten the copy shop phones had caller ID.

"I'm in a library at the University." There was no point

in lying, since it would be easy to check. Any hope I had of concocting a story about a trip the emergency room evaporated. "I lost track—"

"I have *work* to do. Have a crappy life, Ray." She hung up. So did I. Damn.

There was a basket of office supplies on the counter. I took the scraps of paper out of my pocket and set them beside the sink. The spells were powerful, but the paper they'd been drawn on was fragile. I didn't know what would happen to the magic if the paper tore, or if the ink ran. Maybe it would be fine. Maybe it would explode like a bomb. But if it was anything like what happened to the cover of Callin's journal, I didn't want to find out.

I took a tape gun out of the basket and laid out a long strip sticky side up. Then I laid out a second, letting it overlap the first slightly. By some miracle, there were no wrinkles. I laid the ghost knife face down on the tape, then laid two more pieces of tape over the back.

There was a pair of scissors in the basket, too, and they were surprisingly sharp. I trimmed the edges and held it up. Poor man's laminate. Eventually, the tape would yellow and curl, but it would protect the ghost knife for a little while.

I sure as hell hoped I didn't need it longer than that.

I did the same thing to the three steeled glass spells next. As I was slipping them back into my pocket, Hank returned.

"Why don't you eat something?" He set a box on the table. There was a small stack of napkins and a pair of bran muffins inside.

My stomach flip-flopped. I picked up a muffin and bit into it. It was dry and bland and wonderful.

"I didn't realize I was hungry," I said around a mouthful of muffin. As apologies went, it was pretty lame, but Hank didn't seem to care.

"I'm sorry it took so long to return with them. I had a couple things to take care of out front."

I brought out my wallet. Hank waved at me to put it away. "I should pay for this food," I said. The earnestness in my voice surprised me. I wasn't a charity case. I didn't want to owe a debt to this guy.

"They're leftovers from a staff party. If you don't eat them, they'll be thrown out, so please enjoy and don't worry about it." I couldn't argue with that. I shrugged and put my wallet away. "So, Payton," he said, "are you taking any medications?"

It took me a moment to remember that I'd given him a fake name. Luckily, I'd already taken another bite of muffin and had an extra moment to get my thoughts together. "No. I've had a hard couple of days. Seriously, I'm not taking drugs and I'm not high or anything. Just stressed out." I took a small bite. "Why are you doing this?"

"Doing what?"

"Helping me. You don't know me." I watched Hank's expression, trying to figure out his angle. Karl and Theresa had helped me because Theresa was my mother's sister. Andrea had hired me to get close to Jon. Jon had been my friend for years, even if I didn't deserve it. But this guy was a stranger. He didn't have any connection to me and I didn't have anything he wanted. He'd even turned down my money.

He shrugged. "It's the right thing to do," was all he said.

Yeah. Right. I was about to press further when we both heard police sirens approaching fast.

"Wonder what that's about?" Hank said. He stood. "I'll be right back. Do you want some milk? Or a soda?" I shook my head. Hank walked out of the room.

As soon as the door closed, I bolted to the window. The break room overlooked the parking lot and I watched two patrol cars pull into spaces. Four uniformed officers stepped out. One of them was my Uncle Karl and shit, did he looked pissed.

They strode toward the entrance of the library. I had no doubt they were coming for me, and I knew how they'd found me. Andrea had to have tipped them off.

I knew Karl wouldn't have that expression because I'd stayed out and skipped work. It must have been Echo.

I wasn't ready to answer questions about her death. I scooped up my backpack and slipped the ghost knife into my right hip pocket and my three steeled glass spells into my left. Then I pushed a chair up to the window.

I couldn't run out quite yet. I grabbed a pen out of the basket and wrote *Thanks* on a paper napkin. Then I wriggled through the window and ran.

Three damn days and I was already running from the cops, and from my uncle, too, who was letting me live in his home. I jogged to the far side of the parking lot, trying to figure out how I could avoid prison. I hadn't hurt Echo or Payton. I'd tried to save that old man. I'd stolen a book, sure, but the owner had it back already. I didn't *deserve* to go to prison again, but I had no idea how I was going to avoid it.

A light rain fell. I stepped onto a walkway, slowing my pace to a casual stroll. I'd draw less attention that way. Still, I was a pedestrian on the run again. I needed a car.

I set my backpack on a bench, opened it and pulled out one of the practice drawings, letting the rain spatter it. The ink didn't run, but the paper soaked through. I shredded and wadded it, then dumped half into a trash can. I moved on to another trash can and threw out the other half.

I did it again with the next practice drawing, then the next, wandering around the campus and checking out the pretty young women. The last drawing went into a pair of cans by a cafeteria.

I walked down a flight of stairs into a vacant study area. It was a sunken, tiled mini-park with square cement tables and foliage all around. On a dry afternoon it would be filled with students. At the moment it was empty.

I needed a new edition of the paper to see what they were saying about Echo's death. I also needed a way to approach Jon without—

"Ray!" someone said.

Damn. They found me. I turned, prepared to act surprised. But it wasn't a cop who'd called my name, it was Jon Burrows.

CHAPTER ELEVEN

He was wearing the same clothes from last night, but then, so was I. "Jon? What are you doing here? Are you a student or something?"

"Naw," Jon said. "I followed your uncle. We looked for you last night, but you disappeared. What happ—"

He stopped several paces away and sniffed the air. When he spoke next, his voice became low and steady. "You have that smell on you."

I wasn't sure what he meant. I was sweaty from the effort of casting the spells, and maybe I hadn't cleaned my jacket well enough. "I didn't get a shower last night," I said. "Is it that bad?"

He bared his teeth and charged at me, screaming in wild, animal fury.

Before I could blink, Jon had crossed the six yards separating us and slammed his fist into my stomach. It was a stunning, powerful punch and I saw it sink deep into my guts. Too deep.

The force of the blow lifted me off the ground. Curiously, there was no pain, but I felt my body bend around Jon's fist like a car fender wrapping around a pole. I thought for sure there ought to be pain. I went higher and higher, my hips and legs flailing upward as my heavier torso rotated forward. I thought I would fall flat on my face, but the ground just wasn't there. My backpack—and its precious blue pages—was gone, too.

Everything was happening in slow motion. I'd risen up off of Jon's fist and had a moment of weightless confusion. Where was the pain? I was still tumbling, my feet flying upward, my body finally falling again.

I struck my head on a concrete bench and my neck twisted under the weight of my entire body. I felt it turn and compress but I didn't feel it snap. I had no idea that a person could die before they heard their own neck break.

I landed in a jumble of knees and elbows. I rolled out from beneath the study table and scrambled to my feet. I couldn't understand why I wasn't dead and I waited for my nervous system to catch up with the pain I was supposed to be feeling.

I looked at Jon. He'd lifted me off the ground with one punch, and the only reason I was still alive was because I had spells in my pockets.

Jon tilted his head to one side like a puzzled animal. His eyes were strangely flat and glassy.

The bastard had tried to kill me. I grabbed for the taped-up piece of paper in my pocket, finding the corner of the ghost knife poking out. I pulled it free just as Jon leaned forward and bared his teeth.

I wouldn't survive another punch and Jon was too fast for me to let him get close again. As he started toward me, I flung my arm toward him, throwing the ghost knife spell.

The taped piece of paper met Jon just a few feet from my

outstretched hand. Jon stopped his charge and drew back, but the ghost knife entered his breast bone and flew out of his back as though he wasn't there.

He collapsed onto his face like a marionette with its strings cut and didn't move.

I staggered backward then reached into my left hand pocket and pulled out my three steeled glass spells. Two were scorched and useless, but the third hummed with magic.

Damn. All that pain and effort wasted on my friend.

Friend.

"Jon. Oh, shit. What did I do?" I stuffed the spells into my pocket and rushed to him. I'd just used a weapon on him again. My brain and body were still buzzing with adrenaline—*Jon just tried to kill me*—but there was a part of me that thought he had a right to take his shot at me after all this time.

I knelt beside him. The back of his flannel shirt had a slot cut into it where the ghost knife had come out. I spread the cut with my fingers. No blood. The spell had cut his shirt but left his skin unmarked. I turned him over.

He grabbed my wrist. "I tried to kill you." His voice was gentle; all the animal fury had gone out of him. "Dude, I don't know what came over me. Something about the way you smelled reminded me of Echo, and it was, like, fight or flight, you know? I'm really sorry." He struggled to his feet. He didn't seem to be hurt, but he moved as if he was exhausted. He touched the front of his shirt. There was another cut in the fabric there and one of his buttons had been sliced cleanly in half, but the skin underneath was unmarked. "Man, what was that thing?"

I held his arm to steady him, although he didn't really seem to need it.

"A spell," I said. "I don't think it hurt you physically, but I think it cut your... ghost." I felt like a dork just saying it.

"You mean my soul?" Jon asked. "Aw, that is so *cool*. Come on, let's get your stuff."

Jon bent over and picked up a sheet of blue paper. I suddenly realized that the blue pages had fallen out of my backpack and fluttered onto the wet cement.

"Oh, shit! Get those papers! I went through hell to— Don't let them tear or smudge."

We picked up the pages as quickly and as carefully as we could. Jon paused to look at one. "More spells! Where did you get these?"

I remembered his punch going deep into my stomach. "Where did you get your cure?"

"Fair enough," he answered. He gave the last of the blue pages to me and I looked them over. A few were spotted with damp, but none were ruined. "I'll show you."

I put the pages into my pack, then zipped it closed. He started for the stairs, but I wasn't ready to leave yet.

I could feel the ghost knife nearby. I took a moment to get my bearings. If I'd landed beside that bench over there, and Jon had come at me from that direction, the ghost knife would have gone....

I crossed to a set of stairs on the far side of the study area. I could feel the power of the spell as I approached. The railing for the stair was a simple metal pipe, and there, about four feet off the ground, it was cut through. A moment later I found a slot in the concrete steps.

The ghost knife had cut through the cement and embedded itself there. I supposed it could have continued on, cutting through the planet until it skimmed back out of the ground somewhere else, then spun outward into space. I didn't know why it had stopped, but I was glad it had. Because I wanted it, desperately.

The real question was how I was going to get it out. I didn't have a jack hammer handy and the slot was too thin to grab it with a wire or tweezers.

But the magic in the ghost knife carried a trace of me. I held up my hand and *reached* for it with my mind, trying to connect. I willed it back into my hand, and it flew out of the slot in the stairs onto my palm.

The hairs on the back of my neck stood up. This spell wasn't *alive*, was it? It couldn't be.

Jon watched me from the far stairs. He held his cell phone to his ear. "We're set. We're on our way." He closed the phone. Time to go.

As we made our way across campus, Jon touched my elbow and said: "I'm sorry."

I waved him off. "I have a lot to tell you—"

"Save it," Jon said. "The others will want to hear it, too. You should tell us all together."

I imagined us being pulled over and I wanted to talk to him while I had the chance. Besides, no matter how many times he apologized, I still couldn't stop thinking about that punch. "I don't mind saying it twice."

"Bad idea," Jon said. "You shouldn't tell me alone. Tell the whole family together."

I hadn't expected that. I wanted to talk to him and Macy.

She was the other person Annalise and Callin had targeted.

But Jon didn't know anything about that, of course. "Bingo—I mean, Barbara isn't going to pull a gun on me again, is she?"

"Not while I'm around. But I don't mean that family. We're going somewhere else. Then you can tell your story to everyone."

Everyone? Echo was dead and Payton had a broken arm and leg, and maybe he was still in a coma. I hoped he was in a hospital. Were there others beside Jon and Macy?

Jon didn't want to talk. He stalked across the grass toward the street, his head moving from side to side, scanning the campus and the sidewalk beyond. He looked like a panther on the hunt.

We turned a corner and there was Jon's van parked at the curb. I almost grabbed his shoulder and dragged him away. The back corner was smashed in and there were three bungee cords where the sliding side door should have been.

"Oh, come on, Jon. No."

"Let's hurry," Jon said. He climbed in and belted himself into the wheelchair. I looked inside, noting that the hamburger wrappers had been blown, still loose, against the back door.

The cops were going to pull us over for sure.

I laid my hand on the twisted, torn metal. It was hard and unyielding. I closed my eyes, remembering how Annalise had torn it apart like paper.

"Are you all right, buddy?" Jon twisted in his chair and looked at me through the open doorway. I climbed into the passenger seat. I couldn't imagine how an eyesore like this had followed Uncle Karl in a police car without being spotted. Cops were too wary for that. How had Jon managed it?

"I saw this happen," I said by way of explanation.

Jon was wearing his seat belt. I put mine on, too. Jon pulled into traffic and did an illegal u-turn. "Of course," he said. "I forgot. It must have been bad."

I remembered Annalise stomping Payton's bones flat, and Echo slamming her into the metal van. I remembered their furious fight, and the metal lamp post falling, and the thing that crawled out of Echo's throat.

"It was—"

"Remember all those people?" Jon said. "The sick people outside my house that kept trying to beg a cure?"

"Sure," I said. I was glad Jon had bulldozed into a new topic. "Like the guy who shot you?"

"Naw. That guy thought I was possessed. Try to keep them straight." Jon laughed a little. I glanced at his nine-fingered hand and felt a little sick.

Jon grabbed a wrapped-up quarter-pounder off the dash, peeled back the paper and took a gigantic bite. He chewed once, then gulped it down. His face twisted with disappointment and disgust. He threw the rest of the burger into the back of the van.

I twisted in my seat. I hadn't noticed before, but many of the wrappers on the floor of the van still had food in them. How long had they been sitting there?

"Anyway," Jon continued, "one of the sick people out there begging for a cure turned out to be rich. Really, really rich. And he thinks he can put pressure on me, right? So he up and buys the real estate office where Dad works and has him fired."

"You're kidding."

"The sharks are circling, bro."

"What's your Dad going to do?"

"Retire. He's up there already. This just moves his game plan up a few years. He won't have the whole cushion he was planning for, but he figures he'll be okay once they sell a few of the things they were planning to enjoy in their golden years. Mom thinks it's a good thing, actually. She's been worried about his health. Now they're talking about a couple little trips and whatever."

"Still sucks," I said.

"Yep." Jon stopped at a red light. The idling van bounced with each rpm. "I've been a lot of work for them over the years, and I haven't always been a sweetheart about it. Now, even after I'm cured, I bring them trouble."

I nodded and looked away.

"Don't make that face. I told you before, it's all different now. Everything's cool with me. I don't even resent that rich guy. I know what it's like to be less than optimal, you know? I know what it's like to want a cure so bad you feel like fucking crying."

The light turned green. Pedestrians gawked at the ruined van as we drove through the intersection. It was a miracle that the cops hadn't pulled us over already.

Jon wasn't finished. "What cost will be too high? How many people do you hurt to get what you want? Right? Do you know what I mean, or am I talking out of my ass?"

"You're worried about the rich guy's chances of getting into heaven."

It didn't seem funny to me, but Jon laughed. "Maybe he doesn't have a soul. You'll have to give him a paper cut and see if he falls over."

"Point me at him," I said, surprised by the earnestness in my voice. I was ready to take on all of Jon's enemies.

"Christ! I'm sick of talking about this crap. Cure cure cure cure sleep cure cure cure cure food cure cure cure. That's all I talk about these days. Let's change the subject. Tell me what you think of the Mariners' chances this year?"

"Well, I haven't exactly been following them."

"What? Did you switch to another team?"

Jon sounded genuinely betrayed. It was almost as if he thought I had cheated on him. "No, I haven't been following any team. I stopped watching baseball."

"Damn. Even I kept watching the games. You didn't even see the M's in the world series?"

I shrugged. "We had some... trouble. The guards wouldn't let us watch."

"Holy God," Jon said. "Jail must really suck! I can't think what would be worse: no M's or all the ass rape."

Jon suddenly gasped and pulled over to the curb, parking in front of a little house. He turned to me with a pained look on his face. "Dude," he said. "That was a stupid thing to say. I'm really sorry—"

"It's okay—"

"No, it's not and shut up while I apologize. I don't want to laugh at the bad shit that happened to you."

"It's fine. Seriously."

"Good. Great. Thank God. You're my friend, and I shouldn't have made a fucking rape joke. Jesus. It's just that, since the cure, I've felt different. More reckless, kinda. It's mostly a good feeling. I feel strong, ready to take on the world, sharks or no sharks, for the first time in years. But sometimes I'm seriously distracted. Sometimes I talk before I think."

"For the record," I said, "I had people looking out for me, so that didn't happen. We don't have to go further into it than that. Prison was bad, but not as bad as this." I tapped Jon's wheelchair.

"It ain't a contest."

"And you didn't piss me off."

"Cool," Jon said. "I don't want to offend you. You're my buddy and I need your help."

"You got it."

"Cool again." He shut off the engine and opened the door. "We're already here."

I stepped out of the van. We were somewhere north of Ballard on a little block that had missed out on the boom times. Jon crossed the street to a run down little house with a crooked foundation and peeling paint. A downstairs window had been boarded over and the flower garden beneath it had been trampled.

I followed him onto the porch. There was broken glass in the garden. It looked as if something had burst through the window and fallen onto the garden, tearing up the flowers.

The porch creaked as we crossed it. "Whose place is this?" I asked.

"I told you. It's Macy and Echo's house."

I didn't see any point in correcting him. Jon grabbed the knob and strode right inside without knocking. I followed.

We entered a tiny foyer, with cracked, bulging walls that had been painted landlord white. A scarf had been tacked across the worst of the damage in an attempt to pretty it up.

Jon stepped aside, and there was Payton stretched across a yard sale couch. He was pale and covered with sweat and he didn't have a cast on his arm or leg. No one had taken him to the hospital.

Jon lunged at a knee-high pile of pizza boxes and took a slice from the top one. He dropped it when Macy entered.

"Found him," Jon said.

"What's that stench?" Macy said. She recoiled from me as if I had a loaded diaper. Her eyes narrowed in suspicion.

"Forget about that," Jon said. "He's helping us."

Payton stirred on the couch. "No more waiting. Let's do it now." His voice sounded weak.

Jon took Payton by the shoulders and Macy lifted his legs and hips. Both tried to hold his injured limbs motionless and stable, but Payton moaned in agony. The big guy would have screamed if he'd had enough life in him to make the effort.

Jon and Macy carried him into the dining room. I trailed along behind them.

All the dining room furniture had been piled against one wall and the rug had been thrown on top. The bare wooden floor had been painted in red designs, very like the one that made up my ghost knife.

But this spell was huge. It was a circle at least eight feet across, with four smaller circles evenly spaced around the perimeter and another in the very center. Between the circles were an assortment of swoops, symbols, glyphs and shapes.

It was Jon's cure spell, I realized. Years ago, I had fired a gun and crippled my friend. This thing had taken that moment away.

And there, lying in the very center circle, was Echo.

CHAPTER TWELVE

Echo looked twice as dead as she had the day before. I wanted to ask why her corpse was lying in the middle of a cure spell, but I was afraid of the answer I might get.

Macy and Jon set Payton carefully inside one of the perimeter circles. The groans he made as he settled onto the floor made my hair stand on end. Then Macy turned to me and pointed at a circle nearest the kitchen. "Take your spot, Ray."

My spot? Couldn't they tell she was dead? "I don't think we should—"

"Do it!" she roared and rolled forward onto the balls of her feet, her fingers curling into claws. She was about to pounce.

Jon touched her arm, calming her. "Sweetie, he just doesn't understand."

"Guys," I said, keeping my hand close to the pocket holding my ghost knife. "Payton needs a hospital. Echo—"

"Nobody needs a hospital," Macy said. "Not anymore."

"Echo was attacked because of this spell," I said. I already knew they weren't going to listen, but I had to keep trying. "People are trying to kill you."

"Fuck 'em," Jon said. "Bring it on."

"Jon, I saw what came out of Echo," I said, trying to think

of some way to make him listen. "That woman drove out some kind of *thing*."

He took my arm. His expression was so calm and self-assured that I began to doubt myself. "Payton told us about the woman."

"Payton didn't see the half of it. Echo had this *thing* in her."

"The woman put it there."

That startled me. "What?"

"This woman had magic, right?" Jon was placid and confident. Nothing I'd said had surprised him. "And she was trying to kill Echo?"

"Trying?" I said. My voice sounded frail. I stared at a can of red paint and a crusty paint brush in the corner so I wouldn't have to look at Jon.

He continued as if I hadn't spoken. "*She* put the thing inside Echo, not us. Not this." He gestured toward the design on the floor.

I hadn't expected this and the confident way Jon was talking made me think he knew something I didn't. Annalise had draped her firefighter's jacket over Echo, and the creature had crawled out of Echo's mouth. I'd assumed that the sigil on Annalise's jacket had been some kind of exorcism, but it could have implanted that thing. Maybe.

Of course, she'd done the same thing to Payton and all that happened to him was a flash of light just before he passed out.

Had the jacket spell driven out the creature in Echo's body, and had it driven out Payton's... What? His consciousness? His ghost?

Whatever had happened, Echo and Jon had both gotten themselves changed inside this spell. I tried to figure out why Annalise's spell had affected Payton and Echo differently, but my own ghost knife had the same effect on Jon and the library guard.

Too much. I clutched my backpack full of blue pages to my chest. It was too much to figure out with so little real information. I'd been operating on instinct and guesswork; what if my instincts were wrong?

"What did this thing look like?" Jon asked.

I held up my hands. "It was the size of a cat, maybe. It looked like a yellowish worm, but it had long, hard legs, like branches or needles. And it had wings."

"Christ, Ray." Jon shook his head. He looked amused. "If I had a *cat* with needles for feet inside me, don't you think I'd know it? Don't you think I'd feel it in there when I bent over to tie my shoes?"

"That's what I saw, Jon. I'm not making it up."

"I know that. I *believe* that. And I trust you. So the question is: who do *you* trust? Me, or—"

"You."

Jon smiled and clapped my shoulder. "Good. It's time to help Echo. You don't have to do anything at all except sit in that circle right there. That's all I'm asking."

"Jon, I—I just cast a spell, which you know, right? Will there be any fire?"

Jon looked confused for a moment. "What do you mean?"

"When we cast this spell on Echo. Will we burn?"

"Ray, I've done this three times already—"

"Because I'll do it, Jon, I will, but—"

"There's no fire, dude. This is healing magic. Okay?"

"Okay."

I turned and sat in the circle near the kitchen door then put my backpack on the floor behind me. The others sat in their spots, with Macy settling into the most heavily-marked spot opposite me.

Jon winked at me in the same way Arne used to when a job was going well. My stomach knotted. Jon wasn't as slick as Arne, but he'd coaxed and rationalized and played on my loyalty. And I had gone along with it. Jon had tried to kill me less than an hour before, and here I was still trying to pay off a debt.

I pushed those thoughts away. Jon was not Arne. Helping and protecting Jon was not the same as helping and protecting Arne.

Payton propped himself up on his good arm. His whole body trembled; sweat ran down his face. Macy held out her hand to Jon and he took a sheet of folded paper from his pocket and gave it to her. She unfolded it. It was a sheet of blue legal paper, just like the ones I'd used to copy Callin's spell book.

I glanced at the backpack behind me. Jon must have taken that spell while he was helping me pick up the sheets of paper. And the blue pages had come from Callin's spell book.

It was pretty clear that the spell needed four people to cast it on a fifth. Who had been that fifth person?

Someone had given or sold the spell to Jon, and someone had sat in the extra spot when they'd cast it. That someone had to be Callin. I couldn't imagine any other way for Jon to have a spell on the same blue paper except that he stole it from me after I stole it from Callin. I'd thought Jon was talking about me when he'd said "We're set," but he must have meant the spell he'd found.

I wondered how Annalise would feel if she discovered that the dude who closed a door in her face was the same one who had "infected" Echo. Callin was supposed to be on Annalise's side. *Unequal peers*, he had said. Did she know he had created the very situation she was trying to undo? Did she know he had betrayed her?

Macy studied the paper. My stomach was full of butterflies and I was perfectly happy to let her take as long as she needed to get it right. Despite Jon's assurances, I half-expected to burn again, and the prospect of putting my life in Macy's hands terrified me. If she screwed up, it would probably cost my life.

At least, I assumed so. It was possible the cure was completely different from the ghost knife and the steeled glass; Jon didn't seem worried at all. Maybe there would be no fire after all.

Macy cleared her throat. She was ready. She sang a few clear notes that seemed to harmonize and clash at the same time, then silence fell.

Macy's mouth kept moving but no sound came from her; I couldn't hear Payton's labored breathing, either. In fact, there was no sound at all from the whole house. I rubbed my hand against my whiskers and heard nothing. The vibrations didn't even travel along my bones to my ear drums. The silence was complete.

Several minutes ticked by. I glanced at the clock but in my nervousness immediately forgot what it said. I didn't burst into flame and as far as I could tell, neither did anyone else.

Payton's gaze never left Echo. He stared at her, his face deathly pale and sweaty, his mouth set in a grim line. He was enduring a hell of a lot for the woman he loved.

The designs around Macy began to glow. As I watched, the glow spread outward. Two more sigils, then three more, then all of them. Then the silence was broken by the sound of blowing wind that didn't touch anything in the room: no one's hair or clothes fluttered, no papers were carried into the air. The wind, so loud, was only a noise. The glowing designs flared, then turned black.

The floor turned black a moment later. I peered down at it, at nothing. The outer circle around the design was still there, painted onto the floorboards, and the circles around each of the four outer stations remained, but the floor and the designs beneath Echo's body had vanished. There was nothing below us except the void. It was as though a trap door had opened into space.

I leaned forward and squinted into it. Something glimmered down in the darkness. It was a tiny swirling light, growing brighter and arcing wider with each passing second.

After a few moments I realized that it was actually a collection of lights. They spiraled upward toward us, moving very much like a swarm of bees. They came closer and closer, growing brighter and brighter, until I could see that the swarm was huge. There must have been thousands of lights in it.

The lights gathered just below the design. Each was as big as a ping pong ball, and they were all the same icy blue-white color. Their light shone up onto Echo, casting her in a pale, eerie glow. The symbols around Echo, which had vanished when the floor vanished, were illuminated in the weird faerie lights shining from below.

I sat stunned. This was completely different from the dangerous little spells I had created in the library. That had been like forging a piece of metal. This was touching the unknown.

I was looking at the world behind the world, and it terrified me.

One of the swirling lights found a small loop at the edge of Echo's circle and slid upward, floating above the level of the floor. As soon as the first came through, others swarmed after it, streaming through like water droplets shooting up from a fountain. Many more gathered around the loop trying to push their way to the front.

The lights swirled around Echo's body, first moving clockwise, then reversing their direction. They stayed within the edge of her circle, and didn't rise higher than seven or eight feet above her. They spiraled back and forth, making beautiful streams of cool light. It was like watching a school of creatures at the deepest parts of the ocean exploring in a hot water vent. I couldn't look away.

Finally, one of the lights pushed into her mouth and vanished down her throat.

Echo opened her eyes.

The lights flushed out of the loop like water running down a drain. They flowed into the void beneath the floor, and the light they cast no longer illuminated the painted design. I watched them swirl in the darkness, seemingly lost and unable to find their way back.

Echo stood, her movements stiff and awkward; for a moment she seemed to be suspended over the void. Then the glyphs in the design and the hardwood floor began to reappear. In a couple of seconds, the room had become an ordinary dining room with a painted sigil on the floor.

Echo turned to look at us all, twisting at the waist as though she didn't know how to move her neck. She still looked like a day-old corpse. "Hello, cousins," she said in a flat voice. "Thank you for inviting me here."

The hairs on the back of my neck were standing at attention. "What the hell did we just do?"

Macy sprang to her feet and embraced Echo. "Echo! Are you okay? We were so worried!"

Echo seemed puzzled. She looked at Macy, then Jon, then me, then Payton. She was obviously expecting a different reaction.

Payton stared up at her like a love-struck puppy. Tears ran down his cheeks. He gasped, fighting the urge to cry.

Echo looked down at his face, at his ruined arm and leg, and turned away as if they meant nothing to her. "I am fine. You performed your duties perfectly."

"Jesus Christ, Jon," I said. "I barely know Echo and even I can tell this isn't her."

"Shut up!" Macy said.

Jon watched Echo warily. "She's just in shock."

"She's dead," I said. "Whatever you put inside her—"

"Move me into the spot," Payton said. "It's my turn."

I rolled out of the circle and grabbed my pack. As I started to stand, a powerful hand knocked me to the floor.

Macy's voice was low and angry. "You're not going anywhere."

Suffering a threat from Macy would have been laughable under other circumstances. I looked up at her, with her hair curled like a little girl's, and remembered how she'd hit the ball in the cage, and how Echo had moved in the fight with Annalise. I had reason to be afraid of her, and I hate being afraid. "I'm not doing that again. I can't believe I let you talk me into doing it once."

"Payton needs to be healed," Macy said. "We need your help. You are going to help, or I am going to fetch a couple hammers and start breaking your bones."

"Babe." Jon's voice was hard. "Don't threaten my friend."

"Why not?" She sounded annoyed. "We can fix anything we do to him."

"Fuck no," I said. "No, no, no, no. I don't care what you do, I am not going to have one of those things inside me."

"Ray," Jon moved around Macy and helped me to my feet. "No one is going to force you. But listen: Payton wants this. Look at him. Echo nearly died last night, and Payton couldn't do a thing to protect her."

I tried to keep my voice down. "*Nearly*, Jon? Nearly? Echo died last night. The real Echo is gone."

"No," Echo said. She looked around uncertainly, as though feeling blindly toward something important. "I am here. I am just... adjusting to my sudden...."

I watched her search for the correct word. She didn't look confused. I'd seen guys in a drugged-out daze, or who had been beaten up and couldn't remember how they got to prison. I'd also seen my share of liars. Echo looked like a liar, and she wasn't good at it.

"Recovery, sweetie," Macy said. She caressed Echo's arm. "We healed you, and you must still be in shock."

"Yes!" she looked at Macy with a blank expression. "That's it. I was injured."

The others wanted to believe her, and the idea made me sick. "That's not Echo."

"Sure it is. She's in shock." Jon glanced at her again.

"Keep saying that," I said. "Maybe you'll convince yourself."

Macy moved toward me again, but Jon edged slightly closer to her, making her pull back. He was protecting me from her.

"I don't know why you're so afraid," Macy said. "Didn't you see the lights? Weren't they beautiful? Those were spirits of healing. They're the same spirits we put into Jon and me. *Jon can walk because of those lights.* What are you so afraid of?"

"A worm the size of a cat."

Macy shook her head, clearly exasperated.

Jon led me into the kitchen. As I left the room, I saw Echo standing beside the design, holding the can of red paint.

"I didn't see any worms," Jon said when we were alone in the kitchen.

"Is Echo your cousin? Is she Macy's cousin?"

"What?" Jon said. "No, man. She's not. She's just rattled. Confused."

"Jon, I don't have all the answers, okay? I don't. But I don't need all the answers to know there's a problem with this. Why can't we...."

I trailed off. I looked over Jon's shoulder and saw Macy standing in the doorway. She held a carving knife in her hand, and she had an expression I'd seen many times. She was going to kill me.

Jon had started saying something about letting me make my own choices, and how Payton wanted to do the same. Payton wanted the spell because he loved Echo so much, and I would be taking away Payton's choice if I refused to help.

It was bull, but it didn't matter. Macy was waiting for my answer, and she had a weapon ready if she didn't like what she heard. Would she break my arms and legs and pin me into a circle with the knife?

Or she could cut my throat and put me into the center circle. As soon as one of the "lights of healing" entered me, I'd be one of their cousins. My re-animated corpse would be happy to sit in for Payton's spell.

The back door was right behind me, but I knew I couldn't run, not with the way they moved. And while Jon seemed ready to protect me, was I really going to trust my life to him after what he did less than an hour ago on the campus?

They were going to get my help no matter what.

"I'll do it," I said, breaking into Jon's increasingly meaningless argument. "For Payton. I don't want any spirits entering me."

Jon was startled, but then smiled broadly. Macy was no longer standing in the doorway.

When we'd returned to the dining room, Macy and Echo had already moved Payton into the center of the design. "I would like to do the honors," Echo said. "I understand the procedure very well."

"Sure thing, sweetie," Macy said. She sat in Payton's spot. Jon and I took our places.

Echo held out her hand. "I will need to read the music. I can not hold music in my mind."

Macy looked surprised at that, but just bit her lip and handed over the blue sheet of paper.

I wanted that page. When I steal something it belongs to me, and I had to take it back. Callin had done this to my friends, and I needed the spell to figure out how to pay him back, or at least undo this mess.

Glancing down at the design on the floor, I thought it looked different. Was that curling line from the center circle to mine new or had it been there before? I reached out to see if the paint was wet but heard Macy clear her throat. She glared at me, warning me off. I withdrew my hand.

Echo held the sheet music up and began to sing. Her voice was clear and beautiful, but silence quickly fell over the room.

The spell proceeded as before: silence, the roar of a wind that disturbed nothing in the room, a succession of glowing sigils, then the floor opened up into a vast darkness. But this time, the sound of the wind went on and on. The spell kept building, but slowly, as though something was dragging at it. The new curling line, maybe?

When the swarm of lights appeared, they were already close. For a moment they moved back and forth as if lost, then they began to stream through the loop toward Payton's body.

The lights trickled into the space around him, swirling and swarming. Payton threw his head back and opened his mouth wide. A speck of light dove into his throat and disappeared.

This time the lights didn't drain back out into the void. They swam through the air inside the boundary around Payton, then struck the spot where the spiral line of paint connected my circle to the one in the center.

Then a stream of lights rushed along the twisting line of paint straight toward me. I was so startled that for a moment I couldn't move, and that was all the time it took them to come close.

The lights had faces. And teeth.

CHAPTER THIRTEEN

I rolled backward, throwing myself out of the circle. The "spirits" inside the spiral line dissolved in an upward spray of liquid light.

The floor appeared at the outer edge of the design, and the void began to recede toward the center circle. The lights still within Payton's circle rushed through the opening into the void as though fleeing a forest fire. After a few seconds, the void was gone, and so were all the lights.

Echo leaped to her feet and moved toward me. "You burning, lonely squat of shit! What have you done?"

I put my hand on the pocket with my ghost knife. If I survived her first attack, and maybe her second, I might have time to use it. "You tried to put one of those things in me!"

Suddenly, Payton screamed. He clutched his broken elbow and writhed on the floor. The flesh inside his arm shifted and realigned.

"You killed them!" Echo shouted. Her eyes were wide and her teeth bared. "You murdered them!"

Jon rushed to Payton and laid a calming hand on his shoulder. "Hold it together, big guy. I know it hurts—believe me, I know—but it won't take long."

Echo crouched low. Here she comes.

"Stop." One word from Jon was enough. She froze in place, but she still glared at me as if she wanted to tear me to pieces. "What happened, Ray?"

"She tried to cast that spell on me," I said, trying to keep my voice calm. "She tried to put one of those things inside me."

"I didn't see anything," Macy said quickly.

That was it. I'd stayed because I thought it would save my life and how stupid was that? I stood, grabbed my pack and bolted through to the kitchen just behind me.

Jon still beat me to the back door. "Ray, I'll keep them in line. Don't go."

"We're friends," I said, mimicking him as nastily as I could. "I won't force you."

"Sometimes friends fuck up."

Shit. I was suddenly warm with shame. "Who sat in the fifth spot the other times you cast the spell?"

"Ray, I can't tell you. I promised. I got my legs back and all I had to do was not spread around the name."

"Forget it."

"You know normally I wouldn't hold out on you," Jon said. "But I *promised*."

I unzipped the bag and showed him the blue pages inside. "I already know who it was. We obviously got our spells from the same person."

"I guess we did. Look, out of the whole group, I got the cure first. That makes me alpha. I can keep everyone in line."

"Even Macy? What about her hammers?"

"That was just talk," Jon said. "Macy's a therapist. She takes care of people. She heals bodies and souls. That's her whole career. She's a good person, Ray. That hammer thing was just stress."

He hadn't seen her expression when she stood behind him with the knife, but I wasn't going to argue about his girlfriend. "Can I leave?"

Jon looked uncomfortable. "If you want to, of course, yeah. But I hope you don't. I'm so hungry I can barely think, sometimes. I need you here. Do you really want to go?"

"After that?" I said, pointing toward the other room, "more than anything." But Jon needed my help. I still hadn't told him about Annalise and Callin. Did Jon know that Callin planned to kill him and was allied with the woman who'd attacked Echo?

And whatever Macy and Echo had done, Jon wasn't to blame. He was still my friend, and had done the right thing by me at every turn. His family had practically rescued me from mine. I couldn't run out on him now.

"But I'll stick around," I said. "For a while, at least. There's a lot we need to talk about."

Jon beamed. "Perfect!" He clapped my shoulder hard.

Macy entered with a slice of cold pizza in each hand. She gave one to Jon and he bit into it greedily. "Echo and Payton went out for more food," she said. "I ordered another meat lovers'. What about him?"

She took a huge bite of the pizza. Jon talked around the food in his mouth. "He's staying to help us. When the others get back, we'll talk."

"Why not right now? I'll tell you and you can tell them."

Macy shook her head. Jon swallowed and said: "I might forget something. Or something might get changed in the telling. Or they might have questions I can't answer. Besides, they're family. It's not right that we should know something they don't."

I looked at them, hoping they were joking. They weren't. They seriously didn't want to know something the others didn't. It was a strange kind of loyalty, and it didn't make any sense.

"The woman who attacked—" I said, forging ahead anyway.

"Later, later. I need to look at these." Jon snatched the blue pages out of my backpack and walked into the other room so fast that he was already gone by the time I could react.

Macy stepped toward me. I had the urge to step back but I didn't. Her knife lay on the counter; Macy put her hand on it and slid it into the sink.

"I'm sorry," she said. "I shouldn't have threatened you. I know what I did was wrong, but I did it for a good reason. I never... I didn't mean to..." She raised the pizza to her mouth but the smell seemed to upset her and tossed it into the trash. She blinked slowly, her head sagging as though she couldn't organize her own thoughts.

"I've hated violence my whole life," she said. "My father was stabbed to death coming out of a bar. My third stepfather once beat my mom so bad that she bled out of her ears. I've always hated it, always did what I could to help people who had been victims of it."

She took a deep shuddering sigh. "But today, when the stress was intense, I...."

She didn't seem to know what to say next. After a short

while, she said: "I'm sorry I forced you to do what I wanted. I've always tried to be a better person than that. So, I'm sorry. Anyway, I wouldn't have done anything to you that we couldn't undo right away."

I didn't answer. It seemed to me that her cure was worse than anything she could have done to me, including kill me, but there was no point in arguing. She didn't matter. I was here for Jon.

Judging by her expression, I didn't give her the response she was expecting. She moved away. I followed her into the dining room. Jon wasn't around.

But there was the sheet of blue paper sitting on the sideboard; it was different from mine because it had been folded small to fit into someone's pocket, then unfolded again. I wanted to look at it to see if it would match any of the handwriting in the book I'd stolen from Callin, just to make sure.

Macy's back was turned as she headed toward the front room. I picked up the paper.

Macy froze in place and tilted her head like a dog that heard a familiar sound. I didn't have time to pocket the sheet of paper and her body language suggested that she was about to turn around. With a flick of my wrist, I tossed it behind the sideboard.

She turned and studied my face. I tried to look nonchalant but I knew I wasn't doing a great job. She sniffed as though she could smell my fear. "Is there a problem?"

"You can't blame me for keeping a safe distance," I said. She blinked at that, and then moved toward the porch. I followed.

We found Jon squatting on the couch, his shoes squarely

on the seat cushions. He was hunched over a slice of cheese pizza, gnawing and tearing at it without satisfaction.

The stack of blue pages sat on the floor, apparently forgotten. I picked them up.

"Get down off there!" Macy said. She swatted Jon with a little square pillow. "Or at least take your shoes off."

Jon climbed down, still chewing madly. He didn't speak or stop eating. Macy opened the top pizza box, found it empty, then shoved it into a corner with a bunch of others. She opened two more before she found a cold slice with grease congealed on the top.

"Do you want some?" Jon said. "It's terrible."

I hadn't eaten anything except Hank's muffins for most of the day, but seeing Jon and Macy hunched over their greasy food made my stomach twinge. "Pass."

"I don't blame you," Jon said. "This is the worst pizza I've ever had in my life." He took another gigantic bite. His eyes were hooded and distant. He and Macy wandered into the empty dining room and stood beside the design, chewing blankly.

For a moment, I thought they might do more magic, but no. They had simply moved close to the design the way bored people stand in front of a TV without really watching—it seemed to comfort them as they chewed and gulped.

I glanced at the sideboard, knowing I couldn't retrieve the page with the "healing" spell while they were standing there. Maybe, while we waited for Echo and Payton, I should take another look at the pages I'd taken from Callin. Now that I'd seen Macy and Echo cast the spell, something new might jump out at me. "Is there a quiet place I could rest?"

"Yoga room would be the best thing," Macy said.

Jon swallowed the last bite and said: "My thoughts exactly."

He led me up the stairs. There were four doors in the hallway, one of which Jon said was the bathroom. He took me into the room at the back.

It was spare and nearly empty. Foam rubber mats covered part of the floor. In the corner, tiny dumb bells lay piled one on the other the way empty pizza boxes were piled up downstairs. Pictures clipped from magazines had been taped to the walls; all showed women in extremely difficult yoga poses. Any one of them would have eased my long prison nights.

"Will this be okay?" Jon asked.

"Great."

"Okay then." Jon hesitated at the doorway. "I just want to say thanks, buddy. And don't worry. It'll all be cool."

I nodded at him and he left. I sat by the window and watched light from the setting sun reflect off the polished hardwood floor. I was glad I wouldn't have to touch the light switch; I didn't want to touch anything here.

If Jon would only listen to my story, I'd at least feel like we were getting somewhere. I could get away from him and figure out what to do next. But Jon wasn't worried about what I needed or where I needed to go. He had his own agenda.

I sat on one of the foam pads, finding it surprisingly soft. I laid the pages in the sunlight. Echo and Payton would be back soon with more food, and I could explain the situation to all of them while they stuffed their faces.

I turned over the first of the blue pages and saw a spell I'd seen earlier that day. *To Look Into the Empty Spaces and*

See the Great Predators. Below the title were the words *Your enemies are near. You will watch them as a ghost, as they are ghosts to you.*

Design number two was a straight line with a simple curl at the left end. It looked like an easy spell, and I certainly had enemies. If I cast this spell, maybe I'd know where to find Callin and Annalise.

I had a quick mental image of the two of them staking out this house like a pair of cops. It made me uneasy, just as it made me uneasy to think what Jon and the other would do if they knew where to find Annalise. I couldn't picture Macy sneaking out a side door and vanishing into the night the way I would. She'd want to murder them both, and that would make me an accessory.

On the windowsill was a notepad and pencil. Someone had scrawled a list of exercises: weights and sets and reps. I flipped to an empty page at the back, turned it over and sat again.

I practiced the second design quickly. It was easy. Then I studied the first design, the one with "for the mind" written beneath it.

Nearly concentric circles, the smaller covered with crooked lines. A pair of weird squiggles.

The squiggles could be empty eyes. The sphere appeared to have crooked lines across its face. Were those continents? Was this a planet? Two circles could be *the world behind the world.*

The image in my mind glowed silver, slammed together and erupted with power. I immediately began to draw the simple second design, waiting for the fire to hit. It never did.

This time the concentric circles became a long, black tunnel, and I fell through it into darkness.

I was weightless. There was no floor beneath me and there was no sunlight, no window, no yoga mat. I was floating in darkness.

I tried to touch my chest but my hand passed through it as though I was made of shadow. There was darkness all around me but no stars, just faintly-lit mists swirling in the distance.

I looked up. The planet Earth slowly rotated far above me. It was also shrouded in darkness and mist.

Oh, shit. I was dead. I had killed himself—turned myself into a ghost—because I just *had* to fool around with one more spell. I wasn't even sure how it had happened, or if the "how" even mattered.

"So long," I said to the Earth. It looked far away, only about the size of my fist. "It wasn't fun while it lasted." My voice sounded hollow in the darkness.

A sudden, oppressive pressure came over me. It felt as though something was rolling across me, like the mind of God had taken notice of me, and this incredible will was squeezing every thought every living thing was having everywhere into my mind at once. Then the feeling passed, and I was myself again, stunned and disoriented.

I had the odd sensation that something was moving behind me and I turned to look.

A massive *thing* passed by. It was close, only a few dozen yards away, and it was as long as ten aircraft carriers. Its hide was dark and splotchy, with patches of hair and weird, random stripes of black and red.

Oh, Christ, it was some kind of animal, fully alive and

swimming through the void. I peered at it, trying to make sense of the patterns on its skin as it sped by. Then I saw them: Weird alien faces were embedded in the hide, and they looked like they were screaming.

The thing passed by and I watched its stumpy legs and scraggly dragon's tail recede into the distance. I was glad I hadn't seen its head. I didn't want to know what that thing had for a head.

In the distance, I saw wheels of fire rolling through the darkness. Then a group of boulders tumbled below me, and just as I realized the eerie singing was coming from them, they changed direction like a flock of birds.

I'm in hell, I thought. *I died and now I'm in hell. I'm surrounded by demons and I'm in hell.*

A cluster of glowing eel-like creatures approached from beneath my feet, growing larger and brighter with each second. There were no landmarks, and every time I thought they were almost upon me, I realized they were larger and farther away than I'd thought. Hundreds of them.

Then they finally swarmed around me, each as large as a school bus and each with hungry, gaping beaks and wide, searching eyes.

They swam right by as though I wasn't there.

They couldn't see me. If they had, one of them could have turned its head slightly and bitten me in half.

"Watch them as a ghost," I said aloud, testing my hollow voice again.

Maybe I wasn't dead. Maybe the spell had sent me into this void, these "Empty Spaces." I was on the other side of the so-called healing spell Macy and Payton and Jon had cast. This was where the cousins came from, although I didn't see any blue lights or fat worms with wings and spiny legs nearby.

I looked up at the Earth again. The school of eels passed it as though they couldn't see it, either.

Beyond the Earth, and in several other directions, I could see more worlds rolling through the mists. All were obscured and the creatures passed them by. Were the planets camouflaged the way I was, or was there something about the mists that diverted the creatures' attention? Or maybe they could see the worlds but didn't care.

There was a flash of silver light to the left. I glanced over and saw a glowing sigil shining in the darkness. It was a little like the spell Jon had used to summon the cousins, and it had appeared on the surface of a little purple planet shrouded in mist. The sigil burned like a flare.

The eels sped by me, swimming for the glowing sigil. The tumbling boulders changed course and headed straight for the planet. They plunged toward it, then began moving around it in swarms.

I willed myself to be closer and I was. The planet seemed to be growing darker and more of the eels were dropping to the surface. A sound seemed to flow out of the world below like a ripple in a pond, even though I knew it wasn't really a sound I was hearing. But somehow I knew people below were screaming. They were dying in pain and despair, and those emotions echoed out into the void. The little planet grew slightly darker.

Three wheels of fire rolled out of a cloud of mist, drawn by the strange sound. Now that they were close, I saw eyes within the flames. They struck, cutting through the world like buzzsaws. The planet began to burn.

A swarm of tumbling boulders slammed themselves against the world. Their eerie, joyful song halted as they destroyed themselves, but huge sprays of debris were thrown clear of the planet, and each one sang a new song.

The eerie screams finally died away. The purple world blackened and as life left it, I could see it vanishing, as though it would fall out of the Empty Spaces once it was devoid of life.

I'd just seen an entire world consumed and destroyed. These creatures weren't ignoring the worlds around them, they were searching for them, looking for their next meal. And the only way they'd find it was if someone sent up a call for them.

I glanced back at the Earth. A tiny sigil erupted on its face, glowing bright silver. A reddish bolt shot toward it, then the sigil faded. I didn't see the world grow dark and I didn't hear screaming. That time.

My pencil snapped.

I stared down at the broken pencil in my hand. I suddenly felt very heavy and real. I was made of flesh again. The floor was solid and the room was dim.

I was in the yoga room. The sun had gone down while I'd been in the Empty Spaces and the only light came from a shaft of moonlight that fell into the corner.

We were playing with something we didn't understand. Casting these spells was like laying a trail of raw meat from the jungle through the front door of our house. We were calling monsters, and I had fucking helped.

"What the hell have we been doing?" I said aloud.

"Preparing," a voice behind me said.

I jumped to my feet. A tall, slender figure stood in the doorway, lit by the dim hall light. Echo. Her sallow skin and sunken eyes looked healthy again. I'd never been one to go for the plain look in a woman, but she was beautiful.

There was enough light to see that her hands were empty; maybe she hadn't come to kill me. She glided toward me, staring intently into my eyes. "You are alone." Her body was as fluid as a tiger's. She moved out of the hall light and became a silhouette. I didn't move.

Of course I was alone. I'd just spent three years in prison and the only women I saw there were on TV or were taped to walls like a pinup. "Yeah, I—" She leaned toward me, as though she was about to kiss me. "Payton."

She breathed in, taking in the smell of me, and her body language was so smooth that a small part of me was suggesting that maybe she wasn't a monster after all.

"Payton does not matter," she said. "I don't like to share."

That didn't really make sense. I had the sudden intuition that I was being incredibly stupid. It may have been a long time for me, but I wasn't a damn fool.

She leaned close. The tip of her nose touched my cheek and it felt all wrong. I stepped back. "I need to talk to Jon," I said. I realized that I still didn't know where Annalise and Callin were. "We're all in danger."

Echo stepped toward me into the light. Her eyes were wild and starving, and she had a killer's deranged smile.

CHAPTER FOURTEEN

I fumbled for my ghost knife. Echo grabbed my arms, lifted me into the air and slammed me onto the hardwood floor.

It was a bruising impact and I cried out, partly because it hurt like six kinds of hell and partly because I immediately knew that she was too strong for me. The fight was already over, and I hadn't even had time to lift my hands.

I tried to will my ghost knife out of my pocket the way I'd *called* it out of the concrete stair, but I was too panicked to concentrate.

Echo smiled. "If you will not become one of us...." She leaned close to my throat, her teeth bared.

She was suddenly torn away from me, leaving me alone on the floor. She flew backwards and slammed into the wall, cracking the plasterboard.

She fell to the floor, an animal noise of rage and frustration coming from her. Jon picked her up and slammed her against the wall a second time. Plaster dust rained down on them.

"I told you! He's my friend!" Jon pinned her against the broken wall. She struggled, but could not free herself.

"Wake up in there, cousin!" Echo shouted at him. "Wake up!"

Jon shook her. "I *am* awake!"

Payton leaned in through the doorway and switched on the light.

Except for Echo, they were all covered in blood. Their shirts, their pants, their hands and even their faces were smeared with dark blood.

I snatched up my pages and hugged them to my chest. A chill ran down my back. Jon shoved Echo into Payton's arms; he embraced her and began to speak softly into her ear. She glared at Jon.

"Out." Jon slammed the door.

He stalked toward the window. I couldn't see a visible wound on him but, considering how casually he'd taken the loss of his finger, I wasn't sure if he'd even notice one. Had he been fighting? Had Annalise turned up while I was floating around in the Empty Spaces?

"Are you hurt?" I asked.

Jon threw open the window. "You're getting out of here." He climbed out onto the roof.

"That's not your blood," I said. I picked up my backpack, feeling as though I was a step behind everyone else. "Whose blood is that? Is it—"

He reached back through the window and grabbed my arm. His grip was frighteningly strong. He dragged me out the window and onto the roof.

A misty rain had begun to fall. What I'd thought to be a shaft of moonlight was actually a single streetlight. I shoved the pages into my pack.

Jon gasped and clutched his wrist, holding his hand up

to the light. The stump of his missing pinkie finger began to visibly throb.

Something pushed out of the stump of the old finger like a worm crawling free of the dirt and it only took a moment to realize it was a new finger. Jon gasped again. This was hurting him, but he couldn't repress a huge grin.

After a few seconds, it stopped. Jon's finger had grown back. I grabbed his hand and pulled it close.

The regenerated finger looked paler than the others, but otherwise it appeared normal. Jon curled and straightened his fingers. They functioned perfectly.

"Holy God," I said. "How does it feel?"

"Fine," Jon said. "But it didn't hurt when I lost it, either." He held up his hand and made a fist. "I can heal anything now, if I have the right food."

"What food is that, Jon?"

He stopped smiling. "You have to go." He lifted me off my feet and held me like a groom carrying a bride across the threshold. Before I could object, Jon stepped off the edge of the roof.

He shifted his arm to support my head. We hit the ground so hard that I thought momentum would wrench me out of his grip and slam me against the pavement, but Jon held on.

He released my legs, allowing me to stand. The roof was about ten feet off the ground. How strong were these guys?

Through the kitchen window I could see all the way into the dining room. Macy sat hunched on the floor, facing away from me. Her shoulders trembled as though she was crying.

"Get out," Jon said. "Now."

I couldn't read his expression. "I'm here to help you, Jon. There are things you need to know. You're still in danger."

I glanced back into the house. Macy had turned to face us. Blood covered her lips and chin. Her gaze met mine and her eyes widened with shame and horror. She ducked out of the doorway to hide.

There, on the floor where she had been crouching, was a bloody human foot.

"Oh, no." I felt sick at the sight of it, but I wasn't surprised. I should have been surprised, but I wasn't.

Jon grabbed my shoulders and turned me around. "Ray. You're my oldest friend and I love you like a brother. I used to ask my parents to adopt you so you could *be* my brother. Go back to L.A. Go to Chicago or New York. Just get out and don't come back here. Ever."

I backed down the alley. My whole body shuddered with a primal animal dread. Jon was sending me away. Jon was covered in someone else's blood. Jon was eating human flesh.

No. No, no, no. I couldn't allow this to continue. Callin was going to have to take the spell off. I would make sure of it.

Jon stood there, staring at me. I couldn't stay, but I couldn't abandon him, either. "I'm going to make this right, Jon," I called. "I'm going to make it right for you."

He didn't respond. He just watched me jog down the alley and disappear into the street.

At the sidewalk I slowed to a walk. It would take me at least an hour to walk from here to Aunt Theresa's house and while I still had a little money, I didn't want to throw it away on bus fare. Besides, I needed time to think. I stuffed the blue pages into my backpack and slung it over my shoulder.

But there was one thing I didn't need to think about: I'd told Callin that I wouldn't take Jon's so-called cure away if it meant he'd lose the use of his legs again, but after what I'd just seen, I was ready to do it. Hell, I'd do it gladly. Jon didn't just need to be protected from Annalise and her people, he needed to be saved. I was ready to step in and do it if there were no other volunteers, and there weren't.

Was this my life now? Had I somehow gone, in one pivot, from ex-con to... this? I laid my hands against the rough bark of a nearby tree, but there was no comfort in it. It didn't make me feel grounded or sane. My life had gone nuts, and I wasn't sure how I'd get back to the normal world.

Or even if I wanted to. Despite everything I'd seen, I wanted more of it. I wanted more of the world behind the world. It made me feel sick to admit it to myself, but the blue pages in my backpack were worth more to me than diamond. If I studied, went slowly, was careful, I could, maybe have the power of a "peer"—whatever that was—and despite everything I'd seen, there was part of me that wanted it.

It occurred to me that Echo could have slipped out of the front door and come after me. I took out my ghost knife and glanced up and down the street. There was nothing to see, and I realized I ought to be looking out for Annalise and Callin, too.

I picked up the pace, holding the ghost knife so it would stay dry but still be handy, and I had my last steeled glass spell in my pocket.

I was hungry again and my cash was dwindling. I headed home. Karl hadn't been wearing his cheerful face when he came to visit me at the library, but now I knew he wasn't after me because of Echo. With luck, he would be out and I could talk to my aunt alone. Maybe she'd have some food for me.

Maybe, in the quiet of my apartment, I could cast more steeled glass cards. I was going to need them, I was sure, and I needed to find time to study Callin's book again.

And how the hell was I supposed to persuade Callin to remove the spell from Jon and the others? At gunpoint? I wasn't sure a gun would give me the leverage I needed to control him. Maybe I should try it at bombpoint instead.

During the long walk back to my apartment, I turned the problem over in my head but nothing truly workable presented itself. The only thing that came to mind was that Callin and Annalise had been pretty desperate to get that book back. Maybe I could get the leverage I needed if I threatened to staple the spells to telephone poles around town, or upload them to the internet.

It was a bluff, of course. The spells were too dangerous to be shared, but Callin didn't know I felt that way. And the virtue of blackmail was that I wouldn't have to build a goddamn bomb. The real question was whether it would work or not, and whether there was any way at all for me to come through it alive.

Once back in my aunt's neighborhood, I walked an extra block to circle around to the alley. With luck, Uncle Karl's car would still be gone. I'd be able to sneak some food into my apartment. I needed food and sleep as much as I needed a better way to blackmail Callin. I also needed a watch; I had no idea what time it was.

The misty rain had stopped 15 or 20 minutes before, but

the driveway was soft with deep mud. It couldn't have been caused by this misting rain; had someone washed a Mack truck out here?

Then I walked around the high hedges of the neighbor's yard and saw that Karl and Theresa's house was gone. For a moment, I thought I was on the wrong block. All I could see were the houses across the street. But no, this was the right place.

The house had been burned down to its stone foundations. The garage was gone, too. It, and my tiny new home above it, were ashes. The fire fighters were long gone, and there weren't even any neighbors standing around gawking. All this had happened hours ago.

I struck something metal with my foot. It was the tiny bell I had strung beside my door, now charred, dented and missing its clapper.

"Freeze!" a man shouted. "Police."

I froze. I heard several pairs of footsteps approaching, and as they came close, Karl stepped into my line of vision. His expression was grim. This was why my uncle had been hunting for me.

"Uncle Karl, is Aunt Th—"

Karl jammed his nightstick into my stomach. I doubled over and fell to my knees. It wasn't the first time a cop had done that to me, but Karl was damn good at it. More people behind me pushed me down into the muddy gravel and slapped handcuffs on me.

I was handcuffed and processed, and they were pretty professional about it, considering. My blue pages, ghost knife and steeled glass cards were confiscated and I was dumped into a holding cell.

I sat among the other detainees, feeling my hopes sinking lower and lower. No one would tell me if my aunt was alive or dead, I hadn't done any real good for Jon, and I was back in custody, likely to be charged with arson or worse.

And why shouldn't they? I had led Callin and Annalise to Karl and Theresa's home. I might not have started the fire myself, but it had been my fault.

They let me stew in the cell for a few hours, then handcuffed me and brought me to an interrogation room. There was a long, scarred wooden table and chairs, yellow paint on the walls and even a "mirror," just like in the movies. The two detectives with me sat across the table from me, sloppily shuffling papers and looking bored. They had arms a gorilla would envy, but their bellies strained against their shirt buttons. They introduced themselves but I didn't pay attention. To me they were Big and Bigger.

They started by asking basic identifying information like my name and address.

"What happened to Aunt Theresa?" I asked, breaking in on their routine. "Was she hurt in the fire?"

"We'll be asking the questions here, not you," Big said. "Where were you yesterday afternoon between noon and five p.m.?"

I was irritated. Karl had warned me that my debt wasn't repaid yet, but if I was going to be here, opposite these two cops, with handcuffs on, there was no reason to play at being a nice, cooperative citizen anymore. "I was walking around, wondering how my Aunt Theresa is."

"Son, this isn't a time to be a wiseass," Bigger said. "Now answer the question."

"I told you, I was trying to get an answer about my aunt."

"You want to know?" Bigger said, his eyes moving shiftily to his partner and back to me. "She's in the hospital and she's not doing well. If she dies, you could be charged with accessory—"

"Christ! You guys even lie sloppy. Where's my Uncle?"

"What about this?" Big said. He slid a manila folder across the table and opened it.

The blue pages were inside and so was the ghost knife and the steeled glass. I felt a sudden, startling hunger for them. I wanted that power again. I could feel the ghost knife as though it was part of me. All I had to do was will it into my hand....

No. I didn't want these cops to see magic. I didn't want anyone to know about it.

I realized they were staring at me. They'd noticed my reaction to the contents of the folder. I closed my eyes and sat back in my chair. It was too late for a poker face now; the cops knew the papers were important to me.

"Well?" Big asked. "Where did you get those?"

I kept my eyes shut. The allure of those pages was strong, sure, but even stronger was the memory of my aunt embracing me on the steps of her house, or the memory of her lifting that pot of stew with her arthritic hands.

"Where's my uncle?" I asked.

The cops sighed and settled back into their seats. Big closed the manila folder, and I thought he looked a little nervous as he did it. Could he sense the power there?

The door opened and Karl strode inside. He did not look as tall as I remembered, and his weathered face was sunken and shadowy. He looked exhausted.

"Do you know what I lost yesterday, Raymond?" Karl began without any preamble. "Do you know what I lost because I brought you into my home? I lost every picture I ever took of my kids. All of my wife's medications. Every love letter my father wrote to my mother. The rare jazz collection my brother left me in his will. I don't even like jazz, but it was all I had left of him."

Christ, I almost would rather take another night stick to the gut. I laid my face in my hands. "Please," I said. "How is she?"

"She was at the supermarket," Karl said. "She's fine. Did you firebomb my house?"

"No! Never."

"Somebody did. Was it an old buddy from jail, then? Or one of your L.A. crew?"

The urge to blurt out the truth was as strong as my urge to grab up the spells. Didn't Karl deserve to know? I hadn't been able to tell Jon, but maybe the cops would roust Callin out of his hotel, maybe put enough heat on him that he would leave town.

Or maybe they'd arrive at his hotel while he was out, search his room and turn up his spell book. What if one of them had cancer or a dying mother? That would mean more spells, more cousins, more... Who knows what?

I shut my eyes again. My uncle deserved some sort of answer, but there was nothing I could tell him.

The door opened again.

Callin entered. He wore a broad-brimmed hat and a long coat buttoned up to his neck and he was smiling.

"There you are, lively one!" Callin said.

Karl turned and placed a hand on Callin's chest. Karl was six inches taller and fifty pounds heavier but as Karl opened his mouth to order Callin out of the room, I shouted: "Uncle Karl, get back!"

It was already too late. Callin held a handkerchief in front of Karl's face. There was a sigil stitched onto it, but I couldn't see the whole thing.

Karl glanced at it, then his eyes rolled back and he collapsed. Big lunged out of his chair and slammed his body into Callin's back. Unfortunately for him, Callin had braced for the attack and the detective bounced off him the same way I'd bounced off Annalise.

I stood, turned my back and shut my eyes, mentally *calling* my ghost knife. It landed in my hand and I cut through the handcuff chain with a quick twist of my wrist. I heard the unmistakable sound of a taser being fired.

I spun and grabbed the whole manila folder with the blue pages in it, then ducked low beside the cinderblock wall. With the ghost knife, I cut three quick slashes into the wall.

Bigger rolled across the table and struck the wall just behind me, his taser clattering on the floor.

I threw my shoulder against the cut cinderblocks and pushed. Karl lay in a heap beneath the table and I had no way of telling if he was alive or dead. Then the cut blocks slid out of the wall and I followed them into open air.

Instead of coming out into a hallway or office, I found myself six floors above the asphalt parking lot. The weight of my upper body dragged my legs through the hole into free fall. Sky and traffic and the whole world spun around me as I plummeted.

I squeezed the folder, holding the steeled glass against my chest. "Please please please please," I said. The parking lot seemed to rush up at me.

CHAPTER FIFTEEN

The chunk of cinderblock wall slammed into the asphalt only a moment before I did. My whole body jolted and slapped against the broken cinderblocks with terrifying, irresistible force.

Then I sat up. I felt fine. No pain, no injuries. I couldn't see the steeled glass inside the folder but I could feel the magic draining out of it like a water rushing out of a punctured bottle.

I rolled to my feet and wrapped my arms around my chest, hiding the cuffs behind the sleeves of my shirt. Two uniformed police officers ran across the parking lot with their hands on their weapons.

"Did you see that?" I asked as I hurried away from the pile of rubble, getting as far from the building as I could. "Those bricks nearly fell on me!"

The older cop drew his weapon. "Let me see your hands."

"Bob?" the younger cop said. They both looked up.

Callin had stepped through the hole in the wall. He leaned out.

"Sir!" The young cop said. "Don't jump!"

Callin released his hold on the cinderblocks and plummeted six stories into the pile of rubble. The two cops looked away.

Callin's body made a surprising amount of noise when he hit the ground. "Let this one go," I said to the older cop. I had no love for the police, but I didn't want to see them killed. "Let this guy walk away."

Before the older cop could respond, Callin stood up and started brushing concrete dust off his clothes.

"What the hell?" the younger cop said. "Bob, what the hell is going on?"

"You stay right there," the older cop said to me. He turned to Callin. "Don't move!"

They moved toward Callin, both weapons drawn. Callin reached inside his coat.

I turned and ran like hell to get away from the gunshots. Once around the corner of the building I used the ghost knife to slice off the broken cuffs. The gunfire had already stopped but I had no idea who had come out on top. Not that it mattered, really. The police and the peers were after me, and once I started running I wasn't going to stop.

I tried not to think about that. I needed a new backpack to replace the one the cops had taken and I needed it before the rain started again. That was something I could focus on without losing my mind.

I sprinted across the intersection, leaving the cuffs in the gutter. This late at night, there were no pedestrians and no lights in any of the shop windows. There were parking garages all through this neighborhood. Even at this hour, I should be able to steal a car...

I rounded a corner and stumbled headlong into Annalise.

She staggered and caught my wrist, making me drop the manila folder. She spun me against the wall and plucked the ghost knife from my hand. Then she kicked my legs out from beneath me.

I landed hard on my knees. Now that I was closer to her level, she wrapped her arms around my head. "Be still," she said. "I'll make this quick."

"Callin did it!" I shouted before she could break my neck. "Callin cast the spell on my friends!"

I felt her muscles tense but she didn't kill me. I'd startled her. "Callin? Bullshit."

"I can prove it. Get me out of here before he kills me."

After a moment's delay, she let me go. I didn't like the way she was looking at me, but it was better than having her twist my head off. She picked up the folder and looked inside. I didn't think there was any way she could have looked more unhappy, but she managed it.

"Let's go," she said.

She slid a gray ribbon into my pocket, then frog-marched me to her motorcycle. A patrol car screamed down the block, sirens blaring, but they passed us by as if we weren't there.

Once again, Annalise slung me on the back of her motorcycle. She revved the engine and raced down the street, leaving Callin far behind.

Not that I was actually safe. My head and face still tingled where Annalise had held it. How quickly would I have died if she had twisted? In the movies it was like a light switching off, but I suspected it would take a while. Maybe I would have lain on the sidewalk, unable to move as my life drained away.

My hands shifted their grip on the back of Annalise's jacket, and she immediately pulled over to the curb.

"Hold on to me," she said in her weird, childish voice, "Don't shift around and don't try to get away. If you do, I'm going to tear off one of your fingers." She took my hand in hers. God, she was strong. "Now, how are you going to prove Callin is summoning predators."

Suddenly, I saw a path ahead, a way to help Jon and protect us all from the creatures in the Empty Spaces.

I told her about the spells, the blue legal paper, and that Jon had cast the spell again. She didn't like that last part at all, but I explained that it was the only way to keep them from putting a creature in me.

"Show me."

I rubbed my hands together to warm them, but what I really wanted was a second to fish my key ring out of my pocket. I grabbed Annalise's jacket, the ring now looped over my index finger. It had a single key on it, but the lock it went to had been destroyed in the fire.

We drove out into the city, with me shouting directions to Macy and Echo's house. Annalise had a lot of trouble with Echo when they fought the first time; I didn't think she could handle all four of them at once.

We puttered past the house, then rode a circuit of the block just as Arne used to do when he had to visit to someone he didn't like. Everything was quiet. Annalise parked on the corner, then frog-marched me down the sidewalk.

As we approached the house, I threw the key ring as hard as I could, smashing the unbroken downstairs window. Annalise began to run, holding me in front of her.

She kicked open the front door and shoved me inside. I fell onto the couch, smearing cold pizza sauce on my hands and face. Annalise charged in behind me, a ribbon in each hand.

Silence. If Jon and the others were sleeping, surely that would have woken them up. But there was no response. Annalise stalked into the dining room, returned a moment later and raced up the stairs. When she came back down, she was walking.

"They're gone," she said. "But they were here once, so at least that much of your story is true."

Jon and the others had already moved on. It meant they wouldn't be taking care of Annalise for me, but at least I wouldn't have to explain why I'd brought the peer to the house.

Annalise went back into the dining room, and I followed her. The body lay in the corner.

It wasn't the first time I'd seen a corpse but I'd never seen anything like this.

The body looked like it had been flayed open. There was nothing left but congealed blood, bone, and torn clothing. The only reason I could tell this was a guy was because of the shoes in the corner.

I moved closer, taking care not to step into the blood. There was a glass vial on the floor with tiny white rocks inside.

"Drug dealer," I said.

"That's how they start," Annalise said. "It won't take long before they're killing anyone at all, but when they start out they hunt people they think deserve it. It soothes their consciences while they're still human enough to have them."

I looked her in the eye, angry at her for sounding so casual, as though she knew exactly what she was talking about. "What's your excuse?" I asked.

"Where's this proof?"

"Right here." I pulled back the sideboard and was relieved to see the sheet of blue paper was still there. I gave it to her.

She held it up and compared it to the design on the floor then crumpled it into a ball.

"It's one of my own blue pages," I said. Annalise opened the folder. "Look, you need four people to cast the spell on a fifth person. There are only four of them."

"Plus you."

"Plus Callin. I was still in prison when they cast this the first time. You can check. See that paper? Jon helped me pick up these photocopied spells last night. He must have seen the cure spell—"

"It's not a cure."

"Whatever. He saw it among my pages and pocketed it. He got the spell from me and I got it from Callin. Callin to me to them."

Annalise scowled at the crumpled paper. "And the first time Callin cast the spell on them directly."

There was something in her expression I didn't trust. "You already suspect him, don't you?"

Annalise plucked a red ribbon from her vest and threw it against the base of the stairs. It burst into flame, and the fire quickly spread up the banister and across the sigil painted on the floor.

Then she pitched my folder full of blue pages into the fire.

"No, I don't," she said, as though she was trying to convince herself. "Where are your other copies?"

We went back outside to the motorcycle. She didn't have to frog-march me this time, but she stayed close enough to knock me silly if I tried anything. We climbed on the motorcycle again and sped off.

The next stop was the neighborhood post office where I'd rented a box. This time Annalise parked right in front of the building. I felt conspicuous walking around on empty streets at night less than an hour after I'd escaped from police custody. Maybe that gray ribbon made it safe. All the rules had changed. We entered the post office lobby.

I realized I'd left the key in my apartment. I'd planned to add it to my ring but never go around to it. It was probably a blob of melted metal right now.

But Annalise didn't need a key. When I pointed out my box, she glanced around to make sure the lobby was empty, then threw three right crosses against the door until the lock burst.

My second stack of blue pages was inside.

"Is this it?" she asked.

"That's my last backup copy. You burned the one in my apartment."

Annalise studied my face. I was better at spotting lies than telling them, but maybe I'd get lucky. Finally, she exhaled. The tension went out of her shoulders, and I knew she believed me.

"You need to look through these pages," I said. "I could

only skim them, but there was a lot I didn't understand. Maybe you can find a way to undo the spell Callin put on Jon and—"

Annalise threw a tiny streamer onto the pages. They turned gray, curled up and crumbled to ashes.

"Dammit!" My voice was louder than I'd expected. "What I needed could have been right there! *Right there!*"

"Quit your crying," Annalise said. "It's done."

"They were my last chance to find a cure for my friend!" My voice broke as I said it. Of course I did have another copy of Callin's spell book but I couldn't get it from Duncan before Jon killed again. Hell, it would take days for it to arrive in Maine.

"You can't cure your friend," Annalise said.

"Callin must have a way to undo the curse he put on Jon," I said. I had no reason to believe it except that, if it wasn't true, there was no hope, and that was unacceptable. "What can we do?"

"Next we're going to talk to Callin."

Annalise led me out of the post office and plucked the gray ribbon from my pocket. She climbed on her motorcycle and motioned for me to get on back.

I didn't want to go. Callin would kill me on sight but refusing to climb on meant Annalise would probably kill me immediately. Did I want to live long enough for one more ride through the city and a quick trip on an elevator? I got on the bike.

Minutes later we were marching by the front desk of Callin's fancy hotel toward the elevators. I touched the bandage under my ear and shivered. I was being led to my own execution.

"Ms. Powliss?"

Annalise stopped and turned toward the hotel desk. The snooty concierge came out from behind it and approached us.

"What is it?" Annalise asked.

"I have an envelope for you." The man held out a long white envelope. Her name was written on the front, and I was bewildered when I saw that the handwriting was mine.

Oops. I'd forgotten about that. I also hadn't planned to be here when she received that slip of paper. I stepped back but so did Annalise.

"An envelope?" she asked. She stared at the man suspiciously.

The concierge glanced at me but I didn't want to take part in the conversation. The man sighed and said: "Mr. Friedrich left it for you." He made it sound as if Annalise was exhausting him.

Annalise drew her hand from her pocket. I flinched, but she wasn't holding one of her ribbons. She offered the concierge a twenty dollar bill. "Read it to me."

The bill vanished into his pocket. He tore open the envelope and removed the sheet of paper. I could see the faint outline of a glyph written on the other side.

Annalise jumped back quickly, bumping into me.

The concierge glanced at the paper and burst into flames.

CHAPTER SIXTEEN

Flames covered him from his belt to the top of his head and the paper in his hand went up like a flare. He screamed, his voice high, horrible, and choked by fire. The sound echoed in the marble lobby and stunned everyone who heard it. The burning man fell backwards onto the floor.

Annalise grabbed the lapel of my jacket. "Let's go." She began dragging me toward the front door.

I slipped out of my jacket. The other employees were frozen in horror, their mouths gaping. I vaulted over the desk, snatched a sport coat off the back of a chair and wrapped it around the concierge's head. He screamed and struggled against me. I knew I was suffocating him, but better that for a few seconds than for him to breath in flames.

"Call 911!" The woman nearest to me jumped at the sound of my voice and grabbed a phone.

I kept beating at the flames, now working on this shoulders and chest. The sport coat began to flare at the edges and heat scorched my fingers.

The man's clothes wouldn't go out. I'd smothered the flames on his hair and head, but his clothes kept burning. "I'm sorry," I said. "Oh, God, I'm so sorry."

Someone fired off an extinguisher over my shoulder, and I

rolled away. The extinguisher plume doused the flames better than I could have.

The concierge kept screaming. Employees flocked around him, all trying to contain his thrashing while they spoke to him in soothing tones. I stood and backed away. The whole lobby stank. A stick-thin woman sprinted across the lobby with her hand over her mouth.

"Thank you," a woman said to me. She was the employee who had picked up the phone. "You may have saved his life. What happened?"

"I don't know." I didn't even have to lie. I couldn't see the man through the crowd of people helping him, but I'd seen enough to know he'd be scarred for life. I tried to picture him here afterward, in that uniform, but I couldn't imagine it. And I had written Annalise's name on the envelope and given it to him, like handing him a bomb. It was my fault.

Annalise grabbed my wrist and dragged me toward the front door. "I said let's go."

Outside, she slung one leg over the motorcycle and twisted my arm until I had to climb on behind her. Her mouth was a tight, angry line. She was royally pissed, but I couldn't tell if her anger was directed at Callin or me.

We rode south through the city, once again going too fast. I clung to Annalise's back, praying she wouldn't lose control and lay the bike down. She might have been too tough to be hurt, but I sure as hell wasn't.

And now she felt different. I had ridden behind her four times now, and I'd never felt her tiny body this rigid. She leaned forward farther than she had before, angled lower on the turns, and shifted gears sooner.

I'd turned them against each other. I hadn't planned it this way when I'd aimed Callin's envelope at Annalise—I couldn't have. But if it was the only way to convince her of the truth, so be it. Better to have her going after the real cause of Jon's troubles rather than Jon himself.

I just wish she had opened that damn envelope herself. I couldn't get that man's screams out of my head.

I also couldn't forget my uncle's expression as he told me about everything he'd lost in the fire, or that nameless drug dealer, who was probably no different from the dozens of random assholes I'd met in prison, or that old drunk sleeping one off. And there was Echo, killed and brought back to life as a monster.

And Jon was a victim, too.

I hadn't meant for things to go so far, but I had no way to back out now. Annalise was going to be my weapon. She was going to help me get a counter-spell out of Callin.

We reached the warehouse district south of downtown. Annalise braked hard and turned into a narrow side street. I saw her press a button on her handlebars, and a warehouse door ahead of us began to roll upward, opening like the entrance to the bat cave.

She skidded to a halt just inside the door and climbed off the bike. She entered a number into an electronic keypad, shielding the code with her body, then pressed her thumb against a scanner. A light on the keypad switched from red to green and the door began to close.

Annalise walked toward the near corner of the warehouse. A couch and a few tables had been placed on a square carpet remnant. As I climbed off the bike, I glanced at the keypad.

I didn't recognize it, but car security systems were my thing, not home or building systems. The windows were wired and the rafters were littered with cameras. The security setup must have cost six figures, but the couch looked like it had been dragged out of a thrift shop dumpster.

I walked toward Annalise, unable to figure out what she had here that was worth so much protection. Her life, maybe, or her spell book. I wondered what spells she might have, and how I could get at them.

No. I wasn't here to steal, or to acquire power. I was here for Jon. Still, the idea was tempting. The ghost knife was useful—I'd still be cuffed without it—but walking around with a pocket full of steeled glass spells? Or with whatever it was that made Annalise incredibly strong? I couldn't deny that I wanted it.

She picked up a telephone and dialed a long number, then pointed to the couch. "Sit."

I almost told her what she could do with herself, but I held it in. I could swallow my pride to help my friend. I sat like an obedient dog. She held the phone to her ear for a few moments, then, said: "I need you here. It's Lima all over again." After a little pause, she set the phone in the cradle.

"Who was that?" I asked. She didn't like hearing me ask a question, and apparently I wasn't as willing to swallow my pride as I thought because I kept talking. "Because you need to stick a hello or a goodbye on your phone conversations. Manners aren't just for the table."

"Shut up," Annalise said. "Callin just tried to kill me with one of his damn envelopes. That gives your story a little more weight."

I nodded. I didn't mind framing a guilty man. "No shit. But if you hadn't destroyed those pages, we might've had a way to help my friend."

"I'd have destroyed them anyway. Callin and I are peers in the society, and stealing spells from other peers is a capital crime."

That seemed pretty stupid to me. If they all shared all of their spells, not only would they do away with the "unequal peers" Callin mentioned, but they'd know when one of them had a spell that did something dangerous, like summon "cousins."

Annalise was staring at me. Hard. I didn't like it. "What?"

"You tried to save that man," she said.

I watched her closely. Behind her anger at Callin, she was feeling something else. "And you forgot to give a shit," I said. "What does this society of yours do? Because you're not about helping people."

"We help people," she said, sounding almost defensive. "If your friend is left alone, he'll never stop killing. I'm here to prevent that."

"We have to cure them."

Annalise shook her head. "I doubt a cure exists for this."

"No." It was time to push her as far as I could. "You don't get to shrug and say *This was easier* again. You say that too often. It was one of your own that made the mess, and you better step up and fix things. Not destroy the problem. Not kill people. Fix it. We have to make Callin undo the spell."

"'We' can't make Callin do anything," Annalise said. "But when help arrives...." Her voice trailed off doubtfully.

I had to keep pushing her to stand against Callin. "I

want in," I said. "I want to help you against Callin."

Annalise gave me a funny look. It made me nervous. "Will you be my wooden man?"

There was that term again. I didn't know what a *wooden man* was, but I was ready to find out. "To help my friend, I'd team up with the devil himself."

Annalise stood and shrugged out of her fireman's jacket. "Obviously," she said. She draped the coat over me.

I felt a sudden, tremendous pressure, as though my soul was being squeezed out of my body, then everything went dark.

I opened my eyes and saw that the room was still dark. I sat bolt upright, fully awake in an instant. Just as it had with Payton, Annalise's jacket had pushed the consciousness out of me. At least, that's how it had seemed. I felt rested, though, as if I'd enjoyed a long night's sleep. I sat up. My mouth was dry, my stomach grumbling and my legs and back were sore, but I felt pretty good, considering the state of the couch I'd crashed on. It was chilly, though.

I noticed something on the back of my hand. It was covered with tattoos just like Annalise's. They ran over my wrist and up the outside of my forearm to my elbow. I realized that my shirt was missing and that my chest and stomach were also covered with weird black marks.

"He wakes!" A woman's voice said. "Good morning, handsome!"

A dark-skinned woman with a strong Brazilian accent walked toward me. She was somewhere in the prime of her forties, and I could tell, from just a glance at her bright eyes, that she was enjoying them very well. She cut an orange in half with a very large fighting knife and offered half to me.

After a moment's hesitation, I accepted it. "What did you do to me?" I held up my tattooed hand. I tried not to sound angry, but it was there in my voice anyway.

"I have done nothing. She protected you. See?" She grabbed my hand and laid the knife blade against my arm. I dropped my orange half and tried to pull away, but like Annalise, she was too strong. She slashed.

Nothing. No cut, no pain. The knife couldn't penetrate the tattoo.

"My name is Irena," the woman said. She bit a piece of orange. Juice ran down her hand and over her wrist.

"Hello, Irena. I'm Ray." I liked the way she smiled and wondered what she'd be like in bed. *Not now*, I thought. I touched the tattoos on my arm. "I can't feel *anything* here. It's like...."

"Like armor," Annalise said as she entered the room. "Like a shell."

She had taken off her fireman's jacket, her vest and a couple other layers of clothing until all she was wearing was a sleeveless T-shirt and heavy canvas pants. She was even smaller than I'd realized. And the tattoos on her hands continued up her arms over her shoulders and under her clothes. I could see the black sigils through her threadbare shirt.

Like a shell. I'd seen her glow like a star in the parking lot of the sports bar and I'd figured there were more tattoos under her clothes, but I hadn't thought she'd be completely covered. How much of her skin was like dead flesh— completely numb to the touch?

Christ. No wonder she was so screwed up.

I stood and examined myself. The tattoos covered my chest, stomach and outer forearms. As far as I could tell, there was nothing below the waist or above my collarbones.

"I didn't do your back," Annalise said. "When we fight, you'll be protected if you face the danger. If you try to run away...."

"I get it," I said. "Is it permanent?"

"Yes. They'll last as long as you do."

I considered them again. The marks were intricate, meaningless and ugly. I was moving further and further from the seat-belt life I'd hoped for, but it was too late now. I had gone this far and couldn't back out now.

And damn if it didn't feel good. All these marks had *power*. While Annalise and Irena looked over a sheet of paper, I reached out and grabbed a metal table lamp in my left hand. I couldn't squeeze it like tissue paper. Ah well. No super-strength for me.

The bandage Callin had placed on my neck finally lost so much of its glue that it fell partly off and lay against my shoulder. I peeled it away and saw there were two spots of blood on it. "Right here," I said, tapping the spot where Callin had bit me. "I want more on my neck. Both sides."

Annalise and Irena looked at each other. "We move against Callin soon," Annalise said. "We don't have time to put you out again."

Irena pursed her lips. "The process is painful, Raymond."

"Please," I said. "He drank my blood."

Annalise shrugged and took a small paint brush from an end table drawer.

"You will be awake for this?" Irena clucked her tongue and shook her head. "Brave."

Annalise pointed me to the floor and I lay down. She turned me onto my side and knelt beside my back, then wrapped her left arm across my chest, trapping both of my arms. "Take his legs, please."

And I knew this was going to be bad. Irena took hold of my legs and held them tightly. With her forearm, Annalise trapped my head against her knee.

Any enjoyment I might have gotten from the touch of two women—any two—was quashed by the knowledge that something terrible was about to happen. My arms spasmed, wanting to be free, but struggling against Annalise was like pushing against a brick wall.

I couldn't see Annalise's face but I wondered what she was waiting for. Maybe she was concentrating, making sure she got it right. That was cool by me.

Then she touched the tip of the paint brush against my skin and a jet of sizzling black steam blasted out of me.

I screamed. The pain was worse than anything I'd ever felt in my life. Worse that the fire in the library, worse than the beatings in prison, worse than anything. The magic clung to my skin like a living creature and chewed at me. A spider web of pain ran through my whole body like a spreading infection.

I knew a flaw in the spell she was creating might kill me and I tried not to struggle, but my body couldn't be controlled. It bucked and shuddered no matter how much I tried to take deep breaths and relax. There was no Zen meditation for this shit. This was torture.

The women held me in place. I felt woozy and thought I might pass out, but the magic was in my head, keeping me awake and aware as it transformed me.

Then she lifted the brush. It was over. The pain eased but didn't vanish completely. I had never felt anything so terrible in my life.

"Other side," I said between gasps. "Do the other side."

Annalise turned my head the other way and pressed it into place. Irena shook her head and looked down as the pain took hold again. And I screamed. It was all I could do, and I did it with every ounce of energy I had.

When it was finally over, Annalise released me and let me fall onto the floor. Tears welled in my eyes and when I tried to blink them away they splashed onto my face. I should have been ashamed of them, but the pain was still so fierce I thought it might pinch my head off. It was all I could do to hold myself together.

After several minutes, the pain had eased enough to let me stand. I took several deep, steadying breaths, then leaned against a wooden support beam. I slid my hand over the rough texture of it. It helped.

The clock on the wall said it was almost four o'clock. The high windows were dark, so it was a.m. rather than p.m. Annalise brought me here at in the tiny hours of the morning. Had I been out for twenty-six hours or fifty?

The cut orange was face down on the couch. I picked it up and wiped it clean with the side of my hand. I was hungry enough not to care. It was sweet and wonderful in my empty belly.

I noticed an open bathroom door and went inside. The

mirror above the sink was almost too small for me to see the tattoos on my neck.

They weren't real tattoos, of course—they had been painted onto my skin, not injected beneath it—but if Annalise was to be believed they were just as permanent. The spell on my left side was a swirl with a series of dots down one side. I ran my finger over it, thinking too late that I might smear it. I couldn't detect any difference in the way the protected and unprotected skin felt, except that the unprotected skin could feel my fingertip on it, while the enchanted skin could not.

"Where are you?" Annalise said from the other room.

I walked out of the bathroom. Annalise stood by the back door. Irena stood at her shoulder.

"Just throwing some water on my face and looking at my new decorations," I said.

Annalise's expression was flat. "It's almost time."

"Tell him," Irena said. Annalise turned to her in surprise. "He should know what is happening and why we are doing this, yes? You know how Callin steals secrets from his enemies, and so does he. He's just undergone a terrible ordeal for us. He deserves it."

Annalise looked at Irena for a few extra seconds, then turned to me. She was scowling, as she motioned me toward the couch. I tried to work out the relationship she had with Irena. Were they teacher and student? Big and little sister? Some mixture of the two?

I settled onto the end of the couch and Annalise perched herself on the edge of the rocking chair opposite. She held herself very still. "You asked before what we do."

CHAPTER SEVENTEEN

"This world," she began grudgingly, "every world, is surrounded by predators. They're like ghosts who are always near us and they're always hungry, always searching for living planets to devour."

"I—" I stopped myself from saying *I've seen this from a spell in Callin's book*. Stealing spells from a peer would get me killed. "I think I understand." It sounded lame even to me.

She continued. "Certain magic—summoning magic—calls to these predators and changes them. They become partly physical, partly not, like the worm you saw emerge from that girl's mouth. That's what's inside your friends."

"Can you summon these predators?" I asked, thinking maybe she could summon them out of Jon's body.

"No." Her voice was sharp. "Summoning magic is forbidden. We destroy every summoning spell we can find, as well as anyone who knows the spell and anything they might have summoned." She leaned toward me. "I *destroy* predators. I don't call them to this world."

"So, those worms are... demons?"

She shook her head. "I've never seen a demon. Or an angel. I've never visited heaven or hell, and I've never spoken to God. All I know is that humans are prey and we're surrounded by hunters, that the predators like to be summoned, but hate to be held in place, that—"

"Jon and Callin cast a summoning spell." It sounded so simple when I said it that way. So straightforward.

"And now your friend is killing people. He'll keep killing people and summoning more predators—"

"Cousins," I said. "They call each other 'cousins.'"

"Which is why," she continued, as if I hadn't interrupted her, "we have to stop them by any means necessary."

"Do you do this all the time? How often does this happen?"

"You don't need to know that."

"Okay. Tell me more about these predators." She didn't like that question. "Tell me about the first predator you ever destroyed."

She stared at me. I could tell she was doing some kind of calculation about me, but she was unusually hard to read. "I won't do that," she said, "but I will tell you about the second. Did you ever hear about the Torso Killer? The press sometimes called him the Mad Butcher of Kingsbury Run."

I never liked to read the newspapers. "Sorry. Never heard of it."

"He wasn't an 'it'. A man did all those killings. A man with crooked teeth and big round drinker's nose. Don't ask his name because I killed him and burned down his place without asking for it. But he had a predator in there with him. It was hard to see unless it had sopped up human blood... and who knows what else. Some kind of little sponge, I think."

"And this guy was feeding it like a pet?"

"He was."

"Why?"

"I have no idea. It was doing something for him—all these assholes get some kind of power or gift or knowledge for all the killing they do, but I wasn't there to chat with him about it. I was there to start the fire that burned man and predator both to cinders."

There was something more to be said about that story, I could see it in her face. Then she looked at her watch and the moment was gone. "Time to pay Callin a visit."

The three of us did not go to Callin's hotel on the back of Annalise's motorcycle, thank God. Instead we piled into a battered Dodge Sprinter and rumbled through the city.

Annalise drove. Irena sat in the passenger seat. I crouched on the floor beside Annalise's BMW, which was locked into a clever little mounting system bolted to the floor. On the other side of the motorcycle lay a small stack of Irena's luggage.

"Do not open them, handsome boy," she said to me. "The tricks inside are dangerous, and not for you."

"Gotcha," I said, letting the *boy* remark go. I'd sat on the floor of Jon's van, too, but it had been nicer than this one, even with the fast food wrappers. I was again reminded of sitting in the back of Arne's Expedition while we went out to "work." We'd cruise around looking for cars to boost, with Arne dropping one of us off when he'd spotted something worthwhile. Afterwards, he'd drive back to the yard and wait for us to bring in the cars. Then it was back into the Expedition for another round.

I was struck by how much this was like those trips—The tension, the feeling that I was risking myself for a big score. At least Annalise and Irena weren't pounding beers or snorting lines, although Arne would have been furious about the tattoos. He never worked with criminals who wanted to advertise their profession.

Annalise parked on the street. Callin's hotel was just across the street.

"Raymond," Irena said, "please climb out through the front." I moved away from her suitcases and followed her through the passenger door. Sunrise was still an hour away.

Annalise yanked open the back doors of the van and Irena unzipped an outside pocket of her suitcase. She removed a medallion and placed it in Annalise's hand.

"This should allow us to approach him undetected."

"Should?" I asked as she hung one around my neck.

"Callin has been around a long time," Annalise said. Her tone suggested she was phrasing that carefully to avoid saying something I shouldn't know. "He's older than all of us put together."

"And he knows many tricks," Irena said. She hung a medallion around her own neck.

Annalise walked away from us, toward the intersection. She stared up at the top of the hotel.

"Hold this for me," Irena said. I accepted a long canvas gym bag and held the mouth open. Irena took four harpoons from a suitcase and slid them into the bag. I noticed a tiny sigil on each blade. "So, you are Annalise's new wooden man?" she asked without looking at me.

I suddenly felt like a new boyfriend getting the once-over

from the best friend. The idea gave me a perverse thrill. "Apparently."

She looked at me sharply. Should I have sounded more enthusiastic?

"So then, you are a former soldier?"

"No,"

"A policeman?"

"Hell, no." My tone was sharper than I'd intended.

Irena frowned. She seemed to understand perfectly. "A criminal, then. That foolish girl." Irena silently put a small leather case in the gym bag, then a belt of knives, then a coil of rope.

She took an ice pick from a box and, instead of dropping it into the bag, waved it under my nose. "Listen to me, my handsome criminal. Annalise is a very good friend to me, and I have tried to counsel her as best I could. Now she has taken a wooden man, and she has flown in the face of all I have tried to teach her. So be it. Each of us must learn in our own way. But if you betray her, there will be no place on this Earth from which you can hide from me." She dropped the ice pick into the bag.

I'd already betrayed her, of course. I'd written her name on the envelope, fabricating the evidence that persuaded her to make this little attack. It was too late to turn back now. "I hear you."

"You had better." Irena dropped a set of chains into the bag, then took it from me. The bag had gotten heavy, but she hefted it as if it weighed no more than a loaf of bread. "Will this be enough?" she murmured to herself. "I don't think this will be enough." She climbed back into the van.

I had been dismissed. I walked toward Annalise, who was still staring up at the top of the hotel. If she was going to get cold feet, now was the time.

But when I came up beside her, I saw that her face was grim and determined. Apparently, she wasn't the type to back out. She turned and looked up at me. "Has she given you the once over?"

"She doesn't approve."

Annalise looked away. "Neither do I, but you've met the targets, have seen the inside of the rooms, and your appearance might throw him off, so you're in. You won't be much help, but we'll take every little bit we can get."

I nodded again. It occurred to me that she expected me to die in Callin's hotel room.

Of course, she knew better than I did what we were about to face. If I was going to get cold feet, this was the time for me, too. What if I died trying to find a way to undo what had happened to Jon?

The thought should have frightened me but it didn't. It's not like I had something better to do, and I owed Jon whatever I could give him. What's more, I didn't figure my life was worth all that much anyway.

The thought settled my nerves and brought clarity. It was better to decide now that I'd go all the way than it was to wait and wonder how far would suddenly be too far.

"How are you holding up?" Annalise asked.

I looked at her again. She was almost pretty, despite the tattoos and scrawny body and tattered clothes and nearly-shaved head....

Christ. I'd been in prison for too long. "I'm not sure I

know how to be ready for this, but I'm in. Whatever comes up, I'm in one hundred percent."

"Good."

"One thing."

She looked up at me. "What is it?"

"No matter what happens, I want you to try to find a way to undo the spell Callin put on Jon." She frowned and looked away. I pressed on. "I know you don't think there is one. I don't care. I want you to try. Jon is one of the victims here, and I want you to help him if you can."

"Yes," she said. The expression on her pale face seemed to be full of meaning but I couldn't make it out. That made me nervous. "No guarantees, but I'll try."

I couldn't hope for better than that. "Thank you."

We stood in silence for a few minutes, feeling the chill night air while Irena fussed and muttered to herself in the back of the van.

Finally, I said: "This society I just joined...?"

"It's called the Twenty Palace Society."

"It's named after the twenty guys who started it? After their big houses, I mean?"

"Exactly," Annalise said. "They had big houses."

"And I'm a wooden man, now. Is there a story behind that term?"

"Yes."

"Would it scare the crap out of me?"

"Oh, yes."

"Thought so."

Irena slammed the van doors. "There!" she said. "I am ready." Her gym bag bulged but she carried it with ease.

As Annalise turned toward the other woman, she glanced up at me. I saw, in that single unguarded moment, a tiny smile on her face. It was only a flicker, but it was there; I was winning her over, and every step we took closer to Callin's hotel ensured that we were going there for my reasons, not for hers.

I felt a twinge of uneasiness. Yes, she was my enemy, and Jon's enemy, too. She was also a killer. I needed her to get the counter spell for Jon, and I didn't owe her a single thing. But frankly, underneath everything, I was starting to like her.

I shook that off. That had to be my loneliness talking. That, and my hunger for the spells she wore. "Are we ready?" I asked.

Annalise opened her jacket, revealing the ribbons clipped to her vest. Her clothes were thick with them. "No," she answered. "Let's get going."

We approached the hotel from behind. I was glad that we weren't going to walk through that lobby again. Annalise hadn't given me another gray ribbon, but I did have Irena's medallion. Maybe it did the same thing. Maybe it was even better. I didn't know and I doubted anyone was going to fill me in.

Two men lounging at the valet parking station eyed us as we entered but they didn't challenge us. Apathy among low-wage employees was the usually weakest link in any security system.

We entered through a glass door and passed a lounge on the right. On the left was a marble stairway. Annalise sprang lightly up them and I followed.

At the top of the first flight was a bank of elevators and a carefully-groomed young man at a desk. He only needed one glance to decide we weren't guests of the hotel.

"May I see your room keys, please?" He obviously didn't expect us to have them, but at least he was polite about it.

Annalise held up her hand. The young man looked at the white ribbon she was holding. Immediately, his eyes rolled back and he crumpled to the ground the same way my Uncle Karl had. Had Annalise used the same spell as Callin? And had she killed that man?

She knelt and dug a ring of keys out of his pocket. When she glanced up at me she seemed to read my mind. "Don't worry," she said, as she stood. "He's only sleeping."

I nodded and looked down at him. His chest seemed very still. If he was only sleeping, maybe Uncle Karl was still alive, too—still alive and hunting for me.

An elevator dinged. Irena held the door open while we entered. Annalise pressed the button for the highest floor. We didn't speak. At the top floor, Annalise led us up the stairs and used the young man's keys to unlock a security door. We all walked onto the roof of the hotel.

The eastern sky was growing light. Soon it would be day. The three of us stood at the edge of the roof and watched the sun rise. Maybe it would be the last I'd ever see.

I turned to Annalise. "Give it to me." She scowled. "Give it to me," I said again. "It's mine. It's all I have."

"It's stolen."

"I thought you needed all the help you could get."

"It's stolen."

"So what? You can take it from me later. Boss, it's all I have."

Annalise turned away and stared at the horizon. There was an uncomfortable silence.

"Raymond," Irena said, "has Annalise gone over the plan with you?"

"There's a plan?"

"We're waiting for daylight," Annalise said. "It should weaken him. You enter by the living room and run to the bedroom. He follows you. We surprise him there."

"That's it? What do I do once I get to the bedroom?"

"Oh, you won't get to the bedroom. But try. Distract him."

I looked over the edge of the roof. It was a long way to the ground. "Why aren't we going in through the door?"

"He seals it," Annalise said. "We'd have to tear open the wall to get through."

Irena set her gym bag on the gravel roof and unzipped it.

Annalise stepped away from the edge, but I moved into her path. I held out my hand. "It's all I have."

She could pick me up and throw me off the roof if she wanted to and from the flicker of anger in her expression, she looked tempted to do just that. Instead she took the ghost knife from her pocket and gave it to me.

I stepped aside as the others made their preparations, holding the ghost knife to my chest. I felt whole again, as though Annalise had just reattached my hand. Thank God I wasn't going in unarmed—I just wished I'd had time to make some steeled glass spells.

Annalise and Irena walked toward the edge of the building. Irena was pulling on fingerless gloves with sigils drawn on the palms.

"Remember," Annalise said. "The tattoos cover your front, not your back. Try to run away, and—"

"I'm not running away," I said. "He has something I want."

"It is daylight," Irena said. The sun had peeked over the mountains, flooding the city with golden daylight. Had Irena or Annalise arranged for a cloudless Seattle sky in November? Because that would have been powerful magic.

Irena turned her back to the edge of the roof and pulled a fifteen-foot-long rope from her gym bag. She held the ends together until she found the middle point, then wrapped the center of the rope around her neck. After that she handed one end of the rope to me and the other to Annalise. The ends had been knotted into loops.

Annalise stepped to the edge of the roof and slid her foot into her loop.

"Step off the roof at the same time, please," Irena said. She slung the gym bag over her shoulder.

I stood at the edge of the roof, waiting for one of them to start laughing and say they were just fooling. I gripped the rope with white knuckles and looked down at the parking lot below. We were twenty stories up. I slipped my foot into the loop. *You think you've paid your debt, but you haven't.*

Annalise stared straight in my eyes. She wasn't scowling, as she often was. She was simply confident.

Her confidence bolstered mine. I took a deep, calming breath and made ready to throw my life away.

"On three," Irena said. "One. Two. Three."

It sounds ridiculous, but I did my best not to think about it at all. I focused on Annalise and mirrored her movements. She held her foot in the looped rope over the ledge and so did I. She bent her knees and so did I. She held the rope with both hands and so did I. She lifted her other foot, putting all her weight onto the rope and so did I.

The rope went taut around Irena's neck as I slid down the edge of the roof. It would have been a gruesome way to strangle someone, but she didn't seem to be suffering. My knees were at the level of the ledge and I fought the urge to throw my weight onto it and roll to safety. If I did that, I knew I wouldn't be able to climb back out again.

Irena backed toward us. The rope scraped over the corner of the roof as I slid farther down until my stomach was leaning against the edge of the roof.

Then she bent at the waist and laid her gloved hands on the lip of the roof. I slid lower and lower, the lip reaching the level of my armpits, then my nose, then too far above my head to touch with my fingertips. Irena stepped over the edge of the roof and began to crawl down the side of the building. Her legs dangled freely, but her gloved hands held tightly to the wall.

I tried to focus on Irena, but the way the rope cinched her neck made me sick. I couldn't tell if she was strong enough to hold her airway open by flexing or if she didn't need to breathe. Along with that, the way she was lowering the three of us, slowly and carefully, as though she was descending a step ladder scared the holy hell out of me. She and Annalise were incredibly powerful, but they were still afraid of Callin. I was outclassed here and I knew it.

I twisted back and forth, the wall scraping at my jacket. I looked at Annalise. She didn't seem frightened at all, but she could probably survive a fall like this and walk away. I would burst against the sidewalk like a bag of blood.

My panic was revving up and I knew it showed on my face. I wanted to wish it away, to squeeze it down and crush it. Panic might make me freeze or lose my hold. It might make Annalise decide she couldn't use me anymore and cut my rope.

Stop this. My imagination was feeding my fear, and I suddenly realized that it was already too strong for me. I was not going to master it.

"Ray," Annalise said. "Take a deep breath and don't look down."

I looked down.

Dizziness overwhelmed me. My knees grew weak and for a moment I couldn't tell up from down.

Annalise grabbed me and glared at me. I focused on her and slowly came back to myself.

Irena passed a balcony. Then another. Still going down. "We know where he is, don't we?" I asked.

"We do," Annalise answered. She sounded so calm and confident that I wanted to hug her.

Irena suddenly stopped. There was a balcony beside me. A little further away was a second one with the black cloth draped over the railing. That was where I'd dropped Callin's book. We were here.

"Off you go," Annalise said, taking hold of my end of the rope. "Be quick."

I reached for the balcony railing with my foot. Irena couldn't get closer to the window for fear of being seen, but

I couldn't quite reach it. I tried again, leaning farther, and caught the railing with the tip of my boot.

I pulled myself closer. One foot was braced in the rope and holding most of my weight, the other rested on the edge of the railing. Callin's blinds were open, which meant I was exposed, but how was I going to transfer my weight from the rope onto the railing?

Annalise kicked me.

I might have screamed, but I didn't have the breath for it. Just as well, because I fell within the boundary of the railing, landing hard on my hands and knees.

Irena skittered along the side of the building, moving much faster without my weight. Annalise rode on both ends of the rope.

I took out my ghost knife, threw open the balcony door and charged into Callin's living room. I angled toward the bedroom, wondering what I'd do if he was blocking the hall.

Then Callin stepped out of the kitchen, an apple in his hand. "You!" he said. He snatched a towel off a rack and threw it.

In mid-flight, the towel twisted into the shape of a clawed hand. It had started already.

CHAPTER EIGHTEEN

I twisted out of the thing's path, rolling over onto my back and landing hard on the coffee table as it swooped by. One finger of the claw caught the edge of my jacket and ripped through it like an iron spike.

I was on my back like a turtle, and the claw was tearing into the couch cushions; I'd lost track of Callin. I rolled to my knees on the carpet,

The claw rose up—it looked almost like a fancy linen napkin—and zoomed at me again. I saw something red stitched into the heel of its palm. A sigil?

I stabbed out with the ghost knife, striking hard at the stitching. The towel split apart in a burst of light, an unearthly shriek and a blossom of scalding black steam. I staggered back from the heat and saw Callin stumble and clutch at his stomach, as though breaking the sigil had hurt him.

I ran toward the hallway, then realized I'd exposed my unprotected back to Callin. I spun and backpedaled, hoping Irena and Annalise were already in the bedroom.

Callin followed me. He looked calm, as though I was an amusing birthday card someone had sent him. I didn't wait for his next attack; I cocked my arm and threw the ghost knife. It spun flat and quick, headed straight for his heart.

Callin snatched it out of the air with the speed of a striking snake. He glanced at it, holding it between his thumb and forefinger to avoid the edge, then slid it into his breast pocket.

Oh, shit.

"My ghost knife wasn't enough for you," Callin said. The world turned white. Silence fell for a single, hesitating moment.

Then the world returned. Callin, now standing right in front of me, grabbed my throat and slammed me against the door jamb. His eyes were blood red and he leaned toward my throat.

"You had to come back for more."

Damn. I had almost made it into the bedroom.

Callin halted. He looked at the side of my neck in surprise. "Annalise?" His voice sounded small, as though his feelings had been hurt.

The lights went out.

Callin released his grip on me and let me fall to the floor. I pressed my back against the wall.

I couldn't see anything at all. I could *feel* Callin, just inches away, but the darkness was so complete I couldn't even see his silhouette. No sunlight was visible at the end of the hall—Annalise and Irena hadn't cut the power. The darkness was too complete for that. It was as if someone had thrown a blindfold over the building.

The air stirred. Callin had moved away from me. A moment later, I heard the thud of a blunt object striking flesh. It was incredibly loud, almost like the sound I'd made when

I'd struck the ground after falling out of the police station. Callin grunted in response.

Another tremendous thud followed quickly. Then another. In moments, the blows were following one after the other as fast as rounds from a machine gun.

The sounds suddenly stopped. Something changed in the darkness around me; it seemed to *turn around* in some way, as though it was now facing the opposite direction. It didn't make sense, but that was how it felt.

A moment later, the sound of the blows returned, but this time it was Irena's voice after each thud.

I was still trying to figure out what had happened when a huge, fiery sigil appeared in the darkness. It was five feet high and nearly as wide as the hallway. I caught a glimpse of Callin's face illuminated by the flowing, liquid fire.

The burning sigil floated toward the bedroom. I pressed against the wall, making myself as small as possible, but it wasn't small enough; flames from the sigil didn't touch me, but they came close enough to set my shirt on fire and sear my shoulder. Then it glided away.

I slapped at my burning clothes. For a moment I imagined that the fire would burn like napalm, unquenchable, but before that fear had a chance to take hold, the flames were already out.

The sigil was the only thing I could see in the darkness. It drifted away from me and suddenly illuminated Irena. Then it struck her, wrapped around her like a net, and the flames sank into her body.

She screamed.

The darkness receded like a wave, flowing toward the bedroom. I was still on the carpeted floor, completely exposed.

Irena was on her knees, struggling to stand. Annalise crouched beside her, trying to help her up.

Callin stood at the far end of the hall, a white cloth draped over his forearm as though he was a head waiter. There was a sigil was stitched into the cloth. He took a tiny red cloth from his vest pocket and shook it out, revealing another sigil.

A second fiery design appeared and moved toward me.

I rolled to my feet and dove into the bedroom. The twisted, burning shape missed my heel and struck the wall, scorching a huge section of wallpaper.

Annalise dragged Irena toward the balcony. Shit. We were retreating already.

I reached the balcony first. It was a long way down and I wished once again that I'd had time to make more steeled glass spells.

Irena's fingerless gloves lay discarded on the balcony. I snatched them up the way a poor man grabs at a hundred dollar bill, then pulled them on. They might be useful, at some point, in a getaway, but now wasn't the time. Annalise stood beside me now. Irena was coming around, but she was still groggy.

Callin entered the bedroom. "I wonder what the peers will say about this latest escapade. I wonder what they will do to Irena. I know the poor woman loves you like a daughter, Annalise, but she should never have trusted you."

Annalise casually tugged a ribbon off her vest and tossed it at Callin. Callin didn't move. The design stitched on his white cloth suddenly flared, and the ribbon boomeranged back to Annalise.

She caught it casually and clipped it into place. Just testing.

"I'd hoped we'd put our past behind us," Callin said.

"Spare me," Annalise responded. "You've been summoning predators."

Callin's eyes narrowed and he bared his teeth. "How dare you say that to me!" He shouted. "*To me!*"

Annalise started to answer but didn't get the chance. Callin shook another red cloth from his pocket. A burning sigil rushed at us.

Annalise grabbed the lapels of Irena's coat and leaped toward the bed. As she did, she bumped me. I stumbled, off balance, directly into the path of the oncoming sigil.

It was too close. Too close. I could feel the searing heat of it. I felt myself falling forward, into the flames.

There was a wide spot in the design and I dove for it. A flash of heat ran down my arms, hair and face as I lunged. I expected to catch the edge of the design with my shirt tail, knee or shoe, making the flames wrap around me, sink into my body and destroy me.

It didn't happen. I hit the floor and tucked my head, rolling onto my back. My heels swung around and struck the floor. I'd passed through unharmed.

Callin stood over me. "Well!" he said. "No one has done that before."

A glass tumbler struck the side of Callin's head so hard that it shattered into tiny grains of glass. As they fell across my body, Callin tossed a tiny square of blue cloth toward the bed. Bolts of lightning suddenly arced across the room. One struck Annalise and blasted her against the wall.

The lightning set the bed on fire. As I watched, the flames thinned and stretched through the air as though they were traveling up a stream of lighter fluid. The fire swooped toward Callin's back and disappeared, leaving the bed sheets blackened and smoking but the flames had been extinguished.

Callin grabbed my shirt and belt and lifted me as though I weighed as much as a pillow. "Raymond, I've been searching for you everywhere. Even in the *daylight*." He lifted me over his head and began walking toward the balcony.

He was going to throw me over the rail.

There was no point punching or kicking him. Instead, I closed my eyes and concentrated.

"You have been severely annoying," Callin said as he strolled casually toward the doors. "I admit, I've been half-asleep these past few years; I'm ashamed of the way I let you get to my book. But that will all be over in a moment. Also, please consider my offer of employment rescinded."

I *reached* for the ghost knife and it sliced free of Callin's pocket. On its way to my hand, it cut a sigil on his waistcoat, then cut through the sigil on the white cloth, then finally his arm.

The strength went out of him, and he dropped me onto the carpet.

Callin staggered toward the dresser, the broken spells on his vest and white cloth sputtering out black steam. He clutched at his arm, his face pale and slack.

Without taking time to get to my feet again, I swept the

ghost knife through Callin's ankle. He cried out and fell to the floor.

I jammed the ghost knife part way into his foot and began to slide it up his leg. There was no blood, of course, but the pant leg split apart like a tear-away suit.

Callin's face went blank and his eyes rolled back. I scrambled toward him so I could start cutting the spells on his waistcoat. Then, he spasmed; his arm swung out, striking me a backhanded blow on my solar plexus. There was no pain, of course, but I flew across the room and struck the wall.

I hit side-on, luckily, and didn't snap my neck. I fell half on the desk I'd jimmied open, slamming my thigh against the edge, then I hit the floor in a jumble, my ghost knife still miraculously in hand. Just the day before that swat would have crushed my rib cage, killing me on the spot. Even after being cut with my ghost knife, Callin was terrifying.

I couldn't let him recover or he was going to smear me like jelly. I scuttled toward him.

Annalise stepped over me, her clothes smoldering. She flung a pair of green ribbons at Callin which burst into green fire.

Then, suddenly, the flames became stretched out and thin, streaming over Callin's right shoulder and around to his back. His eyes came back into focus just as Annalise stomped on his chest.

The entire floor buckled and tilted. The glass doors to the balcony shattered. Bottles fell off the dresser and rolled toward the balcony.

Callin twisted onto his side and shoved Annalise away. She tripped over me and fell on her back. I scrambled to the side, not wanting to be near her if lightning bolts started up again. Could I get close enough to cut him again without taking a killing blow to my head?

Callin got to his feet like a marionette being pulled upright. He reached toward the pocket of his waistcoat and then the tip of a spear suddenly emerged from his chest.

In the corner, Irena took another harpoon from her gym bag. She laid one weak and trembling finger on a sigil just behind the spear point, and the weapon shot out of her hand, rocketing toward Callin's chest. It struck home, piercing his heart.

Callin pulled out both harpoons at once; he looked more annoyed than injured. Annalise rushed at him, and Callin swung one of the weapons at her with blinding speed.

It struck the side of her head and burst into splinters. I heard the point strike the ceiling above like a sniper's bullet. Annalise toppled to the floor and kicked at Callin's legs.

He fell onto his stomach. A third spear slammed through his kidney and wedged into the floor. Callin reached back and snatched the fourth harpoon out of the air, then flung it at Irena. She waved her hand and it halted in mid-air, dropping straight to the floor.

Callin pushed himself up onto his hands and knees, tearing the spear partially out of his body. Annalise stomped on his back, flattening him again. The floor buckled further and the harpoon shattered. The whole building seemed to shudder. The dresser toppled onto its face and pictures fell off the walls. More glass shattered somewhere. The floor beneath me went soft, as though there was nothing but carpet keeping me from falling into the suite below.

Callin tossed a blue square into the air. Lightning bolts blasted out of it, striking Annalise full in the chest. She flew off her feet and went over me, her wrist colliding hard with my right hand—and in the brief instant we touched I thought it might be a good idea to catch hold of her, and Irena's glove made that happen.

I felt myself yanked off the floor as if by a rope. Annalise went straight through the shattered balcony doors, but the sudden addition of my weight changed her trajectory. I was lifted into the air, my heels briefly losing contact with the floor, and just as I landed solidly enough that I could try to backpedal and take control of my momentum, I fell against the black cloth on the railing. I tumbled, and then there was nothing below me but open air.

Blue sky and tall buildings spun through my vision. I reached out with my left hand and touched the edge of the balcony.

The glove held the concrete. At the end of my right arm, Annalise swung out and down, making me twist over the open air. For an instant I expected her to be ripped out of my hand because there was no way I'd have the strength to hold onto her.

But I didn't need it. The glove had her and I couldn't have let go if I'd wanted to. I braced myself, trying to be ready when her momentum pulled my shoulders out of my sockets, but that didn't happen either. None of the force she exerted from the other side of the sigil was transferred to me; I couldn't feel anything except my own weight.

Annalise arced below me and slammed hard against the side of the building. It made a sickening sound, but it didn't seem to rattle her at all.

"Hold on!" she shouted up at me.

"Good plan," I said. "You always have such fantastic plans." She did a one-handed pull up from my wrist, grabbed my belt and then reached up around my neck. I could feel her weight now, and she seemed so startlingly tiny.

I let go of her wrist and gripped the ledge. I was on the wrong side of the railing and the whole balcony was cracked and tilted. It looked ready to fall into the row of Dumpsters below.

I felt Annalise's breath against my cheek as she climbed over me. For one absurd moment I thought she was going to thank me with a kiss for saving her life, but that was ridiculous. She caught hold of the creaking rail and pulled herself up. I said: "I thought daylight would make Callin weak."

"This is Callin when he's weak." She hopped the railing and ran back to the fight.

"Okay. I'll save myself then," I pulled myself up and peeked into the bedroom. Annalise knelt beside the bed, carefully selecting ribbons from her vest. Irena crouched beside the far wall. Callin stood in the center of the room, and I was startled to realize he had no blood on his clothes anywhere. White spheres the size of small peaches circled him like satellites. Two darted at him and slammed against his back with terrifying force, shattering themselves into dust and white chunks. I recognized the sound as the impacts I'd heard while lying in the dark hallway. Where they cue balls?

Callin had to take a step to shrug off the impacts. "You should not have done this."

Irena drew a claw hammer from her bag.

My ghost knife was lying among the broken glass on

the balcony. I glanced back at the fight and saw Callin lift Annalise over his head and slam her against the floor, then stomp on her.

The entire hotel seemed to shudder and the balcony suddenly lurched and gave a loud crack. I swung back and forth over the long drop, sure it was about to tear free and drop all the way down to the lot below, burying me.

The side of the building was just a few feet away; I only had to reach it. Then I could stick to it like a fly and climb back into the fight, whether the balcony fell free or not. But first I had to get away from where I was.

I tried to let go of the concrete but the glove wouldn't do it. I tugged at it, pulled at it, strained. Irena's glove stuck to the balcony like it had been welded in place.

I heard the sounds of cracking concrete, as loud as a firing squad. The balcony dropped several inches and then stopped.

"Oh, shit. Please, glove. Please please please let go."

I'd already dropped the ghost knife during the fight, and I'd let go of Annalise when she climbed over me. Why couldn't I let go of the balcony? How did the magic work?

I was too rattled to think clearly, not that I was a master of logic in quieter moments. I pulled myself up and pulled open the glove's Velcro strap with my teeth. It would be better to abandon the glove and try my luck with bare hands and the railing.

But I couldn't slip my hand out of the glove. The spell wouldn't let go of me.

The balcony tipped farther.

I was going to fall.

CHAPTER NINETEEN

Something inside the suite crashed like a car wreck. The balcony lurched a little more, and the pitch was far enough that broken glass slid over the edge and fell onto my head. A moment later, Callin's black cloth, whatever it was, followed, fluttering to the asphalt below. I kept tugging at the gloves, mainly because I couldn't think of anything better to do.

I sensed the ghost knife above me and saw it slide over the edge of the balcony. It balanced on the lip for just a moment, then slowly tipped over and fell.

Without thinking, I caught it.

I'd let go of the balcony. I'd wanted to grab something else, and the glove had let go.

I rubbed the Velcro strap against my jaw, closing it, then put the ghost knife into my mouth. I rolled my lips between it and my teeth so I wouldn't bite down on it and destroy it.

I pulled myself up, then picked a spot on the railing I wanted to grab. I did. I pulled myself up again and moved my grip to the top of the rail.

I pulled myself over, feeling almost as though I might live through this whole mess. At that moment, something snapped and the balcony lurched downward.

I threw my body across the broken glass and caught hold

of the metal frame of the french doors. It seemed to be on the safe side of the cracking concrete, and I caught hold and didn't let go.

The balcony didn't fall off the side of the building, but the glass I hadn't trapped with my own body fell away. It hung at nearly 90 degrees now, and I braced my foot against the side railing and pulled myself into the room.

Callin held Irena and Annalise by their throats, their feet dangling in the air. Blue lightning arced around all three of them, but only my allies seemed to be suffering the effects of it. Callin's back was turned to me, and I could see that Irena's face was slack, while Annalise was still conscious enough to be in great pain.

As an experiment, I willed Irena's gloves to attach themselves to the air. It worked. My hands were free. Maybe if I willed them to attach to nothing, I would be able to take them off; that was an experiment for later. I took the ghost knife from my mouth and lunged at Callin's Achilles tendon.

The broken floor shifted, emitting a loud crack. Callin spun and dropped Irena onto my arm, pinning me. Then he threw Annalise against the wall. She hit the floor hard and didn't look like she was going to get up again soon.

I shouldered Irena off of me and lunged at Callin, but he grabbed my wrist and dragged me off the floor. He wasn't tall enough to lift me off my feet, but he was strong enough to throw me off balance.

"And now," he said, "I'll deal with this annoying little object."

I tried to twist the ghost knife to cut his hand or wrist, but he grabbed it too quickly, pinning it between his thumb and forefinger. Once he had it, he had control of it. I couldn't pull it free or push it at him,

Callin pulled on the ghost knife, but it wouldn't come free. His brows furrowed and he pulled harder, but Irena's glove held on. I knew he had the strength to pull my hand off at the wrist, but just as the magic in the glove blocked Annalise's momentum, it blocked his strength, too.

He twisted my hand to look at the sigil on the palm of the glove. From that new position, I was able to bend the back end of the ghost knife just enough to slide the corner into the heel of his palm.

He gasped. His grip on my wrist softened enough for me to pull my hand free. I saw a momentary flicker of apology cross his expression, then it became vague again. I slashed the spell across the chest, cutting deep into his ribcage and bursting several of the designs on his waistcoat.

Callin toppled backwards onto the floor. I dropped to my knees beside him and plunged the ghost knife into his belly. Sigils burst apart. Jets of black steam shot past my face. I leaned away from them and stabbed the ghost knife into Callin's head. His eyes rolled back.

My voice was harsh and low. "You are at a crossroads in your life."

But I was letting myself get clever. There wasn't enough space between winning and dying for me to gloat, and while I was distracted, Callin swung his fist at me, blindly. I rolled away, falling onto my back as the floor shattered under me.

Callin rolled the other way, away from me. What was it going to take to bring this guy down? Then I saw two green ribbons land on his body.

"NO!" It was already too late. I scrambled back as the green fire suddenly expanded around Callin's body. The flames billowed toward me like a sheet blown by the wind, but I just barely managed to retreat beyond it.

Then it did what I feared: it curled up and began to stream toward the flaring sigil on Callin's back.

He was up on one elbow, his back toward me. The green fire stretched like taffy as it streamed over his shoulder and into the sigil. Without thinking, I whipped my hand at him, throwing the ghost knife.

Like a miracle, it passed just above the streaming green fire and cut through the flaring sigil.

There was a sudden concussion, like a small bomb going off, and I nearly fell over. Then Callin screamed, and the stream of fire shot through him like a spike, erupting from his chest like water from a firehose.

It burned a hole through the bed, then through the wall beyond. Callin collapsed onto his back; the fire blasting from his chest scorched a deep gouge into the plaster wall and then punched through the ceiling into the room upstairs.

The flames suddenly grew dark and the harsh sound it made became hollow and echoing, I thought I heard voices inside it, whispering.

The beam of fire sputtered and went out, leaving Callin on the middle of the floor, his left arm and head hanging through a burned hole in the unsupported carpet.

Annalise took a set of shackles from Irena's bag and, after dragging Callin to an unbroken part of floor, began to clamp them around his wrists and ankles. The chains seemed too flimsy to contain a man who had smashed that harpoon into toothpicks with a single blow, but I knew it would be the sigils painted on it that would hold him, not the metal.

I got to my feet, feeling raw and exhausted. We had won, and that meant that Jon had won. Maybe now, finally, my debt would be repaid.

The only light came from the daylight streaming through the huge hole in the wall where the balcony door had once been and from the flames of the burning bed. The thick black smoke billowed through the hole in the ceiling like a smoke hole in a tent.

It was time to get out of here. I could have thrown water on the bed or something, maybe checked the room upstairs for injured people, but my instincts told me that it was long past time we got out of the building. A hotel was a trap; once the cops arrived they'd have very few exits to cover and we'd have no way to slip out unseen.

Maybe that didn't matter to Annalise. Maybe she had another grey ribbon for me to use.

I closed my eyes and *reached* out with my mind. The ghost knife flew into my hand. I looked it over, glad it hadn't been burned by the beam of fire, then slipped it into my pocket. My spell. My power.

The floor beneath me cracked and shifted slightly. I moved closer to the wall where the footing should have been more secure, and that brought me closer to Callin.

From out in the hall I heard someone pounding on the door to the room. Had it been going on for a while? It was possible that I'd missed it in the rush of adrenaline, but I wasn't worried about it. If Annalise and Irena were right, hotel security and the police wouldn't be able to open Callin's door; it was when the pounding stopped and they started peering down through the smoke hole that I'd get nervous.

Callin was still breathing. I stood over him, thinking I should feel triumphant, but instead I was just impatient. He didn't look so tough—had never looked tough—and it annoyed me that he'd made it so hard to get what I needed.

I knelt beside him. His face was pale but otherwise unmarked and his waistcoat had been reduced to scorched threads. There was an untouched sigil on his belt, but I left it alone. I didn't want to kill the guy, I just wanted answers.

I moved his tattered clothes away from his chest and belly. He didn't have a mark on him, not from Irena's harpoons, not even from the gigantic blow torch that had cut through him. What the hell were these people made of, anyway?

Personally, I was ready to start the interrogation, or at least carry him out of here, but Annalise was digging through Irena's bag again. Did she need more chains?

She made a small grunt that suggested she'd found what she was looking for, then took a small clear Tupperware tub from the bag. It was filled with sloshing red liquid and small dark chunks.

Annalise turned to Irena, who stirred, slowing coming back to consciousness. Annalise cradled the older woman's head in her lap, popped the Tupperware lid and slipped a tiny chunk of raw, bloody meat between Irena's lips.

"Slowly," Annalise said. Her voice was gentle. "Take it easy."

I shut my eyes. It was beef—steak tartar. It was raw tuna or pork or dog or *something, anything* other than human flesh. It had to be. I didn't want to think about what it would mean if these people were cannibals, too.

But I had to know. "What are you feeding her?" Annalise ignored me. I was only a wooden man, whatever that meant, but I had to have an answer. "Okay, then. *Who* are you feeding her?"

Annalise glared at me with contempt, then returned to her friend. I took a deep breath. She wouldn't have looked at me with such scorn if she was really feeding human flesh to her friend. I hoped.

The pounding continued. Several people worked at the door now and from the sound of it, they were becoming desperate. Which was too bad for them. I had something important to do.

Callin's eyes were open. "Raymond," he said, as casually as if we were old buddies who'd bumped into each other at a coffee shop. "A ghost knife, eh?"

I didn't answer. Annalise had said her society killed people who stole spells, and I have never been the kind of guy who felt better after a confession.

"On a piece of paper," Callin continued, and shook his head. He looked tired. The fight had gone out of him, just as it had gone out of Jon when I'd used the ghost knife on him. "The spell's name is 'ghost knife,' so naturally I laid it on knives and the occasional saber. Quite effective, as I'm sure you can imagine. Such things are out of fashion now—and they make travel difficult—so I dropped that spell from my arsenal years ago. But putting it on a piece of paper... I should have thought of that myself."

The pounding from the other room had gotten heavier and more insistent. But that didn't matter. "We aren't going to have a friendly conversation," I told him. "Where's the book?"

"Is that why you came here? To steal my book? Again?"

Annalise walked across the shattered floor toward us. "Cut the bullshit. I want to see it. Where have you hidden it?"

Callin glanced at his desk. It was the barest flicker of his eyes, but I didn't miss the significance.

"There?" I asked, pointing. "In that desk?"

Without waiting for clarification, Annalise brought her forearm down on it, shattering it.

Callin groaned. "That was a Wooton."

Annalise shifted the wood aside and drew out a heavy book. She carried it to Irena, who had found the strength to sit up. Looking more alert than she had before she'd eaten, she wiped her hands on her coat and accepted the book from Annalise. Whatever had been wrong with her, eating meat had healed her.

"Are you certain?" Callin said, softly. "This attack could be forgiven. It could be brushed off as bad intelligence or enemy duplicity. There would be consequences, yes, but they'd be manageable. But if you *take my spell book*—"

Irena opened the book. She barely glanced at each page before flipping to the next. She didn't even seem to focus on the page. "Annalise, how can she—"

Annalise glared at me. "Shut up."

Irena reached the end of the book. "Nothing," she said.

"No," I said, the conviction in my voice surprising me. "No, you didn't look carefully enough."

Irena held the book close to her chest. "There are no summoning spells in this book."

"That *can't* be right!" I turned to Callin. "Where's the spell you cast on Jon? I know it was you. I saw the blue page. How do I undo what happened to my friend?"

Annalise shook her head. "Shit."

The pounding at the door stopped.

I turned back to Irena. "It must be a different book! He must have switched them." But I could see where I'd sliced the cover, and I could see the metal plate beneath. "Then he must have a second book around here somewhere." Which didn't make any sense, but I was getting desperate. I stood over Callin. "Listen, you son of a bitch, I know what you did to my friend, and I want you to show me how to undo it. Tell me where that spell is, or—"

Callin laughed. "Please. You wouldn't know how to kill someone like me."

"Boss." I turned to Annalise. I knew I was losing them and I absolutely had to bring her around to my side again. "I showed you the blue page the summoning spell was on. The only place it could have come from was his book."

"Shut up," she said to me. "There's something else that doesn't make sense, Callin: If you haven't gone renegade, why did you try to kill me with that damn envelope?"

"Envelope?" Callin asked, genuinely surprised. "Are you referring to the envelope I gave to him?"

Annalise, Irena and Callin all turned toward me.

I had gambled and lost; I'd failed to save Jon. I would have liked to apologize to him for it, but I wasn't going to get the chance.

Something crashed in the other room. We all turned toward the doorway just as Jon charged screaming through the doorway, an aluminum baseball bat over his head.

Echo, Payton and Macy were right behind him.

Jon crossed the room faster than I could blink. Annalise didn't even have time to raise her arm before Jon began bashing her with it. She fell onto her side just as Payton brought a sledgehammer down onto Irena.

Then with the suddenness of a bad dream, Echo was right in front of me, grinning like a lunatic. She lifted a hatchet and, with terrifying speed, swung for my neck.

CHAPTER TWENTY

Hot pain flared beneath my jaw. Just as I was thinking that she'd cut my head off, I saw her hand rebound away from my neck. The hatchet hadn't cut through.

Echo was startled. She seized a handful of my shirt, making ready for a second swing, and I grabbed her wrist so I could hold onto her long enough to use my ghost knife. The spell on Irena's glove caught hold of her, and Echo *changed.*

Like a picture coming into focus, ghostly shapes appeared around Echo's face, protruding from her mouth, nose, tear ducts, skin, hair. They were like branches, or stick lightning—slender and thinner than pencils, but splitting apart in irregular angles and ending in needle-sharp tips. They shivered as though under the force of a hurricane, and at the same moment Echo threw back her head and screamed. Her knees buckled, but she still had hold of my shirt. I slashed through her wrist with the ghost knife and it passed through her as if she were made of smoke.

Her hand spasmed and she lost her grip on me. I released her and let her fall to the floor at the same moment I remembered Annalise's voice: *Predators like to be summoned, but hate to be held in place.* The ghostly branches vanished as soon as I let go.

Callin moved toward me. Macy stood beside him, an axe high over her head, but she didn't swing it. A glance at her expression told me that she would never swing it.

I had no choice but to take on Callin again, but alone this time. I stabbed at him with my ghost knife and he leaned back, sweeping both of his arms upward. The chain around his wrists struck the ghost knife and a burst of light filled the room. The links of the shackle flew apart.

Broken links of chain pelted my face and chest. Macy tossed aside the axe. Echo looked at me; she wasn't grinning anymore.

Callin's spell book leaped into his hand as he stepped toward the broken edge of the balcony. At the same time, Echo rolled cautiously to her feet, hatchet in hand. At the other end of the room, Jon and Payton were unleashing a furious attack against Annalise and Irena, their blows coming as fast as a drum beat.

Without thinking, I leaped at Callin and caught hold of his torn pant cuff.

He leaped upwards, dragging me along with him. Cloth tore, but before his cuff could tear free, the world disappeared.

For a moment, I was alone in a silent white mist. There was no city below me, no sky above. I could smell icy wind and I held tight to that tiny piece of cloth.

The sound of city traffic washed the silence away and I felt myself falling. Before I had a chance to register that I was back in the world, I slammed down hard onto a flat surface. More tar paper and pebbles: Another roof. It was daytime, but still overcast. Was this the same day? Was I still in Seattle?

"Damned sunlight," Callin said from somewhere close. I rolled over and tried to scramble away, but Callin grabbed my arm and leg. I felt himself being lifted into the air.

"Time to tie a knot in you, my little loose end," Callin said. He marched toward the edge of the roof and I knew he was going to try to throw me off again.

Where was my ghost knife? It wasn't in my hand anymore and I couldn't reach my pocket to check. Had I lost it during the trip? I struggled, but I knew it was no use against someone as strong as Callin. I was panicking; I couldn't calm himself enough to *feel* for my spell.

Of course Callin had the strength to throw me off the roof from right where he was standing, but I guessed he wanted to see me hit the pavement. That thought did nothing to calm me down or help me focus. We passed close to the roof access door but not close enough for me to grab it with Annalise's glove.

Then we were at the edge of the building. "Goodbye, lively one." Callin leaned over the edge and threw me downward just as I grabbed hold of his hair.

Irena's glove held fast to it. For a moment I thought I wasn't going to go over the edge, but then the hair tore free of Callin's scalp with a nasty sound, and I fell over the edge of the building.

I slapped my palm on the stone face and my body slapped against the side of the building. I'd only fallen about five feet, and Callin was a flailing above me, holding his scalp and cursing like a madman. That couldn't be good.

He moved away from the edge of the building, and somehow I suspected that he wasn't heading off to take a relaxing hot shower. I looked down. Maybe if I let go of the wall and dropped a few feet at a time, I could do a controlled fall to the street without breaking any bones.

Above me, I heard the sound of tearing metal. Maybe I could reach a window instead....

Callin appeared at the edge of the roof holding the twisted roof access door. His eyes were wild with anger. He raised the door over his head to throw it and roared.

I was exposed and helpless and I had nowhere to go. That metal door was going to hit, and maybe the force of it would tear my arms off, leaving my hands stuck to the wall while my body splatted on the alley below.

But Callin didn't throw it. While my mind was racing, he took a deep breath, blew it out, and laughed. Then he tossed the door aside. "You are a most irritating boy!"

A smarter man would have said *yes, sir* but what came out of my mouth was "I think I'm an irritating man."

"This anger is invigorating. It's quite a gift for someone who has lived as long as I have."

"Happy belated," I said. "Glad it fits. Give me the cure for my friends and we'll be even."

He smiled at me in a way I didn't like. Then the world became a white blur.

Silence.

And the world returned and I found myself sprawled on the gravel roof with Callin standing above me.

"Lively one, I think you know by now that I don't have the cure or the curse."

"But there's no one else who—"

"You have no idea how much trouble you are in, do you? Did you make a copy of my book?"

That question took me by surprise, and I didn't call up my poker face fast enough. He shook his head and sighed.

For a moment I thought he was going to kill me. "Annalise destroyed them without reading them," I said, for no apparent reason at all. Were those going to be my last words, to help a killer get clear of the trouble I'd caused her?

"She wouldn't," Callin said. He squinted up at the sunlight. My skull stayed refreshingly un-smashed.

I saw the ghost knife lying on the gravel roof, about ten feet behind Callin. I wanted it, desperately, but that was only because I was afraid. I hate to be afraid. Besides, if I took up my ghost knife again, Callin might think the fight had started up again.

But I still wanted him to go away. "Are you going to go back there?" I asked. "Are you going to try to help her?"

"I am not. My first duty is to hide my spell book away so it does not fall into the hands of your infected friends. Protecting my book is a responsibility I have been neglecting lately. I have been sleepwalking through my life, I admit. Irena and Annalise will have to fend for themselves. They're somewhat capable.

"And now that you have destroyed my resting place," Callin continued, "I'm leaving the city. All this leaves me far too exposed. But I'm going to send someone to come and clean up this mess. Someone with *real* power and the will to use it."

"If you're going to send someone, send someone who can

help, not just someone who wants to kill my friends because it's easy."

Callin crouched beside me. "My dear boy, your infected friends could do more harm than you can dream. We peers would destroy this entire city—and every innocent person in it, down to babes in arms—before we would let their infection spread. I'm sending someone with the wit and power to do just that."

"But if your friend is that powerful, why can't he just take off their curse?"

Callin laughed at me again. "You have no idea how much danger you are in, but not from me. I'm not going to kill you. In fact, I'm fighting a powerful urge to apologize to you and to offer you a large sum of money as compensation for all the trouble I've caused while fighting for my life. I'm sure you know what I am talking about. Besides, you are Annalise's wooden man, now, yes? You don't need me to kill you."

The world became a blur of silent white. When I opened my eyes again, Callin was gone.

The first thing I did was fetch my ghost knife. It felt damn good to hold it again, and I was happy that we had both come through the fight with a minimum of damage. Happy? It was a goddamn miracle.

A few hundred yards to the north, I could see a gaping hole in the side of Callin's hotel. I touched the side of my throat and my fingers came away spotted with blood. The spell Annalise had put there had blocked most of Echo's hatchet swing.

My hands started to shake, and I crouched low, moving toward the shadow of the roof access stairs. What if someone was looking out of that ruined hotel room and saw me?

I'd come through that fight with nothing more than a few bone-deep bruises and a set of fear-shakes so bad it made me sick. That was the power I'd hungered for. I'd stuck my neck out for my friend—and, if I was going to be honest, for a taste of the magic Annalise and Callin tossed around so casually—but not only had I failed Jon, I'd failed myself.

God, the fight in Callin's room was the most terrifying experience of my life. I was almost certainly going to be killed in the near future by someone in that room, and, despite everything, I still hungered for more magic.

This was a poison. It was like an addiction. I rubbed at the numb, enchanted flesh on the back of my hand. I had made myself part of the world behind the world, and I hadn't been invited in. I'd lied and tricked my way in. I'd stolen the key, and I had no idea how I was going to survive it.

I was alone now. I no longer had Annalise on my side, and Echo had tried to kill me a second time, despite the fact that Jon had told her I was off limits.

Were the six of them still fighting over there, inside that darkened room? Ordinarily, I'd have put my money on Annalise and Irena, but Callin had done a lot of damage to both of them.

The truth was, I didn't know who would be coming out on top, but I did know both sides were my enemies now. If I was still going to find a cure for Jon—and I was, nothing could change that—I'd have to do it without help.

But where was I going to find a way to undo the curse Jon had put on himself and his friends? I'd been so sure it had come from Callin, once I'd seen that Jon's spell had been copied onto blue legal paper. Where else could he have gotten that if he hadn't pulled it out of the stack of Callin's spells in my own backpack?

Suddenly, everything became clear. I ducked into the roof access stairway, avoiding the jagged edges of the metal hinges where Callin had torn the door off, then hustled down the stairs, heading for the street.

I knew exactly where the spell had come from.

I didn't have any bills small enough for bus fare, so I ducked into the nearest Starbucks. They had only just opened, and I pressed one of their light brown napkins against my neck while I waited in line to break a twenty by buying a cup of coffee.

"Did they get your wallet?"

I turned to the woman who'd spoken to me. She was about sixty and must have weighed nearly three hundred pounds. Her clothes suggested that she worked somewhere formal, like a bank or lawyer's office.

"Worse," I said. "My phone."

She took a smart phone from her pocket. "Do you need to call someone?"

"You know what? Thank you. But what I really need is to look up an address."

Ten minutes later, I was riding a bus out to West Seattle, with an address written on the napkin in my pocket. I had nothing in particular to think about and my mind was clear.

Forty-five minutes later I was standing at the door of an apartment building. I scanned the directory and pressed the call button.

While I waited for an answer, I noticed a small pile of folded newspapers lying in the bushes beside the stairs. The top paper obscured one with the headline: "JAIL."

With a sense of dread, I picked it up. The entire headline was "JAILBREAK!" Right beneath that word was a picture of me.

I threw the paper deep into the bushes without reading any further. Rush hour traffic raced down the street behind me, and I pressed the call button again.

I'd expected to hear a voice squawk at me through the little speaker, but instead the front door swung inward. Wally King stood there, wearing sweats and a bathrobe.

"Ray!" Wally said. "This is a surprise. What's up? Did you get that jay oh bee at the copy shop?"

I looked him straight in the eye. Wally looked different somehow, more haggard and a little wild. I'd seen that expression before, on one of Arne's crew who had been convicted of grand theft auto and was going into prison the next day. It was the look of a man who had lost interest in whatever living he had left.

"Yeah," I said. "I did, but I'm pretty sure I'm fired already. Sorry if I made you look bad."

"I don't give a fuck about that place. But I don't have any other job leads to give you—"

"I'm not here about that."

"Okay. What's up?"

"Can I have a copy of the spell you used to cure Jon?"

He shrugged. "Sure. Why not?" Then he turned around and walked into the building. I followed. "I guess I'm sorry I got you involved in this."

"Mind explaining that one a little more?" We trudged up a flight of stairs. Wally stopped at the first door and fumbled with his keys.

"When I heard you were getting out of the clink I thought you were the answer to my prayers. Stupid me. I was pretty screwed up."

"Because Macy had dumped you."

"Exactly." Wally opened the door and stepped inside, then held the door open for me. His place was a squalid mess. Hard tool calendars and NASCAR posters hung on the walls. The floor was littered with dirty dishes and discarded clothes. I stood in the middle of the floor and tried not to touch anything. Wally locked the door. "Who told you that?"

Echo, when she had still been alive, had said Macy's previous boyfriend had been a charity case, and at the copy shop Oscar had made a crack about Wally stalking his ex. "I saw you standing outside the building where she worked." If Wally was the guy with the spell, Macy was the logical path for it to get to Jon.

Wally was red-faced from the climb up the stairs. It was hard to imagine a loser like him with Macy, but stranger things had happened. Just this morning, in fact, stranger things had happened in Callin's hotel.

"It doesn't matter, anyway," Wally said. "I hoped you were going to reverse-Yoko Jon and Macy apart so I could win her back."

"How exactly was I supposed to break them up?"

"By being Jon's beer buddy. Get drunk and shout at football games with him. She hates that guy stuff because of her dad or whatever." He shrugged. He seemed tired and distracted.

This seemed to be the place where I should have said I was sorry, but there was no way I was going to say those words. "It didn't work."

"So much for my big plan. Guess I'm no Lex Luthor."

"What about the spell?"

He lumbered to the stereo. "It's back here." He shifted a speaker and took out a stack of blue pages. The stack must have been at least 18 inches high.

"Christ, that's a lot of reading."

"It's just copies, dude. I used to work at a copy shop, remember?"

Wally dropped the stack on the coffee table. I edged around him and began flipping through the pages.

"Here," Wally said. He had found the place where the top copy ended and the second began, then offered it to me. "Help yourself."

This stack of blue pages was hand-written like Callin's spell book, but it was thicker. "Thanks." I sat on the couch and pushed aside a plate holding old pizza crusts and a pair of cheese-encrusted scissors. I set the stack onto the cleared spot and began to go through it.

Wally drummed his fingers on the remaining stack of pages and kept talking dreamily. I only half-listened.

"It's hard to remember the guy I was a few days ago. That other me was obsessed with Macy. And stealing from the till. And making moves on customers, like the lady who brought in that book—"

"These aren't spells." The pages I was looking at were

cramped with a large, flowing handwriting, but there were no diagrams.

Wally leaned over and glanced at the page. "That's the true, secret history of the Earth. Spells are in back."

History bored me. I flipped through the pages until I found a large diagram, then began scanning the pages. "Is there a way to undo Jon's cure in here?"

"That doesn't matter," Wally answered. "Listen, I'm telling you something: Woman comes in with her book, and she's not what you call hot but who am I to be choosy? I take a run at her and she shoots me down, big surprise. But she leaves a partial in the trash. It says, *Cure the Lame.*"

I snatched up a page. "Here it is! Cure the lame!"

"Yeah, that's the one."

I scanned the spell, then the spell before it and the spell after it, looking for a way to undo the curse.

Wally droned on. "See, Macy had just broken up with me, and her whole life is helping gimps. If I could *cure* one of them, really and truly, that had to be worth a blow job, minimum, not just the pity sex I was getting before."

"I can't find a way to undo the spell. Is this the whole book? Every page?"

Wally glanced at the stack I was holding. "I think so. I stole it right from her house. She paid by check—like it's 1986 or something—so her address was right there. All I had to do was break in."

Something in his voice broke the trance I was in. There was something wrong with him, and I'd been so focused on the pages that I'd missed it until now.

"You shoulda seen her," Wally said, then he giggled in a high voice. "She had gone nuts."

I put my hands on the stack of pages and looked up at him. His behavior made me feel as though he'd suddenly pulled a gun from his pocket. "What are you talking about, Wally?"

"The not-that-hot chick," Wally said. He smiled to himself, as though enjoying a private joke. "She read the book, but she couldn't handle it. I think it broke her."

"Can I have her name and address?" I stood so I could be on my feet if he started something I didn't like.

The door banged open. The noise was so sudden and so loud that I jumped and yelped.

Macy stood in the room with us. "Wally, I need—" She lifted her chin and sniffed, then turned her gaze on me. "YOU!"

She was between me and the door, so I couldn't run from her, even if I'd wanted to try. I fumbled in my pocket for my ghost knife. I was too slow. Too slow.

"I don't want to fight," she said. Her face was flushed and streaked with sweat as though she'd run a long way.

"Full stomach?" I blurted out.

"That's not funny!" Macy looked like she was about to cry. "I'm cursed!" She turned toward Wally. "You cursed me, Wally!"

Wally shook his head. "It doesn't matter."

"It does! Echo isn't Echo anymore."

"She was already dead when you did the spell," I said. "There's nothing of her left. She's all creature."

Macy wasn't interested in discussing the nuances of her

condition. "Wally, you have to take it back. You have to undo it and turn me back into myself."

Wally shrugged. He seemed bored. "It doesn't matter and I don't know how. And even if I did, I doubt I would bother, anyway. 'Don't tell anyone it came from me,' I said. Was that too much to ask for curing your new boyfriend? But now I have Ray coming around and your other friends, too—"

"Other friends?" Macy said. "Who?"

"You know who wants that cure."

Macy blinked twice. She didn't seem to be thinking very clearly, but she knew what Wally was telling her.

"And you gave it to them?" She sounded horrified.

He shrugged again. "Why not?"

In the blink of an eye, Macy was gone.

Wally turned toward me, a little smile on his face. "Quick, ain't she?" he said, as though talking about a car he'd rebuilt.

I reached into my pocket and touched the ghost knife. The page with the cure the lame spell still sat on top of the stack of pages. I knew Annalise was looking for this. Maybe if I could give her the stack—the whole stack of all the pages—it would be worth my life. She wouldn't trust me, no, but maybe she wouldn't kill me.

"Wally, why do you keep saying *it doesn't matter*?"

"Because I'm going to kill everyone," Wally said.

CHAPTER TWENTY-ONE

I blinked at him. "What did you just say?"

Wally reached down and patted the tall stack of blue pages. "I read the book, too, Ray. I know why we're here, and it's not good. Bad shit is coming, buddy. Shit like you can't imagine. Better if we all die."

"Wally, I think you've gone nuts, too."

He shrugged again, still smiling like a man with a secret. "I think I've gone sane." His dead little eyes told me he was serious... and with the spell book, might even manage it. *Kill everyone.*

No. I couldn't let Wally keep on the way he was, copying spells and sharing them. It wasn't just what he'd done to Jon—I could overlook that, mainly because I assumed he didn't know what he was doing any more than Jon or Macy or I did. It was that he had learned the truth and was going to be sharing spells and taking lives. I couldn't turn my back on this. I looked at Wally's shiny, smug face and I knew he had to die.

I drew my ghost knife from my pocket.

But he was ready for me, almost as though he expected it. He held up a compact disc with a sigil drawn on the blank side and despite myself, I glanced at it.

My body became impossibly heavy, much too heavy for me to stand. I fell forward, hitting my head on the coffee table and slumping on the carpet. All my strength had left me and my vision was getting blurry.

Wally took hold of my arm and rolled me onto my back. I was helpless; he could do anything at all to me, and I tried to use that fear to hold onto consciousness. I wanted to be awake and aware when I died.

"Buddy," Wally said, "I don't blame you for trying to kill me, not at all. I would've done the same thing. Anyway, I'm leaving town in the Accord, but you can have my motorcycle. Key's in the dish."

I couldn't hold on anymore. Consciousness left me in a sudden rush, and I did not dream.

SOMEONE was calling my name. I opened my eyes and blinked away the blinding light. Hands helped me up, and I suddenly had the idea that Wally had changed his mind and come back to kill me.

But that didn't make any sense. Wally wouldn't help me up if he wanted to kill me. I knelt on the carpet and rubbed my eyes. Jon knelt beside me.

"Hey man," he said, "you all right?"

I blinked, trying to adjust to the light. Jon's face was pale and his skin hung loose on his bones, but his eyes were bright. He looked like he'd gone crazy, too, and that that it was eating him alive.

I had to undo that cure as soon as possible.

"Okay," I said. "I'm okay."

Jon helped me to my feet. I touched the sore spot where

my forehead had struck the table. It didn't seem too bad.

Payton and Echo were standing in the doorway, where Macy had stood who knows how long ago. One look at Echo's expression cleared my mind. She had already tried to kill me once today.

"Where's Wally?" Jon said. I didn't answer right away. Had I been on the floor for a few seconds? If so, Wally was just down in the garage. If it had been longer...

Jon stepped in front of me and looked me in the eyes. "Ray, where's Wally?"

I realized I was still holding my ghost knife. Where they going to attack? I really needed more steeled glass. I looked through the window and saw that it was dark outside. Hadn't he talked to Macy? Wally didn't want to take off their curse. "Gone. A while ago."

"We know that," Payton said, impatience rising in his voice.

Jon didn't acknowledge Payton at all. "We need your help to find him."

"My help? You tried to kill me!"

"We didn't mean it," Jon said.

I glanced at Echo. She was smirking slightly, and her eyes were narrow and unblinking. She meant it, all right.

At that moment, Echo noticed the sheets of blue paper on the coffee table. The cure the lame spell sat on top of the stack. She rushed forward, snatched it up, and slipped it into her pocket.

Shit. She was going to cast the spell again. Annalise was right; she was planning to summon more cousins. Time was running out, not just because of Echo, but because Callin's friend was on the way. I wasn't ready to see what a full-scale war of magic would look like.

Jon was still talking. "You smelled like them. You still do. Our sense of smell is very powerful for us now. It's getting stronger all the time, and our noses confuse our eyes. Do you understand what I'm saying? Eyes take longer now."

"And you were with them," Echo said. Her voice was steady and cold.

I glared at her. "They were killing each other because of me."

"Talk," Echo said. She tilted her head and looked away dismissively. "This is just talk. You have done nothing to convince me that you are on our side."

"That's because I'm not on your side!" My temper was getting ahead of me, but I couldn't rein it in. I'd been bouncing from one dangerous situation to another for days, and the fear and stress were wearing me thin. I turned to Jon. "I'm on *your* side. I've always been on your side. Do you think I'd be sticking my neck out like this if you weren't all mixed up in it?"

"I know, buddy," Jon said. "You and me."

"Jon is one of *us*," Echo said. "We are family."

I ignored her and focused on Jon. It was time I got his help. "Jon, I'm sure I can find a way to cure you."

He blinked at me, confused. "I'm already cured."

"I mean cure the cure."

"What?"

Why the hell was he giving me that look? Hadn't he

come here, like Macy, because he was cursed and wanted it taken off? "Jon, that spell turned you into a killer. We have to undo it."

He stared at me in disbelief. "You want to take away my legs? Again?"

We stood there, looking at each other. I waited for him to take it back, call it a joke, something. He didn't.

I waited.

Waited.

Neither of us spoke.

Echo turned to Payton. "Kill him."

In a flash, Payton crossed the room and slammed me against the wall like a tackling dummy. I already had my ghost knife in my hand, but I still wasn't fast enough. Before I could do anything, Payton took a carving knife from the pocket of his jacket and slammed it into my stomach.

I didn't feel any pain, just a strange pressure. I could smell Payton's sweat, could see dried brown blood flecked on the collar of his jersey. There was still no pain and I realized he'd struck the tattooed part of my skin.

He pressed harder and the knife blade snapped. He stepped back and stared at it in confusion.

I glanced at Jon. He was alpha, he'd said, and he could call off the attack.

But Jon just averted his eyes.

So be it. I grabbed Payton's arm with Irena's glove and the ghostly branches appeared around his head. He screamed, then twisted away from me as though he was about to collapse. With my other hand, I plunged the ghost knife into the back of his head, slicing off several crooked branches. They fell away and dissolved into smoke.

Payton's scream stopped suddenly. He gasped and then black blood blasted onto the coffee table. His knees turned rubbery and he fell backwards to the floor. The ghost knife, still inside him, slid along the side of his skull, cutting through his hair, ear and face as he dropped.

I jumped back, shocked and horrified. The severed top of Payton's ear bounced on the carpet and wisps of hair fluttered around it. His eyes were wide and blank, and he wasn't moving at all. He looked dead.

Echo rushed forward, kneeling beside him. She cradled his head in her lap. "Cousin!"

Jon stood over her, then looked up at me. "What did you do to him?"

"It—It never did that before," I said. Jon moved between me and Payton to protect the body. "I swear to God, Jon, I never thought it could do that."

Payton's legs spasmed and his broken skull bulged and twisted. Echo whined like a grieving dog. Payton's face became more and more distorted and his bones made a sound like cracking walnut shells. I had to look away.

The ghost knife hadn't changed; it was the same spell I'd always had. No one had switched it on me and once again there was no way to blame someone else.

But if this was my fault, again, I had no right to close my eyes. I looked down at Payton as his skull split wide open. Spiny legs scraped free and scratched against the coffee table, knocking a black-spattered pizza box onto the carpet. A phlegm-colored worm squeezed into the air, unfurled its wings, then fell onto the floor in two pieces.

Echo tried to scoop up the dead creature, but it dissolved into smoke and disappeared. "You killed him," she said. She raised her hands to show me they were empty. I knew she wasn't talking about Payton. "You killed him!"

I turned to Jon. "I've used this spell before. On you, even. See?" I held up the ghost knife, hoping Jon would recognize it. He only flinched. "Jon, that never happened before—it's not supposed to happen."

Jon backed toward the door, motioning for Echo to do the same. "You keep having these nasty accidents, don't you, Ray?" His voice was low and dangerous.

I stepped toward them. Jon fell into a crouch, shielding Echo with his body. He stared at the ghost knife—he couldn't look away—as he herded Echo toward the door.

"Jon... Jon, just listen to me for a moment. You saw what came out of him. That's the thing I told you about. That's what your so-called cure put inside you."

"No," Jon said, still watching the ghost knife as if it might jump out of my hand and run at him. "Your spell did that. You put that thing in Payton and it tore him apart."

Echo backed through the doorway. "We will be coming for you, meat."

I had lost and she had won. Jon was hers. "You forgot," I said to her, "that you're pretending to be Echo."

She sneered. Jon stepped through the doorway and slammed it shut. They were gone.

I slumped against the wall. I'd screwed up in a big, big way. I held up my ghost knife. It cut through *magic, ghosts and dead things.* It had never cut a person's flesh before. Did that mean Payton was already dead? Had Jon's so-called cure killed him?

That didn't make sense. I'd hit Jon with the ghost knife, and all it had done was cut his "ghost", not his flesh. I'd used it on Echo, too, while holding her with Irena's glove. There had been no black blood or sliced flesh then, either. Just another cut at her ghost.

Not that I had any idea what that meant. In truth, I had no idea what I was doing. Everything that had happened to me since I'd arrived in Seattle had been like a waking nightmare. All I could do was rush from one moment to the next, hoping I could stay ahead of all the people who wanted to kill me long enough to save my friend.

I crouched next to Payton's body. "I'm sorry, big guy."

But not too sorry. Payton had tried to clean me like a fish, which meant this mess in front of me was self-defense. I tried to imagine explaining that to the cops, what with me being an ex-con who'd already broken out of jail after less than a week of freedom.

No, no. Think about cops and prison later. For now, I had to cure Jon, stop Echo from summoning more cousins and head off the peer from the Twenty Palace Society who was coming to "clean up" the mess we were all making. After all that, I'd... What? Change my name and head to Costa Rica, maybe. I sure wasn't going to be a free man in my own country.

And I would have to be more careful with Callin's damn spell. Truthfully, I had no idea what it was doing to the people I used it on. Maybe I'd seal it in concrete and drop it into Elliott Bay on my way to South America.

Ghosts, magic and dead things. Which were the cousins?

I looked down at Payton again, but he didn't look like a human being any more, not with his head deformed that way. And maybe that's what I was missing. The ghost knife had hit Jon in the chest and Echo on the arm, but Payton had been cut on the head. Maybe the cousins—and I might as well start calling them that—lived inside their victim's skulls.

It was an ugly thought. If one did live inside Jon's skull, wouldn't it have destroyed his brain? Jon's personality and memories were still intact, so it didn't seem likely. Then again, when I'd grabbed Payton and Echo with Irena's glove, the weird branches had appeared around their faces and heads.

So maybe they *were* inside Jon, Payton and Macy's skulls. If, as Annalise had said, the cousins were only partly real, it was possible that they could live inside someone's skull while leaving the person intact.

For once I did not have to operate by empty guesswork. If I wanted to know if the cousins could share a space inside a human skull with that person's brain, I could just kneel down on Wally's disgusting living room floor and look for myself.

I knelt beside the body, careful not to get any sticky black blood on my clothes. I did my best not to look directly at his deformed face, only the side and top of his head. I pretended that the hair wasn't really hair, the bone wasn't really bone. I was looking at an open shell, not a person at all.

It was too dark. I took a tissue from a box on the end table and turned on a lamp. It seemed silly to worry about fingerprints now, but the fewer things I touched in this apartment the happier the rest of my life would be.

I leaned over Payton's body again and peered into the split skull. I saw bone, hair and a shadow. It took me a moment to register what I was seeing, but I soon realized I was looking into Payton's empty skull.

I felt woozy and backed away from him. I had the urge to laugh, but I was afraid that if I started I would never be able to stop. There was nothing inside Payton's skull. No brain, no meat, no blood. Not even a whole bunch of rocks. Nothing.

I remembered him standing beside the french fries, saying: "You're wondering why she's with me."

My stomach twisted and I retched against the wall, but I'd spent the whole day lying on the floor and nothing but a thin stream of bitter acid came out. I stumbled away from the body and lurched against the window.

Payton had been acting like himself right up to the moment of his death, but he didn't have any gray matter at all. The cousin had replaced it, had mimicked it, and with it all of Payton's memories and quirks.

Had this already happened to Jon? Was Jon a corpse with one of these *things* inside him, driving his body like a stolen car?

Or had Payton's brain been destroyed when the cousin was destroyed?

That was a thought. Maybe the cousins became truly solid when they died or were forced out of the host's body. After all, when I grabbed them with Irena's glove, the parts I could see were ghostly, hardly real. Something like that could co-exist with an actual, physical thing, couldn't it?

Maybe, up until the point the cousin was killed, their victims could be saved. Maybe if I could find some way to cut them out of their hosts while they were both still alive, I could still save Jon.

I held up my ghost knife. I even had the tool for the job.

There should have been a surge of satisfaction at the idea, but what I got was a sour hollow feeling. It seemed too tenuous, as if I was scamming myself because I just didn't want to face up to facts.

What if Jon was gone, for real? What if the cousin inside him had killed him even before I'd gotten off the bus from L.A.?

The truth was, I wasn't sure what I would do with him. I had too many memories of him and his family to think about cutting him open the way I'd cut open Payton. I wasn't sure I could do that.

But I was getting ahead of myself. Maybe, despite what he said, Wally had a counterspell in his book. If not, I would try the ghost knife. I couldn't imagine how it would actually work, but I had to try.

I was living on hope, and my supply had nearly run out.

I glanced out the window. In the street below, Jon and Echo stood beside a telephone pole. Jon was struggling with his cell phone, as though the numbers were in a different language. Then he held it up to his ear and started talking. Echo stared up at the windows of Wally's apartment. At me.

I bolted from the window. I had no doubt they were calling the cops on me. Jon might have been a cannibal with a monster living inside his brain, but at heart he was still a seat-belt person, and seat-belt people called the cops when they needed help. I yanked the stereo and speakers away from the wall. The stack of blue pages was gone. Wally had taken them.

The copy I'd been reading was still on the coffee table. It was missing the spell Echo had grabbed, of course, but I didn't need that one. I picked up the stack and checked it for splatters of black blood. It was clean. I tucked it under my jacket.

I felt dizzy again. I rushed into Wally's tiny kitchen and scanned the contents. The only thing I felt was safe to take was a plastic bag with four oranges inside. On my way to the door, I did my best not to look at Payton.

There was a little dish on a telephone table by the door, and there was a single engine key inside it. There was also a wad of folded five-dollar bills and a sheet of torn blue paper. I unfolded the paper and saw it was a photocopy of a check written by someone named "Nettle Philips"—if that was a real person's name—with her address printed on it as clear as day. Handwritten beside it was the note: "No hard feelings. Wally."

Wally had given me a motorcycle and the address of the woman he'd stolen the book from. What a pal. I stuffed the copied check, the key and the money into my pocket, then bolted out the front door and down a stairwell. I would have given Wally's apartment the same treatment Annalise had given Macy and Echo's house, if only to destroy any spells he might have left lying around, but I knew I didn't have time.

What's more, I didn't know who else was in the building and if they'd be able to get away. I wasn't going to kill innocent bystanders just because I'd screwed up. I'd just have to believe that Wally was the type to have taken everything magical with him.

There were few vehicles in the basement garage and no people. I passed a battered Toyota and an Isuzu minivan to reach an old Honda motorcycle that was so small it was nearly a dirt bike. I yanked the helmet out of the mesh net on the seat and pulled it on, then lowered the tinted visor.

I revved it and raced out of the garage. As I reached the corner of Wally's block, three police cars raced by. One of the cops looked straight into my blank visor, then straight at my license plate.

Shit. Now I'd have to ditch the motorcycle, and soon. If only I'd gone the other way. I rode away, staying just below the speed limit. Echo had the spell again, which meant I didn't have much time.

Nettle Philips lived on the northern side of the University, in one of those secluded little streets that Seattle tucks away on the sides of hills. It was a wooded dead-end lane surrounded by greenbelt too steep for safe development—it didn't even have a sidewalk. Philips's house was set back from the road and hemmed in by bushes and blackberry vines so high you couldn't actually see it from the street.

I parked the motorcycle down the block and hung the helmet on the handlebars. There was no one around. I double-checked the address and then pushed through the high wooden gate.

Then immediately stopped short. Whatever had happened here, it had been bad.

Philips's house was a cozy little California Bungalow, but something had punched huge holes into the walls, making the roof sag in several places. The building leaned toward the greenbelt slope behind it and groaned like it might collapse at any moment.

I took an orange from the mesh net behind me, peeled it and popped a section into my mouth. I immediately felt better. Whoever this Nettle Philips was, she might have parts of the spell book that Wally didn't, including a way to undo Jon's curse.

There was no other way. I was going into that house.

CHAPTER TWENTY-TWO

I finished the orange, letting the sweetness settle my stomach and give me strength. A strong wind ruffled my hair and made the little bungalow groan. I could picture myself crushed under the timbers in that house when it finally went down, but I shrugged the thought off. If I was willing to face Callin, I wasn't going to back down from this.

The front door bowed out inside the tilted jamb; there was no way I could pull it open. The two front windows were miraculously unbroken, although they also looked as if they were squeezed shut by the crooked frame. The two holes that had been punched through the walls were on the second floor, well out of reach.

I jogged around to the back of the house. The back door was splintering and squeezed shut, but the little kitchen window was sitting open.

I approached it carefully, ready to bolt if it started to fall toward me. There was something strange on the wall above the window—five parallel gouges in the wood. I spread my fingers next to them; the scratches had been made by a claw three times the size of my hand.

And there was something that looked like huge teeth marks on the window sill.

A predator. Someone had summoned a predator. I drew my ghost knife and carefully climbed through the window.

The kitchen was dark and chilly. I eased myself into the sink. Something crashed to the floor nearby. I stepped down from the counter into two inches of water.

All of my thought and energy was turned outward, taking in everything around me. If there was a predator here, I couldn't see it.

The house groaned. The floor shifted and plates slid out of the cabinets, smashing against the counter and bouncing across the wet floor. I jumped away from the rain of flatware and stumbled into the doorway.

By the light of a single desk lamp, I saw that the entire living room was coated with ice. Icicles hung from the ceiling and light fixtures. Books, furniture, TV... everything was covered with a dripping coat of ice.

"What the hell happened here?" I said aloud.

As if in answer to my question, I saw it: Wedged into the wooden banister was a compact disc with a sigil drawn onto the blank side with a Sharpie.

Wally must have been the one who summoned a predator to wreck the place. Had he been trying to destroy the other copies of the spell book, as Annalise had, or was he trying to cover his tracks?

The ice on the stairs was different from the rest. It looked like a single, smooth tube of bluish-white, thicker at the bottom and tapering as it went up. It was shaped like a roll of uncooked dough, but I couldn't tell if it was made of ice or was something else covered with ice.

I did know that it made the hairs on the back of my neck

stand at attention. I laid my hand on the frost covered desk beside me and leaned over, craning my neck to look around the end of the sofa at the bottom of the stairs.

There was more ice there, and it would have taken me a long time to work out the shape if some parts hadn't been stained in blood red. There, on the floor, was a huge hand. The long, curled fingers were like overturned icicles—and the sharp tips were streaked with red.

The hand was palm up and attached to a slender, knobby arm with an extra elbow. The arm connected to the round body, which extended beyond the foot of the stairs to the front door. The body was a continuation of the long tube, without a feather, hair, scale, or other feature on the smooth ice. The end of it—the thickest part yet—looked like a rolled out tube of blue-white clay, and it took me a moment to realize the jagged crack with the red stains over it was not an injury, it was a mouth.

I stared at it, transfixed by its eyeless face and smooth, melting form. For the first time I noticed that the red around its mouth—blood, it had to be blood—seemed to run down inside of it. I tried to puzzle out what it was, because I could not see a physical form beneath that ice—was it some kind of eel or snake?

I didn't know, but I could tell that it was dead, and that was good enough for me.

A beam fell out of the ceiling and crashed against the kitchen floor, bringing a shower of ceiling timbers with it. Both front windows shattered.

I suddenly realized the desk I was leaning over had an

ice-coated stack of paper on the corner. My hand had been resting on it for support.

I smashed it, shattering the ice. The pages at the top hadn't been copied onto blue paper; they were plain white letter paper. The top page was soaked and mashed against the five or six pages beneath it, but I could still read the hand-written ink. There were a lot of nonsense words that ended in "-um" and "-us" and I guessed it was Latin.

I lifted the wet mass of paper, exposing a few copies that seemed to be complete and a spiral bound notebook, handwritten in English. There was a swirly capital "N" on the cover of the notebook that matched the signature on Nettle's check. The mystery woman herself must have trans-lated them.

Something above me cracked. Time to go.

I grabbed a canvas bag off the back of a chair and shoved all the pages into them, Latin, English and whatever else was there.

The way out through the kitchen was blocked, so I crept over the slushy carpet toward a large broken window at the side of the house. I didn't like moving closer to that dead predator, but the only other option was to let the house col-lapse on me.

As I crossed in front of a rocking chair and reached the window, I saw the body.

She'd been a big woman, I could tell that much about her. Her shoulders and arms were muscular and her hair was thick with tight brown curls, but there wasn't much more of her. Every part of her below her ribcage was gone, and the carpet around her was shiny with frozen blood.

Was this the woman who'd turned Wally down for a date? It seemed pretty clear to me that he summoned a predator to kill her, then killed the predator himself, but I had no idea why. Or why he hadn't just bought a gun. Maybe he thought doing this with magic would be cool. I hoped I'd get a chance to ask him about it, at knifepoint.

The building shuddered and a splintering sound echoed around me. I planted one foot on the rocking chair, knocked away a couple shards of glass with the bottom of the canvas bag, then slipped through onto the grass outside.

I was afraid that the pressure of my foot against the sill would topple the building, but it didn't happen. I sprinted away from the house, glass breaking under my foot, until I was safely away.

The house didn't fall. It creaked and groaned, but it held on. I realized I was holding my breath and let it out. There was no reason for me to stand here waiting for it to collapse, even though I thought *someone* ought to witness it.

It felt as though I needed to do something else, but I wasn't sure what. Carry an axe back through the window and hack that big nightmarish thing to pieces? Annalise had burned down Macy and Echo's house, but I didn't have any matches, let alone something that would burn through all the ice inside.

I knew how to set a fire as well as anyone, but so what? I wasn't an arsonist and I wasn't a surrogate Annalise. I didn't want to be her guy, rushing around the city doing her work for her.

A sudden, visceral urge to get out of town burned through

me. I wanted to head south and keep going until I hit Chile. I wasn't meant for this bullshit. I wasn't supposed to be stumbling over corpses of people torn apart by magic. I hated the world behind the world and I wanted nothing to do with it.

But of course I wasn't going to do that. This urge to quit was just another enemy that had to be beaten bloody. I had a debt to repay.

I slipped through the gate and pulled it shut behind me. There was no one on the street—in fact, there were no lights on in any of the other houses. I pulled on the helmet, started the engine and sped away, the little motorcycle buzzing like a chainsaw in the quiet night.

The only problem was that I had nowhere to go. It was already late evening—soon the streets would be nearly empty, and Wally's little two-stroke bike was going to act like a neon sign that said *Hey cops, pull me over.*

I didn't have the money to pay for a motel. With the money I'd taken from Wally, I could park in an all-night coffee shop, assuming I found one. That would give me a chance to read Nettle's pages.

The memory of her body, and of the thing that killed her, flashed in my mind's eye and the motorcycle wobbled. Focus. It would have been monumentally stupid to survive so much only to smash my own brains out on the asphalt.

Once I had a place to study, I could search through Nettle's pages. What did I expect to find there beyond another copy of cure the lame? The spell to summon the ice predator? Maybe a dozen—or a hundred—other ways to destroy friends, ruin lives, and end the world? I was tempted to buy a lighter and torch the whole thing right now.

And at the same time, I wanted to make a special copy all for myself. Despite the tattoos, ghost knife and gloves, I was still the ninety-pound weakling in this fight. The power these pages represented was tempting. Would it give me the juice to take on Annalise? Echo? Even Callin?

No. I wasn't going to summon up more predators, no matter who was coming after me. Not after everything I'd seen.

But there were other reasons to make a copy. Carefully hidden, Nettle's spell book might be a useful bargaining chip if Annalise ever caught up with me.

Without realizing it, I'd ridden to the copy shop. My subconscious seemed to have decided for me. I was going to use what money I had left to copy Nettle's books, and this shop, with its damn blue pages, was the only place I could afford to have the job done.

It was strange to think that the shift I'd worked there had been the happiest time I'd had in years, but it had.

They'd be closing soon, and Andrea would not be glad to see me. Either I'd apologize to her or I'd tear the phone out of the wall and intimidate her. Whatever it took to keep her from calling Uncle Karl again. I'd make my copies, pay for them, then run like hell.

The door to the shop stood wide open. Someone had propped it open with a pack of expensive cream-colored letter paper. I walked inside.

Dried leaves blew across the carpet. A hard-bitten woman in a threadbare suit stood at a self-serve machine, making copies of her resume on cream-colored paper. She added a handful of copies to an eight-inch stack behind her. A homeless man sat on the window sill in the corner. He took a swig out of a bottle in a paper bag, then offered me a smile. Andrea and Oscar were nowhere in sight.

I approached the woman in the threadbare suit. "Where's the staff?"

The woman turned off the copier, slid her original off the glass and hefted her resumes. Her lips were pressed into a thin line and she refused to look me in the eye. "It's not my fault if there's no one here to take my money." She walked out the door.

I went behind the counter. "Hey, buddy," the drunk said. "Can you spare some change?"

There were no jobs running on the expensive copiers behind the counter. The phone was off the hook, and the drawer to the cash register was open and empty.

The office door was closed and locked. I stuck my hand far back into the shelf under the cash register and found the spare key.

The drunk decided to join me. He shuffled around the edge of the counter as I slipped the key into the lock and opened the office door.

We were immediately hit with the coppery smell of drying blood. The wall, carpet, and desk were streaked with brownish-red splashes.

"Holy God," the drunk said. "Jesus, show us your mercy."

I opened the door all the way, revealing a message written high on the wall in blood. It read: *For our cousin.*

I knew I should have just backed away. I should have turned and run out the damn door without looking back. Instead, I stepped into the room. Andrea and Oscar lay beneath the desk. Both had been slashed open and torn apart. One of Oscar's ears, ringed with piercings, lay on the desk calendar.

I staggered toward the door, feeling woozy.

"Jesus smite the devil!" the drunk said. "What happened here?"

I grabbed his grimy sleeve and pushed him aside so I could get the hell out of that room. Andrea and Oscar were dead because of me. They were dead because I had worked here for one damn day.

Jon would never have done this; Echo must have... But Echo had never met Andrea and Oscar, as far as I knew. Only Jon knew I'd worked here.

I closed my eyes, but I could still smell the blood. If Jon had done this, it was because of the cousin inside him. It was like a mental illness; he couldn't be held responsible. If there was some way to drive the cousin out—restore Jon to his old self—and leave him whole...

"What are we going to do?" the drunk asked.

"Do you want to talk to the cops about this?"

"Oh, Good Lord, no," the man said.

"Me, neither." I pressed my knuckle on the phone cradle to bring the dial tone back, then used the same knuckle to dial 911.

I hustled toward the front door before the call connected. The old drunk followed.

This time there were no cops to read my license plate as I pulled away. Not that it mattered. It was getting close to eleven, and I needed to settle in someplace that was secluded and had a light to read by. I ran through all the homes, apart-

ments, and other spaces I'd been to since I got to town, but
they had all been compromised or destroyed. No one had
even *talked* about a place, except...

And then I thought of the perfect spot.

A light rain had begun to fall. I circled the baseball field
once, looking out for a bunch of teenagers sneaking beers or
a homeless guy rolled up in a sleeping bag. Luckily, it was
empty. I rode across left field and parked behind a Dumpster.
It wasn't completely hidden, but it was good enough.

The dugout was just a few feet away. This was the field
where Jon and I had played together as kids. His house was
not six blocks from here. At the batting cages, Echo had told
me that Jon had brought her and the others out to the field
near his house to knock a ball around, and I knew immediately that this was the one. He and I had spent hours here;
of course he'd come back as soon as he could.

I jammed the helmet under the mesh net and went into
the dugout. The shelter was built with cinderblocks that had
been painted blue, and while there was a streetlight to read
by, I was protected from the rain and prying eyes. If it had
walls to keep out the wind, a leather couch and a hot shower,
I'd have been ecstatic.

I took the pages from the canvas bag and separated the
English translations from the non-English ones. Presumably,
I was looking at Latin but beyond *E Pluribus Unum* and
habeas corpus I had no real way to tell.

That left the three copies in English, plus the spiral
notebook they'd been photocopied from, plus Wally's copy.
Each was about four times as thick as Callin's spell book.

I took a deep breath and held the book under the light.

My hands were shaking. Wally had read these pages and had turned into... Whatever he was now. Nuts. A killer. And they had done the same thing to the person he took them from, if he could be believed.

Well, fuck him. Nothing in here was going to get to me. I had work to do.

The first page was a solid block of text. I scanned it, confirmed that it wasn't a spell or instructions for undoing a spell—just a self-important introduction—then moved on.

I turned the next page, and the next. Wally had called this the "secret history of the world" or something, but that didn't interest me. I didn't need to know about the whole world, and I didn't want to know. All I cared about was the one thing in front of me: how to save my friend. Once that was done, maybe I'd read the pages, or walk into a police station, or jump off the Aurora Bridge, or hijack a plane to Cuba. I couldn't even imagine it, because I couldn't see that far ahead.

But what I did know was that I was never going to be a seat-belt person. Never. I'd never have a steady job, a smart wife or a couple of kids. I'd gone too far.

I kept paging through the stack, passing maps, glancing at disturbing sketches in the margins, skimming the cramped handwriting. Finally, I reached the spells.

I laid my hand over the designs as I studied them. Cure the lame wasn't the first spell, but it was near the front. I kept going, carefully not thinking about what each spell did and whether it looked like something I could cast on my own. When I reached the end, I hadn't found what I was looking for.

I did the same thing with the second copy, then the third. Nothing. I took out the copy Wally left for me and the spiral notebook, then compared it to the other three, going page by page. With the exception of the page Echo took, all were identical.

I didn't curse. I didn't shout. I didn't tear the pages apart and throw them on the ground. Instead I carefully turned back to the beginning of the book and began skimming more carefully, searching for references to spell casting—how to undo them, how to find other spell books, anything. I still couldn't find what I was looking for.

Finally, I knelt on the concrete and laid out the three Latin copies of the book with one of the English versions. I flipped through them, comparing the margin illustrations and glyphs. I didn't do more than glance at them, careful not to trigger one when I was not ready. If I could find a page where the Latin and English didn't match, I'd check it somehow, to see if it told me how to reverse a spell. Maybe I'd go back to the University; they had to have a teacher there who could translate Latin. A professor of Latin? I had no idea how it worked, but I could find out.

But it was no use. All the Latin copies matched each other and the English translations. There was no spell to undo Jon's curse.

I stood and walked to the end of the dugout. In that spot, I could be seen from the street but I had to risk it, because the urge to tear all those pages apart was unbearable. I had to take deep, shuddering breaths to control my frustration. I couldn't destroy those books. They contained power. They were tools, and bargaining chips, too, if it came to that. I'd have to find a safe place to hide them.

But they weren't going to help me save my friend. I didn't have any sure, safe, simple way to save my friend.

I drew the ghost knife out of my pocket. As stupid and awful as it sounded, I was going to have to cut the cousins out.

CHAPTER TWENTY-THREE

The first thing I did was eat the rest of the oranges; they were delicious and they made me feel human again. Then I organized the copies and the notebook into the canvas bag, put on the helmet, and rode away.

There was a supermarket relatively close by, and it was busy enough even at this late hour that no one was likely to pay much attention to me. I parked Wally's motorcycle, hurried to the entrance and fished a handful of empty plastic shopping bags out of the bag recycling bin. By some miracle, they were dry. Stuffing all the bags into one, I trapped them under the mesh and rode off to a greenbelt a few blocks from my aunt's house.

There, I wrapped the canvas bag in several layers of plastic to bury it. I had to dig with my hands, because the ghost knife couldn't cut through the tree roots, but I dug deep and, after I filled it in, I covered the spot with a circle of flat stones. Maybe I'd be able to reclaim them someday. Maybe.

I climbed back onto the motorcycle, knowing it was past time to ditch it. Unfortunately, it was already after midnight, and standing out at some corner, waiting an hour for a nearly-empty bus would just get me busted. Walking was just as risky. What the hell. Everyone's luck ran out at some point. It was time to find out how far I could push mine.

I pulled on the helmet. It was time to find Jon, Echo and Macy. They would need floor space to draw out that circle, and privacy, too, in case the society came after them again. I knew where I would do it, if I were them.

Barely fifteen minutes later, I pulled up outside the Hilltop Physical Therapy Center. I parked the motorcycle out front and slid the helmet into the mesh. Wally said he'd given the cure to Macy's friends, and she'd run off. I was willing to bet those friends were co-workers who wanted to cure a few more of their patients.

Ducking under the yellow police tape, I peered through the glass of the front door. It was pretty dark in there; I couldn't see much more than a dim hallway. I walked around the building and found a fire door beside the parking lot out back. It was also locked, but it was not readily visible from the street.

With my ghost knife, I cut a long, thin panel out of the center of the door. No alarm bells sounded, although the metal panel hitting the concrete walkway seemed as loud as a traffic accident in the quiet night.

I slipped into the dark building. My footsteps were nearly silent on the plush carpet, but if they were here, Jon, Macy or Echo had to have heard that panel. I side-stepped so I wouldn't be silhouetted by the parking lot security lights outside. The cold air blew gently through the opening. That meant I was upwind of them and their sensitive noses and there was probably no way I could sneak up on them now. Not that I wouldn't try.

And then there were Irena's gloves. I'd been wearing them

for hours and they'd become a little rank. I held my ghost knife close to my body and extended my gloved left hand in front of me as I went down the hall.

Office doors on either side of the hall stood open. I stepped into the first one on the left. It smelled faintly of stale cigarettes, but it was empty. I checked the office across the hall. Also empty.

I crept to the next one and peered in. Another empty office. I realized I was holding my breath. Arne posted lookouts wherever he went, but I doubted Jon was that organized or experienced. Still, I wasn't about to underestimate him. I didn't want Echo or Macy charging at me from behind.

There was a housekeeping cart parked beside the next door. I figured that was a bad sign, and I was right. As soon as I stepped into the doorway I could smell the blood. Right there in the middle of the floor, a man lay stretched out on the carpet. He looked as though lions had torn into him.

I tried to work out a body count but I was too rattled to make my brain work properly, and thinking of the other corpses I'd seen didn't do much to clear my head. At least I knew they'd been here recently.

I proceeded down the hall, carefully checking each room, but I didn't find any more dead bodies. There were no super-powerful killers, either.

I reached the central reception area, which wasn't as central as I'd thought. The big glass front door with the motorcycle parked out front was just a short way to the left. Another hall like the one I'd come down lay ahead, and beside the reception desk was a bank of elevators and a broad, curving staircase leading up.

I crossed the reception area and walked down the other hallway, just in case one of them was hiding down here. Hell, they might even be sleeping off a big meal.

I wasn't that lucky. Only the first two doors led to offices. The rest were broom closets, bathrooms, tools, a small cafeteria and a padlocked and dead-bolted drug dispensary.

I considered breaking into the dispensary. A hefty sedative would make the upcoming "surgery" much easier, but I wasn't sure they would work on the cousins, which were not even completely physical. And the dispensary was likely to be alarmed.

I skipped it, went back to the reception area and crept up the stairs. I strained to hear a sound, any sound, that would warn me Echo was coming for me again, but everything was utterly still and silent.

The top floor was dark, too, but high, clouded windows along the far wall let in just enough streetlight to see the furniture. To the left was a wide parquet aerobics floor. To the right was a darkened nest of cable-and-pulley exercise equipment. Directly behind me was a row of small examination rooms.

I went toward the parquet floor and the huge sigil that had been painted onto it. I thought it looked very like the design on the floor in Macy and Echo's house, except that someone had added a cross, a star of David and the words "blessed be" to the outer ring.

There were blackened scorch marks in the five places where people were supposed to sit. The methods and goals of the Twenty Palace Society made more sense with every corpse.

"I can smell you."

I spun around. That was Macy's voice, but I couldn't see her anywhere. I squinted into the shadowy, complicated mass of equipment, but I couldn't see her.

"How's my Right Guard holding up?" I said, hoping her answer would give away her position.

"Terrible," she said from somewhere in the darkness. "Their hexes smell like rotting flesh and shit. You're covered with them."

I saw a shadow move in the darkness. Found her. I circled to silhouette her against the windows. As if she could sense what I wanted, she stepped into the light.

This was Jon's girl. If I was going to save him, I should save her, too. "Macy, what if I could remove your curse?"

She laughed. "If Wally can't, you sure as hell can't."

"I think I might have a way. Let me try to help you."

"What am I, a guinea pig? A trial run so you can perfect your technique for your boyfriend?" She laughed again and there was deep bitterness in it. "It's too late for me. Too late for everyone. You seem like a nice guy, Ray. You should go to Rio or Ibiza or something. Maybe you could have a couple happy months before the end."

"Echo's going to cast the spell again?" Of course I already knew the answer.

"And again and again and again until the world is overrun with my cousins and you humans are hunted to extinction."

I moved toward her, my gloved hand and ghost knife held out in front of me. "How could I enjoy Rio knowing that?"

Macy lunged at me. She was fast, so fast I didn't even have time to flinch, but she snapped short of her lunge like a dog on a leash. A bench press machine behind her wobbled.

She was bound by her ankle. I circled back and away from her. "Tied you up, did they? Why did they do that?"

"So I wouldn't be so squeamish about my food."

I looked past her and, for the first time, noticed a body lying at the base of the window. The dim light glinted off the worn reflective stripe of a firefighter's jacket. Annalise.

That's when I noticed a second body lying right at Macy's feet. Irena lay stretched out and torn open like a slaughtered gazelle.

"Oh, shit. You're eating them."

"The smell of their blood was irresistible. I'm getting used to the idea of making meals out of you people. How does Rio sound now?"

"I don't have a passport. And I can't just leave those bodies here with you."

"Whatever. You can be one of us or one of them. I can't bring myself to care the way I used to."

"What about those scorch marks back there?" I asked.

Her silhouette stiffened as if she was surprised by the question. After a pause, she said: "Once they meant everything to me. Now they're just wasted meat."

I tried to keep my voice calm. "Macy, it doesn't have to be this way. You don't have to kill anymore. I think I can cut that thing out of you." Christ. How was I supposed to convince her if I didn't sound like I believed myself?

She lunged at me again. She was fast. Terrifyingly fast. The leash on her ankle jerked at the bench machine and toppled it onto its side.

She leaped again, yanking the machine several inches

across the carpet. Then she did it again, dragging the machine behind her. Her mouth gaped wide—wider than any human mouth should be able to open.

I backed away, cocking my arm to throw the ghost knife. As long as I didn't hit her head, she should survive it, just like Jon. The spell would take some of the fight out of her, letting me close in and immobilize her with Irena's glove. It wasn't a great plan, but it was all I had.

Macy saw what I was doing and crouched down like a catcher. She clapped her hands then held them out, as though encouraging a child to throw a ball.

"Throw it here, Ray. Please. A nice slow-motion throw from a slow-motion human being. I know what you have there—I can smell it—and you know what?" She tugged at her bound ankle. I saw that she was tied with a metal cable. "I could use a good cutting edge."

My guts felt watery for just a moment. If she took the spell from me the way Callin had, she'd be all over me in an instant. How was I going to get close enough to help her?

I tried to sound reasonable and confident. "Macy—"

She leaped again and hissed. "Your voice is driving the cousin inside me wild." She grabbed her tether and pulled at it, dragging the machine over Irena's body.

I ran to my right and ducked among the machines. Macy tried to follow, but the bench machine wedged between two other pieces of equipment. She grabbed the machine and tried to pull harder but she couldn't budge it. She struggled angrily, desperately, like an enraged animal in a trap.

I stalked toward her. If she had carefully worked the machine free, she might already be tearing me apart. Instead she was losing herself in animal blood-lust, pounding furiously on it in frustration.

Several metal plates broke free and fell to the floor. Macy squealed with animal glee, picked one up and threw it at me.

It sailed past my ear and struck a machine beside me so hard the sound was like a gunshot.

I dropped low and scrambled for cover. More plates slammed against the metal equipment around me.

Macy leaped to the top of a lat pull-down machine and crouched low. She held a stack of metal plates cradled in her left arm and began throwing them at me, laughing.

I pressed myself against the floor behind a leg extension machine as plates clanged around me. One rebounded into the air and dropped heavily onto my legs. Another dented the metal post beside my head.

"Hey, Macy, is it too late to go to Rio?"

She laughed and threw all the plates into the air, making me scramble to a new hiding spot as they rained down around me. By stupid luck, none of the plates hit me.

Macy slid out the remainder of the plates, letting them clatter onto the floor. Then she lifted the whole machine.

But it was tangled with other equipment and she couldn't get it more than a couple inches off the floor before it snagged and stuck in place. She screamed with rage and shook the machine, making it rattle like an avalanche of ball bearings, then let it fall.

"Dammit! I didn't want to have to do this."

She bent down, folding her body like a piece of taffy. She twisted her bare, tethered foot, placed her heel into her mouth, and bit down.

Goosebumps ran down my back. "Oh, hell no."

She had to worry her head back and forth a few times, but then it was over. Her heel was gone. She swallowed it whole with a grotesque gulping sound.

My heart sank. Even if she was injured, I didn't have the speed or strength to take Macy in a fight. Hell, I couldn't even run. There was only one thing left to do.

I leaped to my feet and charged at her, ghost knife high and gloved hand out, screaming like a kamikaze.

Macy slid her bloody, mangled foot free of the tether. She smiled at me, glad that I was making it easy to get at her.

A shadow behind her shifted position, then the figure kicked at the lat machine. It toppled toward Macy, who spun and caught it with both hands before it could pin her.

At the same moment, I stabbed the ghost knife into her shoulder, splitting open her sweater. She seemed to wilt, and the lat machine fell across her throat and collarbone, pinning her.

"Ray—" she said.

I hesitated. She sounded different, much more like the woman I had met in Jon's van. "Macy?"

"Ray, you can't cure me. Don't try. There's hardly anything left of me in here."

A chill ran through me. If she really was gone, she wouldn't talk this way. Had the ghost knife brought her real self back somehow, or was this some kind of trick?

It didn't matter either way; I had to act. I grabbed her shoulder with the glove; she screamed. The ghostly branches appeared around her face. I was about to make the first cut by swiping the ghost knife around the outside of Macy's head when one of the branches turned toward me.

At the end of it was a single eye.

It was unbearable to have this thing staring at me and, without thinking, I sliced it off.

Macy went wild. In a burst of hysterical strength, she threw off the lat machine. She was free.

In a reflex born of dumb fear, I threw the ghost knife at her from two inches away. It passed through the bridge of her nose and her forehead and went into the floor. Black blood dribbled from the wound. Macy spasmed once, then went limp.

I scrambled away, cursing myself for my fear. Her skull cracked and bulged. Black, spiny legs stabbed out of her cheeks and mouth, then the cousin fell still. The legs dissolved into black smoke, and more smoke wafted out of the punctures in her face.

I'd failed her. There was black, oily blood on the back of my hand; I wiped it on the carpet. I'd tried to save her, but I didn't have the guts.

"I'm sorry." I touched her hand—it was so hot it was almost feverish. "I'm so sorry."

I looked up and saw Annalise standing beside me. One of her legs was twisted and crooked, and one of her arms hung limp at her side. She stood on her one good leg and held herself steady with her working hand. She didn't have any of her ribbons, either.

She was strong enough to kick over that lat machine, though. I wondered how she'd respond if I thanked her.

She scowled down at Macy's body. "Don't apologize to them. They did it to themselves."

Annalise seemed to lose her balance. I almost lunged forward to catch her but stopped myself. We weren't exactly friends at the moment.

She steadied herself with her good hand. "What you said—about not leaving us here for her to... Why did you do that?"

If she had to ask, there was no use explaining it. "Look, let's call a truce between us, okay? We'll work together to take care of the cousins, and whatever I have coming to me for stealing Callin's book and writing your name on that envelope, we'll deal with it then."

Annalise stared at me. "That sounds like a smart deal to make." Which wasn't exactly a *yes* but it was good enough for now. At least she wasn't grabbing at me, trying to break my neck.

I wasn't sure how I felt about working with Annalise, even now. I'd seen too many dead bodies to question her goals, but I still wasn't cool with her methods. But I couldn't leave her here in this building when Jon and Echo might come back at any moment.

"What were you saying to her about a cure?" she asked, hopping closer to Macy.

"The ghost knife," I said, well aware that she had taken it away from me before. "I don't know if it's possible, but maybe, just maybe I can cut the cousins out of them. Like surgery."

"You have got to be kidding me."

"I know the predators are dangerous." My anger was building and I did my best to hold it in. "I've been stumbling over dead bodies *all damn day*. I know we can't let the cousins bring more of their family here. But I want to stop them and save my friend at the same time, if I can."

Annalise's expression was cold. "This is bullshit."

"I couldn't hold Macy down." I tried to sound as reasonable. "But you're strong enough—"

Annalise grabbed the top of an exercise machine with her good hand and lifted herself a few inches off the carpet. With her good leg, she stamped on Macy's face.

Macy's skull cracked like an empty ceramic bowl and her head sagged like a deflated balloon.

Annalise hopped toward me. "There's nothing left of your friends. Accept it. The cousins killed them."

She sounded like she knew what she was talking about, but I didn't trust her. "Echo, yes. Definitely. But didn't you just hear Macy? She sounded like herself for a—"

"Accept it. They're dead."

"I have to try." I glared at her.

She glared back. "Callin is missing, Irena's dead and I've lost all my ribbons. If we don't kill the creatures that killed your friends—"

"No." I refused to look away from her. "I'm not you! If Jon has to be killed, so be it, but first I have to try to help him. You don't understand! I can't kill my friend just because it's the easiest way to stop him."

She looked startled by that, but only for a second. "When will the fucking light fucking dawn? You can't cure your friends!" She glanced over at the scorched sigil on the parquet floor. "We have to destroy this building so no one else will try the spell, at least."

"That I'll do."

"Good! Get paper to burn. A lot of it."

I ran downstairs. The building was just as empty as before. I sprinted to the office that smelled of cigarette smoke and took a lighter from the top desk drawer. Back out in the reception area, I yanked open a filing cabinet. It was amazing how much paper these places needed. I scooped up an armload of file folders stuffed with computer printouts.

A flashlight beam played across the room. I ducked low and peered around the desk.

A police car stood at the curb, shining a light on the license plate on Wally's motorcycle.

CHAPTER TWENTY-FOUR

I ran up the stairs, cursing myself for my laziness. If I'd parked down the street it wouldn't be such a big deal. But the bike was right out front and the cops were sure to check out this building. And of course I'd cut open that damn door.

At the top of the stairs, I stopped dead still. Annalise knelt on the floor among the exercise machines beside Irena's body. With her good arm, she pulled her friend close, then lowered her face toward Irena's neck.

Oh, no. Was Annalise eating her friend's corpse right here on the floor in front of me? Was there any difference at all between these assholes?

I dropped the papers onto the floor. It was too much. It was all too much and I couldn't let this go on. I took out my ghost knife.

Just then, Annalise sobbed. Suddenly, it was clear to me that she wasn't hunched over to feed; her head was lowered and her shoulders were trembling because she was crying.

I turned my back to give her a semblance of privacy and cut a hole in the parquet floor beside the sigil. There was a ten-inch space between the wood and the cement floor beneath, which seemed like a good thing for the fire I was planning. I shoved piles of papers into the hole, then sliced the cut-out square of parquet into sticks and piled them on the paper.

"Cut another hole over there." Annalise pointed to a spot on the other side of the sigil. She had managed to stand on her good leg. Her expression was stoic, but her cheeks were wet. "For ventilation."

I did. I used the wood to increase the pile. "You know what you're doing," I said.

"I've had practice."

"There are cops outside."

Annalise nodded. "The police can never, ever get anywhere near a spell. Never. Light it and get me out of here."

I lit the paper in three places. There was a closet full of cleaning products downstairs—not to mention a cafeteria that was likely to have nice, flammable oil in it—but there was no time to find a proper accelerant. Luckily, the paper seemed to be doing fine on its own.

I scooped Annalise into my arms like we were entering a bridal suite. She winced but didn't make a sound. Damn, but she had gone pale. I gave her a moment to lay her broken arm across her torso, trying to pretend that she didn't stink of sweat and old laundry.

When she was ready, I ran down the stairs and started toward the fire door at the cafeteria end of the building. At the far end of the hall behind us, a flashlight beam played through the gap in the door I'd cut open. I peeked through the window and, when I saw there was no one in sight, shoved the door open and ran through it.

No alarms sounded but I was sure a silent one was ringing somewhere. The inside of the building was darker than the parking lot, and passing beneath the security lights made me feel exposed as hell, but no one yelled at me to freeze.

At the edge of the lot was a short dirt slope that lead to a fast food parking lot below. I scrambled down it as quickly and as carefully as I could. "Do you have a ride nearby?" I asked.

"No," Annalise said. Her eyes were closed and her teeth clenched. I was trying not to jolt her around too much, but she was still in a lot of pain. "Your friends didn't let me drive to my own murder."

"Well, damn. Aren't you hilarious? We'll just have to steal something." We'd reached the end of the second parking lot. I couldn't carry her down the sidewalk without attracting a lot of attention, so I hustled into an alley instead. We disturbed a guy lying next to a Dumpster but we were gone before he could do anything about it.

At the far end of the alley was a 24-hour supermarket. It was busier than I would have liked. I stayed back in the shadow of the alley while I figured out what to do. "And by the way, I found the real spell book. The one the summoning spell came from."

"Well, damn. Aren't you hilarious?" Her little voice sounded tight.

"I don't expect you to believe me." I told her about Nettle Philip's house anyway, about the weird ice... something in her living room, about the claw marks on the wall, and about the stack of papers. I gave her the information as a peace offering, but it felt like I was shedding a burden, too. Let someone else think about that dead woman for a while.

A cop car raced up the street toward us, its lights spin-

ning but the siren was off. I ducked back farther. We needed
wheels so we could get away from here. I didn't know where
we'd go, but it would have to be private enough to avoid the
cops but not so private that Annalise felt free to pinch my
head off.

Besides, if she was like Irena, I could fetch some prime rib
or something for her and she'd be back at fighting strength
in no time.

Which meant I was an idiot. I should have dumped her
a block back, but I hadn't. There was something about her
that pulled me in. It wasn't that she was beautiful, because
she wasn't. It wasn't that I liked her, because I didn't. It was,
I guessed, because she was so damn powerful that it felt good
to be near her, as if some of her potency might rub off onto
me the way street bums warm themselves by a fire.

"I'm sorry about Irena," I said. "I liked her."

"She understood the risks," Annalise answered. "You're the
only one who didn't—doesn't."

I dropped her and jumped away. She rolled against a
plastic recycling bin, grabbed her injured leg and cried out.
I circled farther from her, putting the corner of a building
almost between us. "Shouldn't you kill me *before* you talk
about me in the past tense?"

She looked up at me, her expression filled with hate.
"You're just as dead as your friends. You're a walking corpse,
just like them." She braced herself against the wall and
struggled upright. I backed farther away—the edge of the
lot was just a few feet behind me. "You lied to me, took my
spells, and worst of all, because of you the only friend I had
in the world is dead."

"I know. I didn't want that and I'm sorry."

"Don't tell me what you fucking want. You're never going to have anything that you want, because I'm going to hunt you down and burn you and all your apologies to screams and ashes."

Time to go. I backed away, quickly, then turned and ran. It should have made me ashamed to run away like that, but it didn't. I didn't have room in me for any more shame.

I slid down the grassy slope at the edge of the lot then through the alley at the bottom. When I came out the other end onto the sidewalk, I slowed to a quick walk.

Maybe there was some way I could avoid the payback Annalise wanted to give me, but I couldn't imagine it. She had power, and "peers," and the resources of a society I knew nothing about. After years of keeping my head down—as a criminal and as a con—I'd finally pissed off the wrong person.

My last hope was that I'd live long enough to save Jon— assuming it was even possible. After that, nothing mattered. Annalise would get her revenge and that would be the end. I was almost tired enough to welcome the thought.

A crowd of homeless teens hung out on the corner, futilely spare changing. Across the street from them, two women in tight clothes idly watched cars creep down the block. Three guys stumbled out of a bar, two of them practically carrying the third.

It was the sort of neighborhood that gets a lot of attention from the cops, and sure enough a police cruiser rolled down the cross street up ahead. I turned into a bus shelter and pretended to be interested in the schedule. The cruiser passed without stopping or chirping the siren.

I didn't like the look of the bar the three guys had stumbled out of, so I went around the corner and found another. The door was open, despite the cold. I peeked in. The music was loud and the room dark. The patrons inside were just shadowy figures nodding over their drinks.

I walked into the parking lot next door. The Dumpster cast a heavy shadow from the streetlight across the way. I crouched down in the dark and waited.

I didn't have to wait long. A drunk staggered out, his sweaty hand clamped around the wrist of a woman with a sagging belly and too many years of booze in her. She giggled as he hauled her toward the parked cars.

I came up on them as the drunk fumbled with his car keys and I slammed him into the side of the car, shattering the passenger window. The woman shrieked. The drunk spun, more confused and hurt than angry, and I hit him with a hard left hook.

He dropped like a sack of old clothes. I snatched up his keys and rolled him away from the tires. Then I gave a hard look at the woman, just in case she was tempted to do something I wouldn't like. "Friends don't let friends, lady."

She staggered back, nearly falling over. She was so drunk she couldn't even look directly at me. I doubted she'd be able to identify me.

The vehicle I'd just won myself was an ancient Cutlass Ciera. I got in and started it up. Some angry idiot's voice blared out of the radio but I switched him off. Instead, I got to listen to the rattle and click of the struggling engine. After I adjusted the seat and the mirrors, I pulled out of the parking lot and made a full stop at the corner. "Hello prison," I said to the car, fully aware that this was a pretty shitty car to risk jail time for. "Hello, old life."

I should have grabbed the drunk's wallet; I was hungry again. On the plus side, the car had just over half a tank. That ought to be plenty for what I needed. Food was overrated, anyway.

There was only one place left to go: I drove to Jon's house.

The news vans were still parked on Jon's block, but the only driver I could see snored behind the steering wheel. An empty police car sat at the end of the street. Directly in front of Jon's house was a limo. Three beefy men in black suits loitered on the lawn, looking like disreputable secret service agents. The house itself was dark.

This was the same house I'd visited many times as a kid. Jon's family had always owned lots of *things,* and I'd grown up thinking they were rich. It was only later that I understood they were very much in the respectable upper middle class; the main difference between their family and mine was that they were sober and sane. Jon's house no longer looked as large and ornate as it had. Still, most of the happiest memories of my life were tied to that house, and to the kindness of the people inside it. Kindness I'd paid back in the worst possible way.

It had all gone away so suddenly. After the accident, Jon's family—the people who'd invited me into their safe, clean home, who'd fed me and helped me with my homework—had nothing but raw hatred for me. That same night Mr.

Burrows had come into the police station in a blind rage: his face red, spit flying from his mouth as he cursed at me. He'd still had Jon's blood on his clothes, and he even threw a punch at me. I'd had too much practice dodging blows from adults for him to connect, and the cops had dragged him away after that, but just like with Annalise I knew no apology I could make would be good enough. I'd been exiled. I went back to my own family, and I would never feel safe again.

I circled the block and parked one street over, taking time to use the sleeve of my shirt to wipe down the steering wheel, rear view mirror, and door handles. The keys I left down by the brake pedal. I doubted I'd need the car again, but it was nearby just in case.

I hurried down the darkened street and ducked into the alley behind Jon's house. The one thing I really wanted to know was this: How long would it take them to recreate the summoning spell? If I was lucky, I'd have a chance to deface the spell when Echo wasn't around, turning her into a scorch mark like the ones on the floor at the physical therapy center.

But there wouldn't be bodyguards all over the lawn unless they were inside the house getting ready to cast that spell again.

Jon's yard was surrounded by blackberry vines, but of course there was no fruit this late in the year. Another shady secret-service type stood alone in the back yard.

I hopped the fence and ran at him. He barely had time to pivot and throw a quick right at me. It was a good punch, too, hard and fast. It was the kind of punch that could put a guy in the hospital. Unfortunately for him, it landed on my stomach, and I didn't even feel it.

I grabbed the wire hanging from his ear and ripped it out of his clothes. I wasn't afraid of this one guy, but if we added the three from the front as well, I was going to be in trouble.

He countered with a quick left that I barely managed to deflect with my forearm. The impact knocked me back, and we had a little distance between us.

The guard squared his shoulders to make himself look bigger, even though he was already the size of an NFL fullback. "One warning," the guard said, and I could see he had several long knife scars on his lips. "Turn around and get lost."

I stepped toward him, holding my hands high so he'd go for my tattooed gut. He did. I took advantage and threw an overhand right at the spot where his jaw met his ear.

He didn't go down—he was tough—but he did stagger. It took three more shots to put him out.

I opened the guard's jacket. He didn't have a holster but he did have handcuffs. Luckily, I couldn't find a badge on him. I cuffed him, gagged him with his tie and dragged him off to the blackberry bushes.

The upstairs deck Jon and I used to play on was dark. The kitchen windows below it were dark. The only difference I could see was that the tool shed at the edge of the yard had been replaced with something larger and newer.

I slowly made my way around the side of the house, keeping low beneath the downstairs windows. None of the front yard bodyguards were visible from this angle, and the police car and news van were out of sight, too.

"How long will they be?" A woman asked. I crouched lower and stepped back into the bushes, but quickly realized the voices were coming from the front porch. It was an old woman's voice, trembling with the outrage that comes from a life of misfortune.

"He said *not long,* Mother," a woman answered loudly.

"Well, you see to it that no one *else* jumps ahead of us. I've waited long enough!"

Damn. They'd already begun.

A light switched on, shining over my feet. I knelt and peered into the basement window. I didn't know the basement of this house. It had been Mr. Burrows's workshop, and none of the kids had been allowed inside.

Three workbenches had been pushed against the wall to clear space for the sigil on the floor. It had been painted in red like the other one, and all of the outer circles were connected to the center by curving lines. This was the slow version of the spell that would summon four cousins at a time, not just one.

Jon stepped into my line of sight, carrying a scrawny little girl in a white lace dress. The girl's legs were twisted and as thin as sticks. An old man with white hair brushed back from his skull-like face followed. He wore a trim black suit with a white silk tie.

Jon gently placed the little girl in the six o'clock position of the sigil, the same place where I'd sat. After doting over the little girl, the old man was ushered into the three o'clock position beside her.

Each of the participants was going to be "cured," whether they realized it or not.

Then, Uncle Karl walked into view with Aunt Theresa on his elbow, going straight toward the center spot.

"Oh, shit," I said, in a soft whisper.

Jon spun around as though he could hear me. I jumped away from the window, rushed into the back yard, and crouched on the far side of the tool shed.

Why in the hell would Jon and Echo recruit my aunt and uncle for their cure? As far as I could tell, neither had shown any interest at all in what Jon was doing... Unless they thought I'd be less likely to go after my own family, and that cousins living inside of them would be protected from me.

And Skullface was obviously rich. Those guards outside—and the little girl in the circle—must have been his. Once they had cousins inside them, they'd be very hard to take out. Not only that, they had the resources to go anywhere in the world. The cousins could start spreading over the planet.

I had to stop them here. Tonight.

The back door opened and Jon stepped onto the porch. I crouched low and put my back against the tool shed. Jon couldn't see very well anymore, he'd claimed, but he could smell like a bloodhound.

A breeze blew on the back of my neck, which meant I was downwind of him. I quietly drew in a breath and held it, in case he could recognize my bad breath. I wasn't ready for a straight-up fight with Jon. First I had to try to save his life.

The back door banged shut. It was eerie how familiar that sound was. I dared a peek around the edge of the shed and saw that Jon was gone. The kitchen light shut off as he moved deeper into the house.

I started toward the house, still without any real plan, and my foot struck something. It was an empty bottle of ammonia, discarded at the foot of the tool shed door.

It gave me an idea. Maybe, just maybe I could get the upper hand with Jon. It would only be for a moment or two, but that should be enough. And maybe it would shock him hard enough that, like Macy, he'd come back to himself again.

I sliced the tool shed padlock off with my ghost knife and opened the door. The stink of rotting meat washed over me and I saw three corpses inside, all hanging like sides of beef. The nearest was a woman, small with dark hair. Despite the blood on her face, I recognized her immediately.

"Bingo." The two bodies behind her had wisps of gray hair above badly-mangled faces, but I knew they were Jon's parents anyway.

God, seeing them there like that was like a knife in my guts. These people had done so much for me, and it had never even occurred to me that they were in danger. *...when they start out they hunt people they think deserve it. It soothes their consciences while they're still human enough to have them.* God help me, I thought I had time.

Had Jon done this? I couldn't believe it. It was an impossible idea. This was a family that took camping trips together. They'd taught their kids to sing Beatles songs. Jon wouldn't turn on them. If there was any motherfucker who was going to murder his family and hang them on hooks, it was me.

Echo must have done this—not that it was really Echo, of course. The cousin inside her had decided Jon's family weren't going to be hosts, so it turned them into meat, then stashed them outside to cure or something. Maybe Jon didn't even know they were dead.

That seemed like a helluva stretch, but it was possible—

stranger things had happened. And it was too late for them anyway. They were dead, and so was any chance I'd ever have to make them understand how grateful I was for everything they'd done, and how sorry I was, too.

Uncle Karl and Aunt Theresa were still alive, and Jon, maybe, could still be saved. I took a bottle of ammonia off the floor, glad that it was full. I didn't want to venture farther into the shed to look for another one. I shut the door, smearing Barbara's blood on the outside. I had no memory of touching her body and had no idea how it got on me.

I ran to the kitchen and peeked in the darkened window. I couldn't see anything, but I knew the basement stairs led straight into the kitchen. If I tried to break in here, Jon or Echo would be on me before I got the door all the way open.

I hooked my index finger into the handle of the ammonia bottle and climbed the post to the back deck above me. Jon and I did it many times when we'd been kids, and I was surprised by how easy it was now that I'd grown up. Irena's gloves didn't hurt, either.

At the lip of the deck, I pulled myself up and swung my foot onto it. There was a moment when I almost dropped the ammonia, but the spell on Irena's glove kept it in place. The deck didn't even squeak as I stepped across it.

I cut the lock on the door to Jon's room and slid open the french door. Like the kitchen, this room was dark, but my eyes were pretty well adjusted by now. I wiped my bloody hand clean on one of Jon's shirts and looked around.

The room was filled with the paraphernalia of a baseball fanatic: Pennants, caps, balls, photos—every shelf, every spare spot on a dresser or desk was devoted to some aspect of baseball.

I glanced into the trash can and saw a picture frame. It was the photo of Jon and me on the baseball field when we were 12, the one he'd shown me in my aunt's backyard. The glass has been shattered and the frame cracked. I left it there.

I spun off the cap of the ammonia bottle and splashed it over everything. I poured it onto the carpet, the shelves, the desk, the folded wheelchair against the wall, the tee ball equipment that must have been twenty years old. Everything. I had to blink tears from my eyes as the fumes built in the room.

When the bottle was empty, I took out my ghost knife and crouched by the door. Then I hurled the empty bottle against a shelf. A rack of baseball cards and a row of signed balls clattered to the floor.

I heard a sudden staccato drumming that had to be a rush of footsteps.

Jon was on his way.

CHAPTER TWENTY-FIVE

The door burst open and Jon charged in, stopping just inside the doorway. He cried out, slapping his hands over his mouth and nose, then wrenched his whole body around.

I drove my shoulder into his low back and knocked him to the floor. His face smashed into the ammonia-soaked carpet and I landed on top of him.

I slapped the heel of my gloved left hand on the top of Jon's shoulder so that my fingers touched the wet carpet. The sigil came alive and took hold of both at once, pinning Jon to the floor. He screamed again, louder this time, and writhing branches appeared around his head.

And my god, there were so many of them. "I'm here to help, buddy," I told him, as much to convince myself I could as to reassure him. I slid the ghost knife through the waving branches and they fell away like cut stalks.

Jon went wild. He kicked against the floor, flipping his whole body into the air, and I flipped over with him.

In a panic, I tried to brace for the fall and lost my hold on him. He bolted away from me, bounding against the wall, then the bed, then the desk, the shelves, the floor—moving too fast for me to keep track of, racing around in a blind animal frenzy to escape.

Then he slammed into me, knocking me against the folded wheelchair. I tripped over it, scattering tee ball bats onto the floor.

I looked up. Jon was gone—he'd burst through the door into the hallway—and I wasn't holding the ghost knife any more.

I rolled onto my knees and looked around. So much baseball crap had been knocked onto the floor that I couldn't see my spell in the clutter. I closed my eyes, concentrated, and *reached* out for it.

There it was, out in the hall. I held out my hand.

Jon stepped on it. "Hey, *buddy*," he said. "You looking for this?"

I started to stand. "Jon—"

I didn't know what I was going to say—or even what I could say that I hadn't said before—but Jon cut me off by pointing a .22 caliber pistol at me.

Then he smiled. "Can you believe this is still in the house? Even after what happened to me—after what you did to me—Dad wouldn't get rid of his collection. Well, except for that *one*."

The inside of the barrel was dark. "Jesus Christ, Jon."

He took a silencer from his pocket and screwed it on, moving so fast that he'd finished before I realized what he was doing. I was still down on one knee, and I tried to imagine a way I could rush someone as fast as he was. Nothing came to mind except all the tricks I'd failed with before. "Cops outside," he said, tapping the silencer. "You know, before we attacked the hotel, I said: 'Let's go get some weapons from my house.' But Echo didn't seem to understand what guns were, and Macy—"

He charged across the seven feet separating us with star-tling speed and kicked me square on my chest. I fell back, spinning, and landed on my stomach. My tattoos protected me from the kick but ammonia smeared across my lips, choking me.

Jon stepped on my back, pinning me. The pressure against my ribs was intense and painful. Then he placed the barrel of the gun against my spine.

"...Macy hates guns. Considering her line of work, I can't blame her."

"Jon," I said, trying to keep my voice calm and failing, "I've been trying to help you!"

"Thank you, buddy. If only I had more people like you *helping* me. In return, you can have my old wheelchair. You're going to need it in a couple—Wait! I have a better idea." He jammed his foot under my ribs and flipped me onto my back. I fell against the desk, a shower of baseball cards falling onto my hip. Jon pointed the gun at my forehead. I shielded myself with my left hand.

"Your aunt is going to be pretty hungry in a few." Jon cocked the hammer. "I should set the table."

My thoughts were all jumbled together in an incoherent mess. My ghost knife was too far away and Jon didn't under-stand that he needed my help to save Karl and Theresa before they were infected but why hadn't Annalise put a spell on my face and Callin's friend was going to destroy the city and I should have been terrified, but all I felt was disappointment that I couldn't set things right and it was all because I had failed to save my oldest—

Jon squeezed the trigger.

It was a tiny noise, like a robot's sneeze. My hand burst into white hot fire just as I thought it would be embarrassing to die without the big, booming gunshot I deserved.

As if in slow motion, I saw the tattooed skin on the back of my hand bulge outward, then snap back with tremendous force, tearing through my palm again.

The sigil on Irena's glove also burst apart in a jet of iron gray sparks and black steam. The jet shot toward Jon's face, and just before he was engulfed, I saw a bullet hole appear in his forehead.

The pain in my hand rushed up my arm, freezing me in place. The jet of ruined magic receded, and Jon staggered backward, bright red blood trickling down his face.

Animal rage surged through me. Jon had tried to kill me. After everything I'd put myself through for him, he'd tried to put a bullet in my brain. I snatched up a tee ball bat with my good hand and rolled to my knees. With all my strength, I slammed it across Jon's shins. He fell to the floor, his expression empty and his face slack.

Then I was on my feet. My left hand hurt so much it might as well have been on fire, but I still held the bat in my right. I smashed Jon's wrist with it, sending the gun bouncing into the hall, but it wasn't enough. My pain and fear had control of me, and the urge to *fight fight fight* was overwhelming. I slammed the bat down onto Jon's head and his eyes fell closed.

I swung again and again. Red blood spattered against the wall and I began to hit his arms and his legs, too, then his battered skull over and over. I realized I was screaming, and as I kept swinging, my scream became words as my terror poured out of me.

"You son of a bitch! You fucking son of a bitch! I couldn't—"

I stopped, then staggered backwards, nearly falling against the wall. My left hand was still in terrible, terrible pain, and that seemed to steal the strength from me. I dropped the bat and cradled it. Tears streamed down my cheeks.

Jon lay still on the carpet, his head a misshapen pulp. "I couldn't save you," I said. My voice was raw and I sounded like the stupidest man alive.

I stumbled into the hall and fell flat on my belly, my face against the carpet. If Echo came upstairs to investigate the fight, I'd be helpless, but so what? I'd failed Jon, just as I knew I would.

But my aunt and uncle were downstairs, not to mention that sickly little girl. I stumbled into the bathroom, yanked a hand towel off the shelf and wrapped it around my gunshot hand. It bled steadily, so I pressed the wound against my ribs. The pain helped clear my head.

On my way to the stairs, I *reached* for the ghost knife, letting it zip into my hand. Then I gripped it between my teeth and picked up the gun.

It was time to put an end to this. It was time to kill Echo.

CHAPTER TWENTY-SIX

I expected to fall on the way down the back stairs, but I held it together somehow. I had blood on my shirt from where it had leaked through the bathroom towel, and I pressed harder against my chest. I was no expert on bullet wounds, but I knew I needed pressure to control the bleeding. My knees were shaking, but whether that was from blood loss or adrenaline, I didn't know.

I stumbled into the kitchen. It was dark, but a dim night light showed me that it had been completely remodeled. I made my way around the table, being careful not to bump the chairs. It was ridiculous to try to sneak around after everything that had happened, but I was doing it anyway.

As I crossed the room, I glanced the length of the house and saw the shadows moving against the frosted glass beside the front door. Was it the bodyguards? The old woman with the bad hearing? It didn't matter to me, as long as they didn't interfere.

The basement door was still in the same place; I pulled it open. It sounded like a gale was blowing down there, but the noise was slowly dying. The spell was almost finished. I hurried down the stairs, my feet clumping heavily on the wood.

Another bodyguard stepped into view. He was the biggest

of all of them, and his big brown eyes and long jaw gave him the good looks of a movie star. Over his shoulder, I could see the painted sigils on the floor flashing as they—and the floor—began to vanish.

I pointed the gun at him to control him, then I spit out my ghost knife and caught it between my gunshot hand and my chest. "I've always heard that shooting someone with a .22 wouldn't kill them, just annoy them."

He backed away as I descended the stairs. I had a sudden memory of Jon at 13, his shirt punching into his belly as the bullet hit him, the sound of the gunshot and the terrible flow of blood. The thought made me dizzy, but I could squeeze the trigger again if I had to. If I had to. "I've heard the same thing," the bodyguard said in a rich, deep voice.

"Well, I have enough bullets in here to be the most annoying guy you'll ever meet in your life."

"Okay, sir, but I'd rather we all kept our cool."

"Good," I glanced around the room. The design on the floor looked even bigger here than it had in the house, but that may have been because, in clearing space for it, Echo and Jon had piled everything into walls of clutter. Cardboard banker boxes had split open from the weight of scrap wood piled onto them, family pictures half-tumbled out of broken laundry baskets, bird houses and wood-working tools both had been thrown onto work benches, all to clear floor space.

Which was barely large enough to accommodate the spell. The circle the little girl in the pretty dress lay in—which was about one o'clock from where I stood—was physically under the work bench—she couldn't have sat upright if she'd wanted to.

Aunt Theresa was in the center and Uncle Karl was over at ten o'clock. The huge plywood model train layouts leaning against the clutter were so close to the outer circle that a cat couldn't have passed through. The only way I was getting to any of them was by entering the circle or hiring a bulldozer.

Neither had noticed me. Both were staring downward, into the Empty Spaces.

But Echo herself was in the seven o'clock position, just on my left. She looked at me with a strange mix of hatred and hunger that made me want to shoot her just on principle.

At four o'clock was Skullface. He was the easy way to break the spell. "Here's the best way for all of us to keep cool, then: Pull your boss out of the circle."

"I can't do that," the bodyguard said. He was watching me warily, waiting for his chance to move, but he was being smart about it.

"You don't understand. What she's doing is going to kill him."

"The man has pancreatic cancer. How much worse could it get?"

Worse than you can imagine, was what I almost said, but that wouldn't have gotten me anywhere. No one else in the room had noticed me yet, and the spell had reached the point where silence had fallen. No one would hear what I said next except the other guard.

"Pull him out of the circle or I'm going to put a bullet in that little girl."

The bodyguard's eyes were wide and blank, but I knew it wasn't shock. He was taking my measure. "Son, you can't even bring yourself to point your gun at that little girl. I don't think you're going to shoot her. I'm guessing you've seen what bullets can do. Am I right?"

I couldn't believe he'd seen through my bluff so quickly. "Are you so sure about that? Are you gonna take that risk?"

"That's my job and I'm good at it."

I glanced over at my aunt and the others. The floor had vanished, and the lights were swirling upward. "Look at this! This is what you're defending?" I was nearly shouting. "Get on your knees."

He did, smoothly. I knew it wouldn't slow him much if he decided to go for me, but I needed every advantage I could get. I pivoted and shot Echo.

I aimed for her head, but my hand was shaking so much that the bullet struck her knee instead. She didn't move, didn't even flinch. My stomach felt hollow. I'd hoped to drive her out of the circle, but I knew that wasn't going to happen, not if shooting her only made her sit and glare at me harder.

There was a shuffle behind me and I turned toward the bodyguard. My look froze him in place. I fired at Echo again—missing this time—and then the gun wouldn't fire again. It had jammed.

Maybe if I'd had both hands, I could have cleared it quickly and kept firing, but it was already too late. The lights swirling below the design began to push against it, then they burst through the floor and floated around Aunt Theresa.

I heard the guard getting to his feet, but I didn't spare him a look. *You think you've paid your debt...* I took one long step toward the circle, and then I jumped.

The circle flashed white as I passed through it, and suddenly I was inside the void.

It wasn't cold, or hot, or any other feeling I could identify. There was a sense of deadness against my skin, as though my sense of touch had been switched off. After an instant of weightlessness, in which it felt as though I was falling from a great height, I realized I was simply floating toward my aunt. There was no gravity here and I might have floated across the room if not for the sigils inside the central spot, drawing me in.

It seemed as though I was moving slowly, terribly slowly across the open space. I made progress, but each moment felt as wide and as deep as the universe. *I* felt as wide and deep as the universe, my mind and my senses expanded to fill so much space that I lost all sense of myself. My every thought, memory, and emotion broke apart into tiny specks and flew away from me until they were like single dust motes hanging in the spaces between galaxies.

And still I floated forward, feeling like a wave so small it was indistinguishable from its surroundings.

After an eternal second, I broached the edge of the circle my aunt was sitting in, and I suddenly collapsed in on myself. It was like returning to consciousness from a moment of blessed oblivion, and I could suddenly see, smell, touch, everything. My whole life rushed back at me, every fight, every fuck, every moment of shame or fury. I became myself again.

But on a conscious level my thoughts continued uninterrupted: Aunt, cousins, Echo, ghost knife. My feet silently struck the invisible floor inside the central circle—as I'd hoped, it had been large enough to hold Echo's corpse, so it was large enough for two people—and I found myself standing over my aunt.

She looked up at me, as shocked as if I'd flown down out of the sky, and I saw her say my name. I still couldn't hear a thing. She gaped at the sight of my bloody hand. A glowing light circled near her mouth.

I bit down on the Velcro strap holding Irena's glove on my right hand, yanked it off, then stuffed it into my mouth with the palm—and the sigil on it—facing outward.

The circle was full of the glowing lights, now. They spun around us quickly, excitedly. I pulled the ghost knife from beneath my bloody hand, sliding it over my clothes to wipe it off, then crouched down to pull my aunt closer to me. Just as her weight braced against my legs, one of the lights entered her mouth. At nearly the same moment, I slid the ghost knife into the back of her neck.

The ball of light burst into a sickly mist. Theresa slumped against me, her whole body going slack. Other cousins, already fighting for position, dove toward her. With my injured hand, I supported her head, holding it so I could keep the ghost knife in place. The pain was like being shot all over again, and I shouted through the glove.

Immediately, a half dozen cousins swarmed toward the sound, even as more and more dove into Theresa's mouth and burst into greenish-black mist. They followed each other in a steady stream, pushing up through the opening in the floor as though they couldn't sense each other and had no idea what was happening to the rest of their swarm.

A half-second later, the cousins who responded to the sound of my voice rushed toward my face. It took all my self-control not to reel back and dodge away from them; I let the first enter my mouth and strike the glove.

The impact was solid. The spines of the cousins' crooked legs scraped at my lips and gouged the roof of my mouth. A second, then a third struck the spell, all of them taking up the same space, all of them digging at the inside of my mouth. A fourth hit, a fifth.

The awful mist nearly obscured my aunt's head, but I could still feel, through some connection I didn't understand, the cousins throwing themselves blindly onto the ghost knife. I didn't have to endure the pain in my mouth forever. I just had to hold on until every cousin had come into our world and destroyed themselves.

A sixth hit the glove.

The balls of light floating around me suddenly dissolved upward in a spray of liquid light. Someone had broken the circle. I looked downward and saw two dozen or so swirling lights still out in the Empty Spaces. I'd been so close to getting them all. So close.

I slid the ghost knife from the back of my aunt's neck. It came out clean, and after a moment's shock realized there was blood all over the back of her neck.

Only my blood, I hoped, not hers, but there was no time to check now. I pivoted inside the circle. The spell must have been broken a few seconds before, because the floor had returned before I even had a chance to look up. The passage into the Empty Spaces was sealed.

Echo leaned to the side, her hand planted on the concrete beyond the circle. She'd broken the spell while there were still cousins safely in the Empty Spaces; if she'd waited a few seconds longer, they would have all died, every one. The only ones left were the ones stuck to the glove in my mouth, who were still panicked and attacking me.

Echo rolled over, getting her good leg under her. The gun-shot knee didn't seem to bother her, but she clearly couldn't use it. Even so, her movements were quick and fluid, and I could tell by the look on her face that she was coming for me.

I took a deep breath. There were others in the room—my uncle, the bodyguard, Skullface—who might be coming after me, but I didn't pay any attention to them. I had one chance to take on Echo and live, and the winner was going to be decided in the next quarter second.

She bent her good leg, ready to jump, and I started moving my right hand—and my ghost knife—forward. Her eyes darted toward it. Just as she pushed off, I let out that deep breath I'd just taken and spit the glove at her.

She came at me fast, but not as fast as she had before. And although she couldn't change the direction and momentum of her jump, she did reach out quickly and easily to snatch the glove out of the air.

The cousins were still attached to it, and they thrashed and gouged at her skin. The small injuries they gave her made her wince in pain in a way the bullet hadn't—because the predators were still mostly magical? Whatever caused it, she paused just long enough for me to slap my injured hand over hers, and Irena's glove.

Her whole body stiffened, and the crooked, branching limbs of the cousin appeared around her head, whipping and twisting under the strain.

Ignoring my pain, I threw myself at her and plunged the ghost knife into her left cheek, then slicing upward.

She fell onto the floor and the side of her head broke

open, just like the others' had. Except this time, my aunt and uncle, Skullface, his bodyguard, and the little girl all saw the creature that came out of her.

I staggered to the side, feeling suddenly woozy and fell to my knees on the concrete floor. The red circle was just there, beside me. I'd have to destroy that soon. Very soon. And just behind the circle where Echo sat, a plastic supermarket shopping bag lay on the floor. Amongst all the clutter, something about it called for my attention

My mouth was full of blood, but not as much as I'd expected. I let it run onto the floor because it was disgusting to swallow it.

"Karl, no."

That was Aunt Theresa's voice, just behind me, breaking through the silence; suddenly, I could hear everything around me, shuffling feet, harsh breathing, the little girl calling for Daddy.

I turned and saw Karl pointing his gun at me.

"Karl," Theresa said again. "Ray just saved me. Those lights... I saw them up close. I saw them. They were...."

She turned to me, hoping I would finish the sentence. I could have said *alive* or *hungry*, but what I said instead was: "Hallucinations." It was hard to talk, but they seemed to understand.

She looked disappointed. "Oh, Raymond."

Uncle Karl didn't lower his weapon. "What do you mean, *hallucinations*? I saw that! We all did!"

I was too tired to argue. Footsteps thundered across the living room floor above. The guards from out front were on their way. Skullface and the others were watching us with wide eyes, as if we were juggling hand grenades.

I spit blood on the floor so I could talk to Skullface. "Keep those motherfuckers out of here, or else."

The bodyguard leaned close to him. "Sir, I think we should leave."

Skullface agreed and they met the guards halfway on the stairs, ordering them all to back up.

My uncle was still angry, but the barrel of his gun was no longer pointing at me. It had wandered off to the side a few inches. "How could that have been a hallucination?"

"What other explanation are you going to give?" I asked, loud enough for Skullface to hear me. "There was no cure. There never was. It was just a drug that liquefied your brain."

Karl shook his head. "I've seen Jon's medical records. His spine was healed."

I shook my head and spit again. "It was a con."

The old man stopped at the top of the stairs and stared at me. Did he believe me? I hoped so. If the guy put his fortune into finding another spell, he just might succeed, and who would be around to clean up that mess? Not Mr. "I gave my word" over there.

"They tried to get me involved," I continued. "But fuck that. They used hallucinogens to make you see things—to make you think they were doing magic."

When Skullface spoke, his voice was thin and nasal. "My people checked him out, too. His medical records—"

"All they would have given you is poison."

"But—

Karl pivoted toward the stairs. "Do you have a better explanation?"

Skullface shut his mouth. The little girl in his arms looked at me over her wasted legs. Her eyes were wide but her expression was calm. Whatever she was feeling, she wasn't showing it. They disappeared up the stairs.

Karl had put his gun away and helped Theresa to her feet. I pocketed my ghost knife and picked up the supermarket shopping bag.

Inside was Annalise's vest and all of her ribbons.

Theresa hugged me, briefly, then walked quickly around Echo's body. Karl led her toward the stairs.

On a shelf beneath the stairs, I found a can of turpentine and an old mop. I screwed off the top and started pouring it over the painted floor.

"Hey!" Karl growled. "You're destroying evidence!"

I didn't turn around. I just began mopping the chemical around, destroying the design.

"Hell," Karl said, resignation in his voice, "Good thing I wasn't here to see that." They continued up the stairs.

The blue sheet of paper with the summoning spell on it was lying under the shopping bag. I dropped it into a puddle of turpentine, then took out one of Annalise's a red ribbons. Would it even work for me? I had no way to know except to try. I willed it to ignite and threw it into a corner. It struck a pile of magazines like a dart and burst into flames, setting fire to a stack of magazines beside the design. Then I lit the end of the turpentine-soaked mop and tossed it into the pile of clutter. Go, fire.

Of course, I was still holding a bag full of Annalise's spells. There was a lot of power in here, even if I didn't know what it all did. Strangely, though, holding the bag of spells was like standing beside her, in some weird way. I could sense her in the magic.

And while I wanted power, I didn't want hers. I wanted my own. I threw the bag into the flames.

There was a loud crash and a scream from upstairs. I ran upstairs as quickly as I could, but I was weak from exhaustion and it took me too long. Much too long.

In the kitchen, I found Karl lying on the floor, holding the side of his head and moaning. Skullface stood in the corner, the girl in his arms.

I knelt over Karl. "Where's Aunt Theresa?"

"He took her," the little girl said.

The garage door opened outside. I ran to the window and yanked the curtains back. Jon's van rumbled out of the garage, steadily picking up speed. Through the windshield, I caught a glimpse of him, his head mashed and swollen like a pumpkin, at the wheel. As the Savana passed, I looked through the ragged hole Annalise had made when she tore off the side door and saw my Aunt Theresa lying there, bound hand and foot, and terrified.

CHAPTER TWENTY-SEVEN

The van rumbled down the driveway toward the street. I hissed out the word "Shit" and sprayed blood onto the window.

A hand clamped down on my shoulder. "Son, you have some explaining to do."

It was the bodyguard. I yanked the ghost knife from my pocket and slid it through the end of his finger. He yanked his hand back. "That man's a cop," I said as I ran out of the room. "Make sure he gets out of the building."

I sprinted toward the front of the house. Every drape and curtain in the house was shut tight, so I couldn't see the van. I did hear the thick, metallic sound of two vehicles slamming into each other outside.

In the living room, hanging over the fireplace just where I remembered it, was the thirty-ought-six Barbara had promised to use on me. I leaped onto the couch and yanked it off the wall. As I ran for the front door, I slid back the bolt. Still loaded. Thanks, Bingo.

I burst out of the house and ran down the porch. An old woman in a wheelchair shrieked as I passed, but she was just a blur to me. At the end of the drive, Jon's van backed away from a news van, then turned hard onto the narrow street.

The three bodyguards heard the woman's shriek and spun around toward me, but drew back when they saw the rifle in my hands.

Jon started down the block, braked, straightened out, then started down the block again. Even with the delay from his fender-bender, he was too far and too fast for me to catch on foot.

I ran between two cars and knelt in the street. There was no way I could brace the rifle with my injured hand, so I laid it in the crook of my elbow and aimed down the length of the barrel. Absurdly, it felt like I was hugging it.

I knew that make and model of van and I knew exactly where the gas tank was. But Aunt Theresa was in there, and I had already accidentally shot someone I...

I squeezed the trigger before I could think about it more. A bullet hole appeared low in the fender and gas began to leak onto the street.

"FREEZE!" a man shouted from behind me. "DROP THE WEAPON!"

I tossed the rifle away and looked over my shoulder. Cops. Perfect.

"Don't turn around!" another voice shouted.

At the far end of the block, two police cars skidded to a halt, blocking the street. The van braked hard.

I raised my hands and lay down on the street. The two cops pounced on me, hard. One knelt on my shoulders and neck while the other twisted my arms around my back and cuffed me. My injured hand flared in pain at every jolt. "The guy in the van has a hostage," I told them.

"Don't struggle. Don't!"

I wasn't struggling. "He's killed a lot of people."

The cops weren't listening. "You have the right to remain silent. You have the right—"

"I know the drill." I let myself go limp. I'd known this would happen eventually. There wasn't much point in fighting.

Gunfire erupted from the far end of the block. Then screaming. The cops manhandling me froze; those were not good sounds. The gunfire kept going, fast and futile. Another man screamed.

"Charlie?" one of the cops said. He stood and took a couple of steps toward the gunfire. The other cop stood, too.

"You don't understand—" I said.

The bigger cop turned and pointed at me. "You! Stay!" Then they trotted toward Jon's van. The screams and gunfire had stopped.

The cops spoke into the radios on their shoulders, but I couldn't make out what they were saying. They spread out and moved along either side of Jon's van.

I dug the ghost knife out of my back pocket and sliced through the handcuff chain. I rolled onto my good hand and pushed myself onto my knees. At the end of the street, Jon's van was still idling. I couldn't see any people.

A bright light shone into my eyes, blinding me. A man circled me with a camera on his shoulder, his bright light beaming at me and my broken handcuffs.

"The real news is over there," I said.

More gunshots—the camera swung toward the sound. I tried to blink the spots out of my eyes, but I couldn't see anything ahead, but I could heard the screaming.

I pushed myself up onto my feet, holding my bloody hand against my bloody shirt. I still couldn't see clearly, and I felt vulnerable as hell. Down the block, the van revved its engine and backed up. It pulled up into a driveway, rumbled over a lawn and drove around the blocking police cars.

Jon was getting away with my aunt.

Behind me, the police car sat parked with both front doors open. I ran around to the driver's side and there were the keys, right in the ignition. I was willing to bet every penny I had that was against regulations. I climbed in and started it up.

The light shone on me again; the cameraman had picked the perfect moment to catch me on video. I waggled the fingers of my good hand at him as I drove by, hoping the jurors at my trial might find it charming.

I drove down the street. The light was dim at the end where the police cars—the other police cars—blocked the intersection, but I could still see several silhouettes sprawled across the asphalt.

How many deaths had Jon caused so far? I'd lost count, and now that he'd attacked a bunch of cops, things were going to get *really* ugly. I drove up the driveway over the lawn, following that damn van.

I can heal anything now, with the right food. And the right food was people. As soon as Jon found a place he felt safe, my aunt was going to die.

There was the van ahead and I fell in behind it. The police car had a full tank, and soon Jon would be running on fumes. I just had to stick with him until that happened.

He suddenly slammed on the brakes. I couldn't stop myself fast enough, and the police car slammed into the back of the van, lifting the back bumper and jolting it to the side. I felt a sudden clutching terror that my aunt would roll out the open side door and splash onto the street, but it didn't happen. In trying to right itself, the van side-swiped three parked cars, scraping off their side-view mirrors, then swerved into the middle of the street.

I slowed down to put some distance between us, but Jon took off as fast as his lumbering broom closet could go. Shattered pieces of tail light fell into the street, and I sped up to keep him in sight.

The van swerved onto the sidewalk, still accelerating. I could see strings of colored lights hanging in the yard and a crowd of people on the grass. There was music, a picnic table, a barbeque grill.

I slammed on my brakes, but Jon just plowed through.

In the movies, the camera is always set up so the audience can see stunt people diving out of the way of a vehicle just in time. But from my position behind the van, I couldn't see any of that. I saw the grill slammed into the air, gray charcoal falling onto and against the house next door. I saw the stunned faces of the people not in the van's path. I heard screams and the sound of heavy impact. I saw the van jolt from side to side as it went up the gently-sloping lawn, looking for all the world as though it was navigating a piece of rough road.

Then the van swerved into an alley and disappeared.

There was nothing for me to say. There was nothing I *could* say. I threw the car in reverse and backed into the street. Blood ran through my gritted teeth as I lined up the car, threw it into drive, raced along the street in the same direction Jon had gone.

I remembered, him, only 12, standing on the pitchers mound. I remembered him lying on his back deck, a bloody exit wound in his back. I remembered all kinds of things about him.

But none of it mattered anymore, because he was going to die. I didn't care what he had inside him or whether he was a victim who needed saving. I didn't have room in my head for any of those thoughts, because it was all crowded out by a white hot rage filling me up like an inflating balloon.

This had to stop. I was done trying to save my friend. Finished. I didn't care about being a hero to him or making amends. All I cared about was killing him.

It was a simple realization, very clear and very powerful. I was going to murder my friend and I was going to do it very, very soon.

I reached the end of the block, but the van was nowhere in sight. I went around the corner and peered down the alley, but I didn't see him. I couldn't even find a trail of gas on the asphalt.

He had to be close. I knew that much. That battered van of his attracted too much attention. It was going to run dry soon, and he'd have to switch to another ride or go to ground. Me, I was ready to bet he'd go to ground. But where?

I had to be the one to find him. What could the cops do? Shoot him? Arrest him? There was only one thing that had stopped the cousins so far, and it was sitting in my back pocket.

But where would Jon go? Breaking the law, hiding from

cops—this was all new to him. He must know that his van was too conspicuous. He might as well hang a "Call the cops" sign on the side.

But he also needed to feed. He needed to take my aunt somewhere he felt safe, kill her, eat her, and then venture back out into the world. Once he looked like a normal human, he could carjack someone and run for the border.

Mexico, probably. Somewhere he could summon more cousins, if he still had a copy of that damn spell. Or maybe he'd seek out Wally...

I stopped myself. It wouldn't do any good to start imagining some other trouble in the future. I had to fix the problem in front of me. Jon would go somewhere he felt safe, but where? His parent's house was on fire. Macy and Echo's house had already burned down. Payton's home, whatever that was? No; the cops had to have found his body by now. He wasn't thinking clearly but I figured he knew better than that.

Then I realized exactly where he would go.

Fifteen minutes later, I found Jon's van crookedly parked in the shadow of an old oak tree. Across the street was the same baseball field where he and I had played as kids, rain or shine. It was also the same field where I'd hidden out to study the stolen spell books.

There was no one in sight. I could hear sirens in the distance and I knew time was running out. I pulled close to the van, wondering how long it had been there. It was dark and still, with nothing visible through the gaping hole in the side but shadow.

There was a big flashlight mounted on the dash, so I yanked it free and shone it into the van.

Jon immediately bolted from the vehicle. His head was still a bloody mess, and even with Theresa slung over his shoulder, he ran like a horse at full gallop.

I threw the car in reverse to line him up in my headlights, then drove onto the sidewalk after him. He was already part-way up the grassy slope, and I raced after him. I didn't have a lot of weapons left, but this car was one of them.

Jon looked back at me, then shrugged Aunt Theresa off his shoulder. She fell onto the grass. Hard.

I swerved to avoid her, getting a feel for the car's sloppy handling on the muddy field. Unencumbered, Jon ran even faster; I stomped on the accelerator.

He was headed for the right field fence and the trees beyond it, but I caught up with him in center field. I felt the car surging forward, and I was aching to see him vanish under my hood, just as those party-goers must have gone under the van.

Jon glanced over his shoulder then spun, jumped to the right and bounded over the roof of the car.

I looked in the rear view mirror and saw him fall onto the grass. I slammed on the brakes and twisted the wheel, letting the car fishtail, scraping up turf, so I could come at him again.

I felt a twinge of guilt at ruining the field, which was so absurd that I laughed out loud. It didn't sound like the laugh of a sane person. I pressed the accelerator all the way down and started after him again.

In the distance, I could see Aunt Theresa on her feet, hobbling toward the sidewalk. Thankfully, Jon was running in a curve, away from her, heading for the cinderblock dugout.

He wasn't going to reach them. The police car was heavy and full of power, and I was gaining fast.

He glanced back at me again, and I suddenly remembered the chase games we'd played as kids. Jon never dodged the same way twice in a row. With my good hand, I reached across my body and grabbed the driver's side door handle, steadying the steering wheel with the forearm of my left hand.

Jon faked right but jumped to the left; I was already opening the door, bracing it with all the strength I had left. They collided with a crunch that filled me with an ugly happiness. Jon smashed through the window glass, toppled over the door and landed on his neck. It was a gruesome fall that would have killed a normal man.

I slammed on the brakes. Aunt Theresa was still limping away; she didn't look back and I was glad of it. The police sirens became louder as though someone had turned up the volume knob, and I saw them racing down the street toward us.

There wasn't much time. I threw the car in reverse and leaned out the open door to see where I was going. Jon tried to scramble away, but it was pretty clear his legs were broken, along with one of his arms.

I hit him with the bumper and felt the car lurch as the back wheel rolled over him.

I rolled out of the driver's seat, suddenly exhausted again. There wasn't much more left to do. The wheel sat squarely on Jon's abdomen, and the way it flattened his crushed torso was as sickening as his bloated, misshapen head.

I took out my ghost knife.

Police cars skidded to a halt on the grass around us. A

woman shouted "FREEZE! Don't you make another move!" I could hear their equipment jangling as they ran toward me, but I didn't glance up at them.

"Ray," Jon said, meaningless red blood dribbling from his lips. "Ray, don't do it. Despite everything, there's still a bit of me in here."

With my ruined, bloody mouth, I said: "I know, Jon. And you have a debt to pay."

I threw the ghost knife. It plunged through his forehead into the ground. A geyser of black blood burst out of him.

There was a gunshot, and everything became dark and cold.

CHAPTER TWENTY-EIGHT

I was surprised to wake up in a prison hospital—I'd expected to be put out of my misery right there in the grass. I slept as much as they would let me. I answered their questions in a deliberately groggy and incoherent way, and the injuries to my mouth helped make it convincing. Eventually, they left me alone.

Two cops had fired a total of twelve shots at me. One skimmed across my biceps, barely furrowing my skin. A second grazed my temple, giving me a serious concussion and hairline fractures in my skull. The doctors told me I would recover completely if I took it easy.

My shirt had seven additional bullet holes in it, but because I had not been harmed, the police decided that those other shots had missed me. They offered no explanation for the holes. Annalise's spell had saved my life again.

I went in and out of consciousness for the next few days, and at some point I had surgery on my gunshot hand. I didn't know about it until after I woke up and saw the new bandages. A trustee told me I was lucky, but I couldn't concentrate on him long enough to find out why.

It healed pretty well. I'll never play guitar, but I can make a fist, which is better than I had a right to expect. One of the nurses told me that, when I was older, it would probably ache before a storm. She didn't understand why I laughed.

Before I was even able to sit up in bed, a tall, slender blond man struck up a conversation with me while he was mopping the floor. He dressed as a trustee, but his glasses were very thin and very expensive, not prison-issue at all. I figured him for an informant.

I was right, but he didn't work for the police. He turned out to be Callin's friend—at least, that's what he claimed. He was the friend with enough power to destroy the city and everyone in it.

He didn't look like much, but neither had Callin.

He asked for my story. I figured he was really there to kill me, but maybe, if he heard the truth, he wouldn't make the whole city slide into the sea or something.

I told him everything, leaving out one detail: The copy of Callin's spell book I sent to my cousin Duncan in Maine. I didn't want Duncan killed just because he got an envelope in the mail.

He listened intently, his expression nearly impossible to read. Maybe he was a great poker player or maybe he didn't have human emotions. I didn't ask. In any event, he heard the story from front to back, only nodding at a couple of points, then, instead of killing me, he promised to visit again.

After he left, I realized I hadn't asked his name. Probably for the better.

A few days later he turned up again. The cops had been trying to get me to sign a statement saying that I killed Jon, Macy, Echo, Payton, Andrea, Oscar and a lot of other people. They were hot to find someone to prosecute because they lost six of their own in that fight on Jon's street. It was a bad scene and a tragedy for the city. As the most disreputable survivor, I was supposed to be the scapegoat.

But I resisted. I figured it was only a matter of time before Callin's friend—or Annalise—returned and pulled my head off. I didn't have any hope of getting out of this mess, but I sure as hell wasn't going to cooperate, either. They were going to have to tie the noose without my help.

When Callin's friend returned, he was dressed as a lawyer, and he had brought another lawyer in an Armani suit with him. Callin had hired Mr. Armani for me; I felt like the proverbial fattened calf.

The friend told me he'd recovered the spell books I'd buried. They were a real find, he assured me—copies of a book the society had been hunting for centuries. He assured me I'd given them "an important lead," whatever that meant.

He made me retell Wally's part of the story, and the trip to Nettle Philip's house, too. We talked about where Wally might have gone and what he looked like. I had the impression my old friend was a new priority for the Twenty Palace Society. Good. I hoped they made life interesting for him. Interesting and short.

We also talked about the cousins, how they behaved and what they looked like. Maybe he was putting together a pamphlet.

Again I expected to be put out of my misery at the end of the meeting, and again it didn't happen. This time the friend left me alone with his associate. I had a lawyer.

We worked out a story that played off the throwaway comment I'd made to my uncle and Skullface: Jon and his

friends had gotten a mysterious designer drug from their pal
Wally. It made people hallucinate and eventually drove them
cannibal crazy.

What the hell. It wasn't too far from the truth.

Finally, at my arraignment, all the charges were dropped.
If there's an ultimate improbable miracle in my whole story
of magic and strangeness, that's it.

The police had too many loose ends they couldn't explain.
Jon's, Macy's and Payton's bodies were in a condition no one
could satisfactorily explain. The police reports *said* he was
running across the field but the coroner's report said he was
a corpse without a brain, and that he'd been one for days—
days in which he'd appeared on the news, on hotel security
cameras and in which he'd killed his whole family.

Autopsies on Jon, Macy, and Payton revealed human flesh
in their stomachs. While I was unconscious, my stomach had
been pumped, too, but nothing had been found but bile.

The police car I'd stolen was full of bloody fingerprints,
but apparently none of them matched mine. They even ran
DNA matches, but for whatever reason—their own incom-
petence, I assumed—they couldn't place me in the stolen cop
car. What happened to the footage of me waving at the news
camera from behind the wheel, I never found out.

Finally, there were the numerous witnesses, from the
homeless guy at the copy shop to Hank. I found out
Skullface had spent an afternoon sipping lemonade with
Aunt Theresa, and whatever she told him, he left believing
that I'd saved him and his daughter from madness and can-
nibalism. He'd been the one to hire a hand surgeon from

somewhere back east to reconstruct my hand.

I learned all this after the fact, when my lawyer let me watch the video testimony he'd given. He even did a couple bedside TV interviews, going on the news several times to call me a hero.

That was not something I expected to hear. No one should be called a hero because he'd killed his oldest friend. No one should be called a hero because he promised to save someone and failed.

Of course, if I'd turned Jon and his friends over to the society right away, I would have saved the lives of Andrea, Oscar, Bingo, and thirteen other people—some I hadn't known anything about. But I couldn't betray my friend.

I didn't feel like a hero. Still, I never got the chance to thank Skullface; his cancer took him before I got my walking papers.

So the case against me was full of holes, I had a wealthy supporter, and a high-priced lawyer. On one sunny spring afternoon, I walked out of the courthouse a free man, squinting from the sunlight. The lawyer (I had never thought of him as "my lawyer") shook my hand and hustled down the steps, no doubt to make up his bill.

I looked around, amazed to be a free man again. There, at the curb, leaning against her motorcycle, was Annalise. She was watching me. Waiting for me.

I wasn't surprised. The society sprung me from jail so they could dispose of me in private. Fine. I expected it.

Uncle Karl and Aunt Theresa met me at the bottom of the steps. Uncle Karl shook my hand. Aunt Theresa threw her arms around me. The cast had come off her arm, but it still looked like skin stretched over bare bone. She didn't complain.

She pressed a ring of keys into my hand. It was a copy of the keys to their rebuilt house. I gave it back. "I'm sorry," I said, and I walked toward Annalise.

She scowled at me as I approached. I wondered if she would kill me right there in front of the courthouse or if she'd take me somewhere first. "Thank Callin for my lawyer," I said.

"Thank him yourself." She took my ghost knife from her pocket and offered it to me.

I didn't accept it. "You're not going to kill me?"

She took a helmet off the back of the motorcycle and tucked it under her arm. "No. Those are my orders—my punishment, actually, for attacking Callin a second time. And, according to the peers, you've earned a second chance. You're still my wooden man.

"But," she continued, "if you refuse to work for me or don't do what I tell you to do, I have the society's permission to kill you."

I took the ghost knife. I felt something that might have been relief, but it was too mixed up for such a simple label. I noticed she had a second helmet and I put it on. It sorta fit.

"I have a job right now," she said as she pulled on her own helmet. "It's a dangerous job. Very dangerous." She looked at me like I was an undercooked piece of meat.

I climbed on. She revved the engine, sped off down the street and we headed into traffic.

ACKNOWLEDGEMENTS

I'd like to offer special thanks to my agent, Caitlin Blasdell, and to the editor of the other books in this series, Betsy Mitchell. I feel extremely lucky to be able to take credit for all the good ideas they've given me. I'd also like to thank Elizabeth Glover for her help in typesetting the interior, and to George Cotronis for the terrific cover.

Child of Fire, the next Ray Lilly novel, was published by Del Rey and was named to Publishers Weekly's Best 100 Novels of 2009. The sequel, *Game of Cages*, was released in 2010 and the third book, *Circle of Enemies*, came out in the fall of 2011.

Harry lives in Seattle with his beloved wife, his beloved son, and his beloved library system. You can find him online at:

http://www.harryjconnolly.com

37863616R00178

Made in the USA
Middletown, DE
07 December 2016